Slay It with Flowers

A Flower Shop Mystery

Kate Collins

A SIGNET BOOK

SIGNET
Published by New American Library, a division of
Penguin Group (USA) Inc., 375 Hudson Street,
New York, New York 10014, USA
Penguin Group (Canada) 10 Alcorn Avenue, Toronto,
Ontario M4V 3B2, Canada (a division of Pearson Penguin Canada Inc.)
Penguin Books Ltd., 80 Strand, London WC2R 0RL, England
Penguin Ireland, 25 St. Stephen's Green, Dublin 2,
Ireland (a division of Penguin Books Ltd.)
Penguin Group (Australia), 250 Camberwell Road, Camberwell, Victoria 3124,
Australia (a division of Pearson Australia Group Pty. Ltd.)
Penguin Books India Pvt. Ltd., 11 Community Centre, Panchsheel Park,
New Dehli - 110 017, India
Penguin Group (NZ), cnr Airborne and Rosedale Roads, Albany,
Auckland 1310, New Zealand (a division of Pearson New Zealand Ltd.)
Penguin Books (South Africa) (Pty.) Ltd., 24 Sturdee Avenue,
Rosebank, Johannesburg 2196, South Africa

Penguin Books Ltd, Registered Offices:
80 Strand, London WC2R 0RL, England

First published by Signet, an imprint of New American Library,
a division of Penguin Group (USA) Inc.

First Printing, March 2005
10 9 8 7 6 5 4 3 2

PUBLISHER'S NOTE
This is a work of fiction. Names, characters, places, and incidents either are the
product of the author's imagination or are used fictitiously, and any resemblance
to actual persons, living or dead, business establishments, events, or locales is
entirely coincidental.

Praise for *Mum's the Word,*
the first Flower Shop Mystery

"Kate Collins plants all the right seeds to grow a fertile garden of mystery. . . . Abby Knight is an Indiana florist who cannot keep her nose out of other people's business. She's rash, brash, and audacious. Move over Stephanie Plum, Abby Knight has come to town."
— Denise Swanson, author of the
Scumble River mysteries

"An engaging debut planted with a spirited sleuth, quirky sidekicks, and page-turning action . . . Delightfully addictive . . . A charming addition to the cozy subgenre. Here's hoping we see more of intrepid florist, Abby Knight, and sexy restaurateur, Marco Salvare."
— Nancy J. Cohen, author of the
Bad Hair Day mysteries

"Kate Collins' new Flower Shop Mystery is fresh as a daisy, with a bouquet of irresistible characters and deep roots in the Indiana soil."
— Elaine Viets, author of the
Dead-End Job mysteries

"A bountiful bouquet of clues, colorful characters, and tantalizing twists . . . Kate Collins carefully cultivates clues, plants surprising suspects, and harvests a killer in this fresh and frolicsome new Flower Shop Mystery series."
— Ellen Byerrum, author of A Crime of
Fashion mysteries

"A charming debut . . . Abby makes for a spunky, feisty heroine, her sidekicks are quirky, and Marco is suitably hunky . . . well-fleshed-out, witty characters."

—The Best Reviews

"This amusing new author has devised an excellent cast of characters and thrown them into a cleverly tumultuous plot. . . . Readers will savor Abby's courage as she confronts corruption, violence and evil. The pacing is brisk, with parallel plots that intersect in interesting ways. A terrific debut!"

—*Romantic Times*

"This engaging read has a list of crazy characters that step off the pages to the delight of the reader. Don't miss this wanna-be sleuth's adventures."

—*Rendezvous*

"The story was cute and funny, had a good plot line, which entwined a lot of interesting threads, and although the mystery was somewhat easy to figure out in some respects there were still twists that I didn't see coming. . . . The shop and its associates sounded darling. I'd love to visit there for a cup of coffee. I also enjoyed Simon the cat, though non-cat lovers might not feel the same. . . . *Mum's the Word* is an enjoyable read and a fine debut for this new mystery series."

—Dangerously Curvy Novels

As always, a big thanks to my home support team—my husband, Jim; children Jason, Julie, and Tasha; and my away team, Lacinda, Damian, Tamara, Wolfgang, and of course, baby Niobe. I thank you all deeply for your understanding and encouragement.

To my mother, for your patience and support, and for *not* being like Abby's mom.

To my late father, a cop with a sharp sense of humor and an Irish temper, for inspiring the character of Abby's father.

To all the dedicated "Men in Blue" who have the integrity and backbone to stand up for what is right.

And to Karen and Julie at Expressions for their valuable assistance.

CHAPTER ONE

Just for the record, I am not, in the true definition of the word, a meddler.

According to my dictionary, a meddler is one who involves herself in a matter without right or invitation. *Phfffft.* Isn't me at all. I am a naturally curious, caring individual strongly opposed to two things: tyranny and injustice. That strong sense of right has been with me as far back as third grade, when I first strode the halls of Morton Elementary School with my-hall monitor sash strapped across my chest.

I inherited these traits from my father, Jeffrey Knight, who was a sergeant on the New Chapel, Indiana, police force until a felon's bullet put him in a wheelchair. He firmly believed that his badge stood for honesty and right, and because of that he refused to play politics, which took a lot of courage but cost him many promotions. He has always been my hero.

But after the previous week—when my beloved 1960 yellow Corvette and I were run off the road, my flower shop was burgled, and a homicidal garden center owner decided to put a stop to my breathing capabilities—even my father had determined that I'd put my safety in jeopardy once too often.

As my assistant Grace, who had a quote for everything, was fond of saying, "If we don't learn from history, we are doomed to repeat it." Grace was usually right.

That week was behind me now. The bullies had been caught, the innocent cleared, and I had sworn offf what my friends termed my *meddling,* a vow they did *not* have to twist my arm to get me to make.

This particular Monday started at the customary time of eight o'clock in the morning—or ten minutes past four by the clock on the courthouse spire. The clock had stopped running in either 1997 or 1897, but none of our elected officials were willing to take a stand on the matter—or find someone to fix it. When asked, their usual response was, "What clock?"

I pulled the Vette into a space two doors down from my floral shop, landing it directly in front of the town's local watering hole, the Down the Hatch Bar and Grill, owned by the sexiest man who has ever worn a uniform, Marco Salvare, a former cop turned bar owner who dabbled in PI work on the side. Out front, Jingles the window washer was already hard at work with his trusty squeegee. Jingles was a friendly retiree whose goal in life appeared to be to keep every window and door on the square squeaky clean. His nickname came from his habit of jingling coins in his pocket. I wasn't sure if anyone actually knew his real name.

I gave Jingles a wave, then continued down the block, stopping on the sidewalk outside the old brick building that housed my shop to gaze up at the hand-lettered sign that proudly proclaimed my ownership. Even after two months, I was still in awe. Me, Abby Knight, a businesswoman. All grown up and in debt up to my eyebrows.

I traced a finger across my left eyebrow. The ring was gone. I had truly crossed the threshold into adulthood.

Bloomers was the second shop from the corner on Franklin Street, one of the four streets that surrounded the courthouse square. The store occupied the first floor and basement of the three-story building and had two bay windows with a yellow-framed door in between. The left side of the shop housed our flowers and the right side was our coffee and tea parlor, where customers sat at white wrought-iron tables and watched the happenings on the square.

The courthouse, built in 1896 from Indiana limestone, housed the county and circuit courts, plus all the government offices. Around the square were the typical assortment of family-owned shops, banks, law offices, and restaurants. Five blocks east of the square marked the western edge of the campus of New Chapel University, a small, private college where I would have graduated from law school if I wouldn't have flunked out.

Because I *had* flunked out, I'd had to rethink my career plans to find something I could do successfully. It had been a very short list. Then I'd learned that the quaint little flower shop where I'd once worked part-time was for sale—a stroke of luck for me because I loved flowers and actually had a talent for growing things. So I used the rest of my grandfather's college trust as a down payment and had an instant career, which mollified my stunned parents. It also saved the owner, Lottie Dombowski, from bankruptcy caused by her husband's massive medical bills. Now Lottie worked for me, doing what she loved best, and I worked for the bank, trying to make the mortgage payments.

Inside the shop, my assistant Grace Bingham was preparing her coffee machines for the day. As soon as I stepped inside and shut the door, she sang out in her crisp British accent, "Good morning, dear. How are we today?"

Grace spent years working as a nurse and sometimes still spoke in first person plural. I met her the summer I law clerked for Dave Hammond, a lawyer with a one-man office on the square. Grace was his legal secretary at the time. After she retired and found herself with too much time on her hands, I persuaded her to work for me at Bloomers. It was a perfect fit.

"We are in a good mood," I called back. "The sun is shining, the temperature is just right, and it's Monday. The only way it could get better is if twenty orders came in overnight." I peered into the parlor. "They didn't, did they?"

"No, dear, only five."

Grace handled as many tasks as I cared to load on her. Since she was an expert tea steeper, coffee brewer, and scone baker, her main job was to run the parlor. It was one of our many efforts to lure in more customers. We were in dire need of more customers, especially now that a gigantic floral and hobby shop had opened on the main highway.

At that moment Lottie came bustling through the curtain from the workroom in back, a bundle of white roses in her ample arms, her usual pink satin bow pinned into the short, brassy curls above her right ear. It was a daring look for a forty-five-year-old mother of a highly embarrassable seventeen-year-old boy. Even more daring considering that she had *four* highly embarrassable seventeen-year-old boys. Lottie's opinion on that was simple: Suck it up.

"Oh, good, you made it before Jillian did," she said to me as she stocked a container in the glass display cooler.

The gray clouds were moving in. I almost expected to hear ominous music in the background. "Jillian is coming? Now? Something dreadful must have happened to get her up before noon."

Lottie rolled her eyes. "She's got another bee in her bonnet about her wedding plans."

Grace handed me a rose-patterned china cup filled with her gourmet coffee, fixed just the way I liked it with a good shot of half-and-half. "Drink up, dear. You'll need the fortification. You know how tiring your cousin can be."

Grace phrased it so politely. My term would have been *pain in the ass,* which Jillian had been since she hit puberty and discovered that boys adored her. Jillian Knight was twenty-five, tall, gorgeous, and one year younger than me. She was also the only other girl in the family, which was about all we had in common.

My father was a retired cop. Jillian's was a stockbroker. My mother was a kindergarten teacher. Jillian's mother wielded a five iron at the New Chapel Country Club. I paid the mortgage on a floral shop. Jillian got paid to shop for other people's wardrobes. As children, my brothers, Jonathan and Jordan, and I worked for our allowances. Jillian allowed their maid to work for hers.

The only justice in our separate worlds was that my two brothers became successful surgeons, while Jillian's brother waited tables in a Chicago diner. For years, our families spent all holidays together, and that had given Jillian and me a siblinglike relationship: we loved each other but didn't get along.

"I'm telling you, Abby, don't pay for that bridesmaid dress," Lottie warned.

I waved away her concern. "Jillian won't call off *this* wedding. She wouldn't dare."

"Ha! Look at her track record."

Lottie had a good point. Jillian got engaged once a year—it seemed to be a hobby of hers. Her list of ex-fiancés read like a travel brochure: an Italian restaurant owner from Chicago's Little Italy; a moody Parisian artist named Jean

Luc; an English consulate Sir Something-or-Other; and a Greek plastic surgeon with an unpronounceable name. This was the first time she'd ever made it to the actual choosing-of-the-flowers stage.

Jillian's current groom-to-be was Claymore Osborne, who, coincidentally, was the younger brother of my former fiancé, Pryce Osborne the Second. Claymore was every bit as boorish and snooty as Pryce was, but that didn't matter to Jillian. What mattered was that Claymore stood to inherit half the Osborne fortune. Jillian always did go after money.

The wedding was set for the Fourth of July, three weeks away. At first Jillian wanted to hold it in a field of daisies, but having none in the area suitable for a wedding ceremony, she settled for a hotel ballroom that she believed had daisies in the carpet. Somewhere.

On top of choosing me as a bridesmaid, Jillian had also asked me to do her wedding flowers. I had agreed because Jillian's wedding would most certainly be lavish, and that meant expensive flowers, which translated into money to pay my bills. I really needed to pay my bills.

"Here are your messages, dear," Grace said, handing me a small pile of memos. "Lottie has breakfast ready in the kitchen."

Monday breakfast was a tradition at Bloomers, and I was already drooling in anticipation. There were four messages: three from my mother and one from a client named Trudee DeWitt, or "Double-E Double-T," as she called herself, who needed to know when I was coming over to consult with her on decorations for her party.

The three messages from my mother all said the same thing: "Call me. Urgent." Nearly all her messages claimed urgency. One of these days, I've told her, it really will be urgent and then won't she be sorry? The Mother Who Cried Wolf.

I took the memos and the coffee and headed for the workroom, a gardenlike haven where I've spent some of my happiest moments. As soon as I stepped through the curtain I had to stop to inhale the aromas—rose, lily, eucalyptus, buttered toast, scrambled eggs. It didn't get any better than that.

I dropped the messages on my desk—a messy affair littered with a computer, printer, phone, a pencil cup shaped like a grinning cat, a few framed photos, and assorted office items—and went to the kitchen to grab a plate of food. While I ate, Lottie and I went over the orders and discussed the coming week so we could make a list and call our suppliers. After washing my plate in the tiny kitchen sink, I tacked the orders on the corkboard and sat at my desk to call Trudee.

I had just punched in her number when I heard the bell over the front door jingle, and a moment later the curtain parted and the bride-to-be swept in, pausing to look around the room in confusion. I could understand her bewilderment. The workroom was a riot of color and shape and texture and scents. Dried and silk flowers sat in tall containers, ribbon-festooned wreaths adorned the walls, and brightly hued foil and painted pots lined the shelves. A small person like me, even with my red hair, could blend right in. A female Waldo.

"Abby!" she cried dramatically when she spotted me, brushing a silken strand of copper hair off her face. Jillian never did anything without drama. "Thank goodness you're here!" She threw her long, tanned arms around my shoulders and sobbed hideously, ignoring the phone pressed to my ear.

"Trudee? This is Abby Knight. You called?"

"It's horrible, Abby. I just can't bear it," Jillian wept. She lifted her head from my shoulder to stare me in the face, and since she was taller than me—everyone was taller than me—it required her to bend her knees to put us at an even eye level. She cupped my head with her hands. "Abby, you have to help me."

"Wednesday at four o'clock?" I said into the phone, giving my cousin a hard glare while trying to maintain a smile in my voice. "It's on my calendar. I'll see you then."

Jillian took the phone from my hand and put it in the cradle. "Are you *listening* to me?"

"No, I am *not* listening to you. I'm seething with fury and that tends to make the blood pound in my ears. Did you happen to notice I was on the phone?" I turned to write Wednesday's meeting on the calendar hanging on the corkboard.

"Irate customer?" Jillian asked, settling herself on a stool at the worktable. When I looked around at her to see if she were serious or just really stupid, she had crossed one linen-clad leg over the other and was gazing at me expectantly, her tears magically gone.

I saw Lottie hovering outside the curtain and knew she was waiting to get on the computer. "Let's go to the parlor and talk."

We settled at a table in front of the bay window in the cozy Victorian-style parlor. Once Grace had brought coffee for Jill and refreshed my cup I said, "What's the problem?"

"Claymore. He's being completely unreasonable. He insists that Punch be his best man even though Punch dumped Onora and now she refuses to walk up the aisle with him. And please don't tell me to switch my maid of honor. I simply must have Onora as my maid of honor. I mean, look at her name, for heaven's sake. Abby, what are you staring at? Have you heard a word I've said?"

I dragged my gaze from the scene across the street, where sheriff's deputies were moving prisoners from a van to the courthouse for hearings. "Sorry. You lost me after you said Punch. Who's Punch?"

"Claymore's best man, former fraternity brother. You met him."

We paused as three middle-aged women came into the parlor and took seats at a table nearby. Grace immediately breezed over to take their orders. "I haven't met any of the wedding party," I said to my cousin.

"Right. Okay, Punch, Flip, Bertie, and Pryce are the groomsmen. They were in the same fraternity at Harvard, except that Pryce graduated two years earlier."

"With names like those I would have guessed the Ringling Brothers School for Acrobats."

"The Ringling what?"

"The Ringling Brothers . . . Barnum and Bailey . . . A *circus,* Jill. Did you grow up in Azkaban? Never mind. Hand me the pitcher of cream. And the bridesmaids?"

"Onora, Ursula, Sabina, and—" She paused to count them on her fingers. "There's one more."

"Me. The one without the *a* at the end of her name."

"Of course it's you, silly."

"Your sorority sisters, I assume?"

"Yes. Well, except for you."

I was so glad she pointed that out. "So getting back to Punch," I prompted, liberally lacing my coffee with swirls of creamy calories, which helped subdue the urge to choke her.

"His real name is Paulin Chumley, so they call him Punch. Everyone went by a nickname in the frat house."

"He's lucky they didn't call him Chump."

Jillian didn't get my joke. She wasn't real swift on the uptake. "Punch fits him better. He's a brute who likes to use his fists and thinks he's God's gift to women."

"The kind of guy I love to hate."

"Exactly. In college he drove a genuine army Hummer. Now he owns a swanky sports bar. You know the type. He always has to prove he has the Y chromosome. He even wears a solid gold punching bag earring. He says it's his logo."

"Kind of carries that theme thing a bit too far, don't you think? Just out of curiosity, what's Claymore's nickname?"

"Clay."

"That's original. Can't Punch be a plain old groomsman instead of the best man?"

Jillian heaved a big sigh. "That's what I keep telling Claymore! Onora would be fine with that arrangement as long as she doesn't have to stand anywhere near Punch. She detests him. I mean, she really, really *detests* him. And to tell you the truth, I can barely tolerate him myself—he's such a chauvinist. But Claymore says he can't drop Punch's rank because that would show a lack of moral fiber, whatever that means."

It would have been pointless to try to explain it to her. The only fiber she understood was listed on the labels sewn into her clothing. And I was the one who had flunked out of school. I rested my chin on one hand and gave her a glazed look. "Just what exactly do you want *me* to do?"

"Talk to Pryce. Claymore looks up to Pryce. If Pryce tells him to switch men, Claymore will listen. Pryce should be the best man anyway. I mean, he's his brother, for pity sake."

"I have two questions. First, what would make you believe that Pryce would listen to me? He dumped me, remember? Two months before the wedding? When I failed to meet the Osborne standard of excellence? And second, if you can't come to some resolution with Claymore now, what does that bode for your future?"

"You obviously don't know anything about marriage."

"Neither do you. Hand me the cream."

"I know this much," she said, pushing the little ceramic pitcher toward me, "Claymore hates making decisions, so once we're married I will make the decisions for both of us. See? Problem solved."

Poor Claymore would never know what hit him.

"Besides, Pryce still carries a torch for you, so of course he'll listen. He'll hang on your every word."

I glanced over at the three ladies, who had stopped talking and were now quietly stirring their lattes so they could hear more about this so-called torch.

I leaned across the table to whisper, "If Pryce is carrying a torch it's so he can tie me to a stake and set fire to my feet. His parents will provide the kindling." They were still trying to live down the ignominy of my having been booted out of law school while engaged to their son.

"Silly! All you'd have to do is crook your little finger and Pryce would take you back just like that." She snapped her fingers and all three women gave a start. "Besides, you love to help people. So help *me*." She grasped my hand. "Pu-*leez*, Abby. I'm desperate!"

"Fine. I'll talk to Pryce." Anything to get her off that topic so the ladies next to us could resume their own conversation. There was nothing like a juicy bit of gossip to start tongues wagging around this town. "Can we discuss your flowers now?"

Jillian held up a hand to catch Grace's eye. "More coffee, please," she mouthed.

"Picture this," I said. "You're floating down an aisle strewn with rose petals. In your arms—"

"Am I beautiful?"

"In your arms," I continued, giving her a scowl, "are long, luscious, creamy peach callas, their lovely dark green leaves splashed with flecks of white, all tied together with a luxurious white satin bow."

"Calla lilies?"

"Callas. Not lilies. Callas."

"Katharine Hepburn called them Calla lilies."

"Katharine Hepburn was not a florist. Callas are from the *Zantedeschia* family, whereas lilies—" Noticing that Jillian's attention was fixed on a point somewhere beyond my left shoulder, I turned to look.

Coming up the sidewalk toward my shop was Marco Salvare, moving with a sexy swagger most women—and I include myself in that group—found terribly exciting.

"Who is *that*?" Jillian said in awe, and I could almost see the drool forming on her lower lip. The three women next to us craned their necks for a look, too.

"That's the new owner of the Down the Hatch."

Five of us watched him pull open the door. The bell jingled to announce his arrival, and suddenly tiny bottles sprang from the purses behind us. Hair spray, perfume, and breath freshener quickly filled the air. I waved away the cloud, coughing, as Marco strode into the parlor, grabbed a chair from another table, pulled it up beside me, and straddled it.

"Hey, sunshine. How's it going?" The mist settled and Jillian came into view. He stuck out his hand. "Hi. I'm Marco."

She wrapped her long, graceful fingers around his. "I'm Jillian Knight. *Very* pleased to meet you, Marco."

"Would you care for coffee?" Grace asked coolly, placing a cup and saucer in front of him. Grace was the only woman I knew who seemed impervious to Marco's charisma. He was impervious to her imperviousness, so it didn't really matter.

"No. Thanks anyway." Marco looked from Jillian to me. "You're not sisters, so you must be cousins."

"How did you know we were related?" Jillian asked, prompting Marco to shoot me a look that said, *"Is she clueless?"*

"The last name was a dead giveaway, Jill," I said.

She nodded sagely. "That's true."

Our surname was the *only* thing we shared, a fact that was both a blessing and a curse. On the curse side, Jillian was a head taller, had a well-proportioned body rather than a top-heavy one, and had long, shimmery, copper-colored hair, as opposed to my shorter, fiery red, blunt-edged bob. On the blessing side, I was smart—regardless of what my law professors thought.

"Jillian is getting married July fourth," I said, just in case Marco had any ideas about dating her. "I'm doing her flowers."

He eased his hand from Jillian's hot little paw. "Congratulations."

Jillian lifted one shoulder in an effortless shrug. "*Maybe* I'm getting married. *If* Abby helps me." She rose and put the strap of her Ferragamo purse over her shoulder. "I have to run. Let me know what Pryce says." Her voice dropped to a sexy purr. "It was a pleasure meeting you, Marco."

As soon as Jillian had gone, Marco turned a highly skeptical brown-eyed gaze on me and topped it off by raising one dark eyebrow. "If you help her?"

"She wants me to talk to my former fiancé to convince him to convince the groom to—well, it's a long, complicated story that will only bore you. The bottom line is that if I want to salvage the vanload of callas I ordered for this wedding, I have to make sure there *is* a wedding." I took my cup over to the coffee counter for a refill, where Grace was also giving me that doubtful look. "I'm not meddling," I assured them both.

"That's good," Marco said when I returned to the table, "because less than forty-eight hours ago you swore off meddling."

"Did you come to harass me, or did you have some other goal in mind?"

"Harass you." He picked up my coffee and sniffed it, obviously trying to decide if I had poisoned it with artificial sweetener. "Did you put that dead bolt on your apartment door?"

"Oh, right. I meant to do that."

Wrong answer. Counting on his fingers, Marco began to list why I should have a dead bolt, most of which came from the unfortunate events of the past week. I had to tune him out, though, when my ears picked up the threads of a much more interesting conversation the three ladies were having behind me.

"If it's a massage parlor, why don't they advertise? And why do they cover their windows with butcher paper?"

"I heard that a woman tried to get in and was told it was for men only."

"Well, look at their sign, for goodness sake. EMPEROR'S SPA. What does that tell you?"

"It's open twenty-four hours, seven days a week. Would a legitimate business do that?"

I grabbed Marco's wrist. "Did you hear that?"

"Hear what? I don't know what I'm supposed to be listening for."

I leaned closer to whisper, "What the ladies behind me are talking about. Remember those five Oriental women in their skintight Mandarin dresses who came into your bar Saturday night? Remember we heard that they work at the Emperor's Spa, and give a whole lot more than massages?

Remember me suggesting that we investigate? *That's* what they're talking about."

"Remember your promise not to meddle?"

I should never make promises for something I'm inherently unable to do. "Come on, Marco. New Chapel is a very conservative, very clean college town. We don't want prostitution going on here. As concerned citizens, it would behoove us to expose it."

"As a former law school student, it would behoove you not to jump to a conclusion without having all the facts."

"But it all adds up. They don't advertise. Female customers aren't allowed in. The windows are covered with paper. . . . I know there's something fishy going on. I have a sixth sense about these things."

One corner of Marco's mouth quirked, like he had a secret.

"You found out something about that spa, didn't you?" I said.

"I figured you'd try to snoop, so I did a preemptive investigation."

My eyes got very wide, then narrowed suspiciously. "You went in that place?"

"Yes, Miss Marple, I did, and I got a very thorough *back* massage."

"By one of the Oriental women?" I fairly seethed.

"By a large European woman with hairy arms and a mustache. I didn't see any women from the Far East."

"That's because they smelled cop."

He gave me a look that said, *Yeah, right.* Marco had left the force because he didn't fit the police mold. It had been a mutually acceptable decision. "I think you should know," he said loud enough for the eavesdroppers to hear, "a new restaurant called the China Cabinet had their grand opening this past weekend. The waitresses wore Chinese costumes for it. I'm guessing they were the ones who came into the bar Saturday night."

At that, the three ladies behind us gathered their purses and shopping bags and left, obviously in a rush to broadcast the new bit of gossip. I watched them through the bay window as they met briefly on the sidewalk outside, then headed off in three separate directions like a trio of female Paul Reveres. *The China Cabinet has opened! The China Cabinet has opened!*

"Let's see if I have this right," I said, turning my attention back to Marco. "Those five women at your bar Saturday night are waitresses, not masseuses, and the Emperor's Spa is a legitimate business?"

Marco sat back in his chair and crossed his arms over his chest, ready to declare a victory. "That's what I'm saying."

"Then what do you call *that*?"

He followed my pointing index finger to a police van that had pulled up across the street, where, at that moment, two cops were dislodging five hissing, spitting, handcuffed Asian women wearing ankle-length, formfitting, brightly hued Mandarin dresses and four-inch spike heels.

Must have been tough serving food in that getup.

Chapter Two

In the two minutes it took us to exit the shop and cross the street, a crowd had formed on the courthouse lawn, gesturing, whispering, and making rude comments as the five women were herded to the rear of the building. Marco told me to stay put and went to find someone he knew to ask what was going on. I glanced around, spotted Deputy Prosecutor Greg Morgan near the front entrance, and made a beeline for him. Morgan prided himself on having a finger on the throbbing pulse of New Chapel.

I'd known Morgan since high school, when we'd both had a crush on the same person—him. One thing he was not known for was his modesty. He was a handsome man, though a little lacking in intelligence. He'd made it through law school by the skin of his capped teeth and was now the courthouse staff's golden boy, always radiating an angelic charm that was hard to resist.

Even the defendants liked Morgan. And Lottie absolutely adored him. She had made it her goal to see us hitched, even though I'd told her that being hitched was for donkeys and wagons, and if I were to marry Morgan I'd be the ass on that team.

Sadly, now that I no longer had a crush on him, he had suddenly discovered me, a little fact I'd used shamelessly to my advantage. Like now, for instance. "Hey, Morgan!" I called.

He looked around, saw me, and smiled, and I could almost hear a chorus of angels singing a capella from the clouds above him. "Abby! Wow. I heard about what happened to you last Saturday night. You look pretty good for someone who was drubbed two days ago."

"I'm resilient." I nodded my head toward the circus act. "What's that about?"

He looked over at the five women. "They're being brought in for an arraignment."

"What are the charges?"

"Intimidation and resisting arrest."

"I *knew* they weren't waitresses. And that Emperor's Spa isn't a massage parlor, is it?"

Morgan's wide, smooth forehead crinkled in bafflement. "What are you talking about?"

"I'm talking about the so-called massage parlor where those women work."

"Massage parlor?"

"Weren't they arrested at the Emperor's Spa?"

"No, at that new restaurant, the China Cabinet. The girls had a beef with the owner and decided to stage a protest in costume to draw attention to themselves. There was an altercation and someone called the police."

"Those women *are* waitresses?"

"I haven't seen the report yet, but supposedly they attend New Chapel U."

Had my sixth sense failed me? "You aren't aware of any gossip about the Emperor's Spa?"

"Never heard of the place."

So much for Morgan's pulse on the town. He glanced at his watch, grimaced, and started walking backward. "I'm late for court. Why don't you check your calendar and see when you're free for lunch?"

"Will do." Only because I could pump him for information. I gave him a little wave and swung around to find Marco leaning against a tree not ten feet away, watching me with that knowing male gaze that said, *Aren't you ashamed of yourself for your coy, feminine manipulations?* Silly man. Of course I wasn't.

He pushed away from the trunk and joined me as I headed back to Bloomers. "New boyfriend?"

"Old crush. Greg Morgan, deputy prosecutor."

"Aha! Your secret source. Did he tell you about the women?"

"Yes." I tried to sound unconcerned, hoping he wouldn't rub it in.

"Satisfied now?"

I shrugged a shoulder. What a absurd question. I was never satisfied until I had all the facts. We stopped at the street and waited for two cars to pass. "See you later," I called and dashed across.

"Hey! Remember your promise!"

Rats. My promise. Talk about a short memory.

The bell jingled as I walked into Bloomers. Grace was at the front counter waiting on a customer who was buying one of my latest wreath creations. I greeted her with a cheery hello—customers always made me cheery—and continued into the workroom where Lottie was arranging yellow and orange Gerbera daisies in a glass vase filled with yellow marble halves.

"What happened across the street?" she asked, as I pulled an order and gathered my supplies.

I gave her as much information as I had, including the info about the Emperor's Spa that I'd heard from the ladies in the coffee parlor. I stopped short when Grace walked in.

"You needn't stop on my account, dear," Grace said. "I could hear you from the other room."

"Before you say anything, I do remember my vow, and I intend to stick by it."

I glanced at Lottie, who was trying hard not to laugh.

Lottie had already finished the first wire order and was nearly done with the second, so I tackled number three, plus a phone-in order. By noon we had finished them and broke for lunch. I grabbed a turkey sandwich at the corner deli, then, because it was such a beautiful day, I hopped in my Vette and took off for a quick spin on the highway.

I thought best when I was sailing along the open road with the top down and the radio on. Since I was still puzzling over how to approach my ex-fiancé about the groomsman situation, going for a drive seemed a good idea. I took Lincoln Street, the main road east through town, passing neighborhoods of old Victorian houses, aluminum-sided ranch homes, and cedar two-stories, past a park with baseball diamonds, tennis courts, swing sets, and sweaty kids, to Highway 49. From there I headed north toward Lake Michigan and the Indiana Dunes State Park, where I'd spent many summer afternoons swimming, sunning, and climbing the sand hills.

The Indiana Dunes covered more than two thousand acres of primitive landscape on Lake Michigan's southern shore, most of which were wooded and contained the most diversified flora and fauna of the Midwest. I knew this because I had to memorize it for a forestry course in college. What I learned from actually hiking those woods was: 1) use a trail map so you don't get lost; 2) wear long pants to protect against poisonous vines; and 3) always use insect repellent.

Besides its proximity to Lake Michigan, New Chapel was also an hour's drive from Chicago—as long as there was no snow, construction, traffic, sun spots, or anything else that could prevent a driver from reaching a cruising speed of fifty-five miles an hour. New Chapel had the advantage of being near a big city without the disadvantage of *being* a big city.

Getting back to Jillian's dilemma, as I saw it I had to convince Pryce that it would be in his best interests to keep my cousin happy and therefore engaged. Why? Well . . . because Claymore would be heartbroken without Jillian.

Claymore? The original tin man? Pryce would get a good laugh out of that.

Okay, then, because Pryce deserved to be best man and Punch didn't.

Too egotistical on Pryce's part.

Because if she called off the wedding, Jillian would keep her three-carat diamond ring.

Bingo.

The next problem was when to talk to Pryce. My preference would have been Friday night at the country club because it would have presented the perfect opportunity to corner him without the rest of the bridal party in attendance. But Jillian would never have the patience to wait until the end of the week. She could barely make it to the end of a sentence.

Every Friday my family ate dinner at the country club, mostly because my mother had always dreamed of being able to. For a girl raised on a farm, being a member of an exclusive club was the epitome of high society. For the wife of a cop, however, it was an unattainable goal. But now that her sons were members, my mother considered herself as good as in. As she put it, "Blood is thicker than thieves." She'd always had a problem with metaphors.

Coincidentally, the Osbornes also ate dinner there on Fridays, which was convenient when Pryce and I were engaged and awkward thereafter. Because his parents were still horrified that their son had almost married a law school reject, our families had taken to sitting at opposite ends of the dining room so we could politely ignore each other. Thanks to Jillian, that was no longer possible.

Friday night dinner was out, as was a phone call. Pryce hated receiving personal calls during business hours, and I couldn't call him at home because he'd blocked my number. Like I would ever phone him again. That left showing up at his condo, the place where I was to have resided with him in holy matrimony, and I really didn't want to do that.

Still without a solution, I reached the end of the highway, did a U-turn at the entrance to the state park, and headed south again. Ten minutes later my cell phone rang, so I exited onto a side road and pulled over to answer it.

"Abigail?" my mother said breathlessly, as though she were on her treadmill. She hated to waste time on the phone, so she usually combined it with some form of exercise.

"Hi, Mom. What's up?"

"Aunt Corrine is having a get-together for Jillian"— pant, pant—"and her bridal party tomorrow evening. You'll be able to come, won't you?"

There it was—my opportunity to talk to Pryce. "You bet I'll be there."

"Seven o'clock. Oh, and Abigail, I'll be by the shop later this afternoon. I have a surprise for you."

I gasped inwardly. Not *this* afternoon! Not when the Monday Afternoon Ladies' Poetry Society would be meeting in the parlor. "Mother!" I called. "I have to meet with a customer this afternoon. Can you make it tomorrow instead? I'd sure hate to miss your surprise."

I winced, expecting a lightning bolt to zap me for lying.

"Abigail, how sweet. Of course I can bring it tomorrow. I'll see you then."

I dropped my phone in my purse with a groan and made a mental note to warn Lottie and Grace that another surprise was on its way. At least I had averted one potential disaster.

In addition to being a kindergarten teacher, my mother fancied herself a clay sculptress and used my shop as her private art gallery, expecting me to sell her creations for her. I humored her because she was my mother, but Lottie felt no such loyalty and usually managed to sneak the worst of the lot to the basement storage area.

Two weeks ago my mother had brought over a circle of neon-hued, anatomically correct, male monkeys doing the hula, with their hands raised over their heads to hold up a circle of glass. We'd dubbed it the Monkey Table. She'd unveiled her creation just as the poetry society adjourned, and we'd almost had to perform CPR on several of the members. The sight of those cavorting, naked apes was just too much for them.

Since I'd turned off the highway short of my usual exit, I took a different route into town and ended up on Concord Avenue, a north–south business thoroughfare that happened to pass right by the Emperor's Spa. I got a red light and stopped. On the opposite corner, set far back on the lot, was a very drab wood-framed house separated from the beauty shop next door by dual gravel parking lots.

I wouldn't have noticed the shabby building if it hadn't been for the plain white sign on a tall post near the street that proclaimed in bold blue letters EMPEROR'S SPA. There was a phone number underneath but nothing else, not even the normal items you'd expect to see, such as, *Facials: 20% off*. That was definitely odd.

The light turned green, and I pulled forward with traffic, doing a quick check of the spa's parking lot. No cars. The windows were covered on the inside with white paper, so it was impossible to tell if the spa was open. Then I spotted a tiny cardboard OPEN sign someone had slipped beneath the white paper on one of the windows. They certainly weren't going out of their way to attract customers. Or maybe they didn't have to.

Just as I was about to pass I caught a glimpse of black hair and a bright flash of color on a small form darting from the rear of the old house across the gravel lot to the rear of the beauty salon. One of the masseuses going for a haircut?

I was tempted to pull into the salon's lot and check it out, but I recalled Marco admonishing, *"Remember your promise not to meddle."*

Just to prove I was a woman of my word, I didn't stop. Instead, with one last wistfully curious glance, I drove on.

When I returned to Bloomers, Grace was serving tea and scones to the poetry group in the parlor, and Lottie was hard at work in the back, where I could hear her humming a Willie Nelson tune. I tiptoed past the parlor doorway—I always avoided the parlor on Monday afternoons—stuck my head through the curtain to wave to Lottie, then, for the next hour, I manned the front counter.

As I rang up a credit-card purchase for a young couple, I could hear the particularly loud voice of one of the poetesses as she shared her newest ode:

"Canned tuna, canned soup, and some cheese,
And carrots and onions and peas,
Make a casserole dish
That is mighty delish.
The leftovers you can easily freeze."

After four more verses on the delights of casseroles, she received a hearty round of applause for her efforts, and even a few *"bravas."*

That was why I avoided the parlor on Monday afternoons.

The rest of the day zipped by as Lottie and I put together more orders, including an arrangement of colossal proportion for the New Chapel Savings and Loan. They had redecorated the lobby and were having an open house to celebrate. I'd had to practically beg for the job, but I wasn't above a little humble begging if it would bring in more customers. I hummed along with Lottie as we worked together on it, already hearing the *ka-ching* of the cash register.

"Three more customers came in today with the coupons you had printed up last week," Lottie told me as I stripped a long-stemmed Abraham Darby rose of its thorns. The apricot yellow flower with its unique, fruity fragrance was one of my favorites. "The coupons seem to be working."

"That's good, because the contest is a bust." I'd tried two new promotional gimmicks, a coupon for ten percent off a purchase of twenty dollars or more, and a contest called "What's My Vine?" The person who came up with the cleverest name for an ivy in a hand-painted sprinkling can won a bouquet of flowers on the date of their choice. In the three weeks the contest had been running we'd had only eleven entries, and the drawing was two days away.

"Live and learn," Lottie said. "Your cousin's wedding will give us more exposure. How many people are invited?"

"Two hundred for the wedding, four hundred for the reception."

"And her father has to pay for all those mouths?" Lottie let out a low whistle. "I'm glad I have boys, even if there are four of them." She stripped more roses, muttering, "Four, big, loud, brawling, eating machines who think the floor sweeps itself, the food cooks itself, the clothes wash themselves . . ."

Grace came through the curtain to hand me an order and a wicker basket. "Mrs. White would like to pick this up at four o'clock today. Will that be a problem?"

I looked at the order. The woman wanted a summery table centerpiece in pink, yellow, and white. I had just the combination in mind: a variety of buttercup called *Ranunculus asiaticus,* and a creamy pansy called *Viola x wittrockiana* for the yellows; dark pink Gerbera daisies and pale pink peonies for the pinks; and scented jasmine and Madonna lily for the whites. It would be gorgeous. "No problem," I said.

"Also, I have a hair appointment at noon on Thursday. Would you mind if I switched lunch hours with you?"

"Not at all."

As Grace turned to go back through the curtain, I asked, "Isn't your hair salon right next to the Emperor's Spa?"

"Yes, it is," she replied carefully. "Why?"

Who better to ask what was going on at the spa than the girls who worked at the hair salon next door? But could I tell Grace that? Only if I wanted a lecture. "How are their manicures?"

"You don't get manicures."

I held out my stubby nails. "It's high time I started."

CHAPTER THREE

At my announcement, Lottie and Grace glanced at each other. They knew I'd never waste precious dollars for fingernails I'd only break anyway. I winced as Grace went into her statesman's pose, holding the edges of her sweater as though they were lapels. "It was Samuel Johnson who said, 'Curiosity is, in great and generous minds, the first passion and the *last.*'"

Lottie clapped enthusiastically. We were always impressed by Grace's ability to find a quote for every occasion. Usually I joined in the applause, but this time I pretended to be absorbed in picking goo off my knife, hoping to avoid further lecturing.

"You know what that means," Grace said, unwilling to let it go.

"I have a great and generous mind?"

"It means curiosity will be your undoing." With a final nod, Grace marched through the curtain.

"You can stop picking at that blade," Lottie said quietly. "I'm not going to ask why you suddenly need a manicure. You know what my motto is. Don't ask, don't tell."

"You're a wise woman, Lottie Dombowski." I couldn't see any reason to burden her with my plans anyway. With four teenaged sons, she had enough on her plate.

At five o'clock, after Grace and Lottie had gone home for the day, I made a manicure appointment at First Impressions Beauty Salon for Thursday afternoon. Then I set the newly installed alarm system and took off for home.

Home was a second-floor, two-bedroom apartment I shared with my longtime friend Nikki Hiduke and her white cat Simon. Living with Nikki was supposed to have been a temporary arrangement, but after Pryce called off our wedding I stuck around. It worked well because our schedules meshed perfectly—I worked days, and Nikki worked the four o'clock to midnight shift as an X-ray technician at the county hospital. We had our privacy plus weekends together for excursions to the local shopping mall or the beach.

I parked in the lot, let myself into the vestibule of building C, and checked the mailbox, dumping the catalogs and junk mail into the trash container and tucking the rest under my arm. On the steps I met our neighbors, the Samples—a middle-aged, childless couple, and their annoying Chihuahua, Peewee—coming down for a walk. Mr. Sample was a laid-back guy who always had a smile and never said more than two words. Mrs. Sample was an intense, nosy chatterbox. They were the yin and yang of the apartment complex.

Because Peewee's favorite activity was to try to bite my ankles, I normally kept our encounters as brief as possible. Today, however, as I muttered a greeting and prepared to scuttle past, Mrs. Sample blocked me.

"Peewee, tell Abby that her cousin is waiting for her upstairs," she said, holding the dog under the front legs like a child and waving a paw at me. I had to wonder: Does she speak to her husband through the dog, too? *"Peewee, tell Fred that his supper is ready."*

She leaned closer to me to say in a low voice, "Your cousin is such a lovely young woman, and how nice that she's getting married to such an upstanding young man, but honestly, she is a talker!"

Her husband took her arm and tugged her down the steps, still chattering, while I nodded at every third word and backed up, wondering what the heck Jillian wanted now.

"Finally!" my cousin exclaimed, rising from the floor outside my apartment. She made a show of dusting off her slacks and straightening her black silk tee. "Where have you been?"

"At work."

"That was ages ago."

I put the key in the lock and opened the door. "It was ten minutes ago. Hello, Simon." I stopped to scratch the cat under the chin, but upon seeing my cousin he fled to my bedroom, where he would stay until Jillian left the building. Simon hated all men except Marco and loved all women except Jillian. I'd say he was smart, but he was also afraid of throw rugs.

Jillian opened the fridge, found a partial bottle of white wine, and rummaged through the cabinets until she found a wineglass. She refused to drink from a glass that didn't have a stem, yet she had no problem drinking orange juice from the carton. "You've got to talk to Pryce soon, Abby, or I swear Onora is going to kill Punch."

"Want a grilled-cheese sandwich?"

"Sure. I honestly don't understand why Claymore puts up with Punch. He's rude, egotistical—even Flip can't stand him anymore, and Flip gets along with everyone. He and Punch used to be best friends."

I spread butter on slices of whole-wheat bread and slapped them on a hot skillet. "Does Flip have a real name?"

"Phillip Whitcomb."

"What is it that Punch is doing, other than being rude and dumping Onora, that even Flip can't stand him now?"

"Being more obnoxious than usual. He has this big secret he keeps hinting at but won't tell anyone. . . ." She paused to watch me place slices of American cheese on the bread. "Don't you have anything French? Or Dutch at least?"

"You'll survive the cheese, Jill. As far as Pryce is concerned, I'll talk to him tomorrow night. You'll just have to be patient until then." I flipped the sandwiches to brown the undersides, then slid them onto two plates and took them to the living room, where we sat on the sofa and ate to a rerun of *The Simpsons*.

"What do you think Punch's secret is?" I asked, licking the last bit of all-American cheese off my thumb.

"A new girlfriend. He won't tell anyone because he's afraid of Onora's reaction. She has a volatile temper. The way he's been strutting around, though, it's pretty obvious. The whole wedding party came to town two weeks ago and usually they hang out together in the evenings. But for the past week Punch has been leaving around nine o'clock. Flip says he doesn't stagger in until after three in the morning, reeking of flowery perfume."

"Are he and Flip sharing a hotel room?"

"And Bertie. The whole wedding party is staying at the New Chapel Inn and Suites."

"What does Bertie have to say about Punch's behavior?"

Jillian shrugged. "Not much. But you know how Bertie is."

"Jill, I don't even know *who* Bertie is."

"You'll get your chance to meet him tomorrow night." Jillian took her plate to the kitchen, then headed for the door. "Thanks for the sandwich, but honestly, next time make it Brie."

On Tuesday morning, as I walked the track around Community Park, I rehearsed how I was going to broach the best-man problem to Pryce, which caused early-morning joggers to give me wide berth.

"Listen, Pryce, I know you hate my guts, but—" No good. Never assume the worst.

"Hey, Pryce! How's it hanging?" Way too personal.

"I really need your assistance, Pryce." Blink, blink. He'd never go for the helpless routine. I'd just have to play it by ear.

I showered, ate a quick breakfast of cereal and toast, and indulged Simon by tossing a rubber band for him to chase. He was the only cat I'd ever seen who would play fetch, but only with rubber bands and plastic straws. We usually played until he decided the game had ended, which he signaled by suddenly plunking down on the floor and licking himself in areas better left unmentioned. Today, however, I had to end the game so I could make it to work by eight o'clock. Simon's look as I left said, *"Deserter! See if I torture any flies for you today!"*

"Good morning, dear," Grace called from the parlor. She sailed out with a cup of coffee for me. "How are we today?"

"Bracing for a visit from my mother." As I savored the new blend Grace had concocted, I couldn't help but notice the way she floated back to the parlor.

Lottie came out from the workroom with a wrapped bouquet in her hand and nodded in Grace's direction. "Guess who had a hot date last night?"

"Really?" Grace had lost her husband years ago to cancer and until two weeks ago had shied away from dating, claiming a woman in her sixties was beyond such nonsense. Apparently she had changed her mind. I leaned closer to whisper, "Who was it? Mr. Bowling Alley?"

That was our nickname for Richard Davis, owner of Mini-World, a complex that included a miniature golf course, a twenty-lane bowling alley, an arcade, and a fast-food restaurant. He also owned—this is what impressed me most—a 1971 fire-engine red Eldorado Biarritz Cadillac convertible with monster fins on the back.

"You know Grace never tells me a thing," Lottie whispered back. "I happened to hear her on the phone this morning thanking someone for a glorious evening."

As far as we could tell, Grace had been on two dates with Mr. Davis, which was remarkable since he was Grace's exact opposite in terms of temperament and breeding. Where Grace was soft-spoken and genteel, Richard was outspoken and somewhat ribald. Lottie thought it was hilarious, which was why Grace wouldn't talk to her about him.

Lottie set the package on the counter. "A customer by the name of Morelli is coming at nine to pick this up."

"Duly noted. I should warn you that my mother is coming, too."

"What a shame," Lottie said dryly. "I'll be out making deliveries."

"If you'll stay for the art show," I said quietly, "I'll pump Grace for information about her date."

Lottie's mouth pursed as she weighed the offer. She stuck out her hand and we shook on it. I finished my coffee and took the cup to the parlor, where Grace was setting out her bud vases, singing what sounded like an English tune. From what I heard, it was quite bawdy.

"So," I said, following her around the room, adjusting the vases, "how are you?"

She gave me a curious look. "Just fine, dear. Thank you for asking."

While she prepared her machines, I sat at the coffee counter trying to think of something to ask that wouldn't sound obvious. "Good coffee. New blend?" Well, *that* was ingenious. Like she would ever reveal her secret recipes.

She stopped what she was doing to peer at me over her glasses. "I played mini golf with Mr. Davis last night, if that's what you're after."

"You did? Good for you!" I raised my hand to give her a high five.

She didn't raise *her* hand but she did raise an eyebrow, haughtily. "Good for me?"

"I meant good for *him*. He's darn lucky to be going out with you. So, are you . . . ?"

"Going out with him again? Yes, this Saturday he's taking me to dinner. Anything else, dear?" She smiled tolerantly, and I, feeling like a child who'd asked too many questions, slunk away to the workroom.

Lottie looked up from the roses she was trimming. "Well?"

"Richard Davis. Miniature golf. Dinner Saturday. No more questions."

Midmorning I heard the bell jingle, followed by a familiar "Yoo-hoo!" that signaled my mother's arrival. Lottie and I looked at each other across the table, and I could tell she was ready to bolt for the back door. "Remember our deal," I warned her.

Lottie took a deep breath, then we rose in unison and

marched bravely through the curtain to see what latest monstrosity my mother had wrought.

Maureen Barnett Knight—Mo to her friends—was calling directions to a deliveryman as he maneuvered a large, sheet-draped object through our door on his dolly. "More to the left. That's it. Now straight . . . straight . . . a little to the right. There!"

She had on a colorful short-sleeved shirt and coordinating slacks, and her light brown hair was gathered at her nape and held by a gold barrette. She handed the man a tip and turned to us with a happy sigh. "Are you ready?"

Grace joined us, and we all held our breaths, hoping for the best, expecting the worst.

"Voilà!" My mother whipped off the sheet and there it was: a seven-foot, faux-pineapple-barked palm tree—and when I say palm, I don't mean those beautiful fan-shaped green branches. I mean the inside of a green hand—or, in this case, many green hands—on the ends of many bark-coated, curving arms, complete with elbows, stretched out in three directions, front, right, and left, as if begging for alms. The base of her tree sat in a wicker basket complete with tufts of artificial turf sprouting around the trunk like armpit fuzz.

"How clever," Grace said admiringly, while Lottie and I threw puzzled glances at each other.

"Abigail?" my mother said, waiting for my opinion.

"Creative. Very, *very* creative." It was the best I could do.

"I agree," Lottie said quickly. The phone rang and she and I nearly collided in our eagerness to grab it and escape further questioning. She got to it first, put her finger in her ear, and turned her back to us.

"Now, then," my mother said, eyeing the room, "where best to display it?"

Antarctica?

"Why not beside the wicker settee?" Grace suggested, pointing to one of our display props. Unlike me, she seemed to recognize the purpose of the object.

My mother made a face. "Back in the corner?"

"Shading the corner," Grace corrected. "To complement the tropical theme."

I waved at her behind my mother's back and mouthed, *"What is it?"* Grace very subtly mimed putting on a shirt— no, not a shirt, make that a jacket.

Aha! It was a coatrack.

My mother and I tugged and pushed and swiveled her creation into place, then she stood back with her hands on her waist to admire it. "Ideal! Good idea, Grace. Now then, who can use a cup of Grace's wonderful cappuccino? Abigail?" She gave me that guilt-ridden look mothers have perfected, the one that says, *"Say no and trample on my heart."*

"I have five minutes," I warned. "We're very busy today."

If only.

"Your aunt hired a caterer for the bridal soiree tonight," my mother told me as we sipped sweet, foamy coffee by the bay window. "Isn't that just like her to call it a soiree? You will wear something nice, won't you?" By nice, she meant not jeans.

"I'll wear something very nice."

"And don't forget about the bridal shower on Sunday afternoon."

"I'd better not forget. I'm doing the centerpiece for the head table." And that was all I was doing, because Jillian had decided she wanted fancy crystal votives with gold-flecked candles for all the other tables.

"Would you like to ride with me?" Mom asked, her stare boring straight through to the lie that was trying to form in my brain.

The liquid in my cup sloshed at the mere thought of getting into a vehicle with my mother. It would be safer for me to ride a unicycle down the middle of the interstate highway in heavy traffic than to strap myself in beside Mad Mo, whose pleasant demeanor vanished when she got behind the wheel of her monster van. "No, thanks. I have to be there early."

Mom took a sip of coffee and sighed in satisfaction. "It should be a fun afternoon."

"Right. For three hours I get to sit in a room with chicken-salad-and-banana-cake-stuffed women, watching another woman tear her way through wrapped packages while making inane comments."

"Be nice, Abigail. This is your cousin's bridal shower."

I was well acquainted with Jillian's bridal showers; I'd sat through many of them. In all cases it had taken her less time to return the gifts than it had to open them. And then, of course, there were *the games* that preceded the opening of the gifts. Her favorite one was: Make a phrase from the letters in *Jillian Knigh* *Whatever,* such as, "Never will kin jag that hi." The most creative answer won a kitchen towel and dishcloth sewn together to look like a bride. I've never won one. I hope I never do.

My mother patted my cheek. "I'm so pleased you'll be getting to know Jillian's college friends. Who knows? Perhaps you and Pryce will be able to mend fences, too."

I smiled benignly and made a grab for the cream. Mend fences with Pryce? Those fences had not only been dismantled, but the wooden slats had been burned and their ashes scattered over the ranch. This filly was free.

*   *   *

My Aunt Corrine and Uncle Doug lived in a small, exclusive subdivision on the north side of New Chapel, where the streets were curved instead of straight and nothing as common as a sidewalk was allowed to mar the rolling green lawns. Their large, two-story brick home was built on a hill and had a walk-out lower level that opened up onto a brick patio in the rear.

That was where I found Jillian and her bridesmaids, their tall, lithe bodies draped over chaise longues, wearing gauzy blouses and silk pants, their nails done, their hair perfect, the toe rings on their manicured feet glittering. I had on a pale blue denim skirt and white peasant blouse that had probably gone out of style the day before I bought it, and my toes sported nothing but a few stray hairs.

Jillian handed me a chocolate martini and introduced me to the girls. There was Onora, the finicky maid of honor, with red, pouting lips, porcelain skin, and sleek ebony hair to her waist, giving me a bored nod of acknowledgment; Ursula, perched at the foot of Onora's lounge chair, with her angular Germanic looks, pale lipstick, and light blond hair, giving me a friendly but distant smile; and Sabina, a bubbly, dishwater blonde with rosy cheeks and lips, and blue eyes that seemed a little too bright as she hopped up and came over to shake my hand.

"Abby, hi! I'm Sabina. I've heard so much about you. A florist. That must be really exciting."

More exciting than this evening would be.

"The boys aren't here yet," Jillian informed me. "They went golfing today." At twenty-five, they were hardly boys. Then again, I hadn't met them. Some boys never grew up.

She tapped the face of her slender watch. "They should have arrived six and a half minutes ago. But you know how old college chums are when they get together. Oh, I'm sorry. I know that's a sore subject for you."

"I graduated from college, Jill."

She patted my arm comfortingly. "But it was such a struggle."

I took a gulp of martini to keep myself from strangling her. I sat down on a wicker settee next to Sabina, who seemed the friendliest of the lot, and spent the next half hour nursing the drink—which, if not for the fact that it had chocolate on the rim, would have been in the nearest potted plant. From the talkative Sabina I learned that Onora ran an upscale boutique in Manhattan, Ursula managed a home health care business, and Sabina worked as a stockbroker trainee. Not a flunk-out among them.

I was saved from the tedium by Claymore, who walked out through the patio doors followed by Pryce and another of the "boys."

Claymore and Pryce were easily identifiable as brothers. Both wore tasseled leather loafers, crisply pleated slacks, Izod polo shirts with matching sweaters draped over their shoulders, and had perfectly tonsured brown hair and fair skin. Both were also anal-retentive. The only difference between them, other than age, was that Pryce was a corporate lawyer and Claymore was a CPA. I couldn't help but contrast their garb with Marco's standard outfit: black boots, tight jeans, and tighter T-shirt. In my mind, Marco had them beat hands down.

Jillian jumped up and flew into Claymore's arms as though he'd just returned from a two-month walkabout. "I've been worried sick, thinking something terrible had happened to you."

She had certainly hidden it well.

"We were waiting for Punch and Flip," he told her, craning his neck out of her way as she straightened his collar and adjusted the drape of the sweater. "Are they here?"

"Of course not, silly. They're with you."

"As you can see, dearest," he said tensely, "they're not. Flip had mentioned wanting to take photographs around town, and you know how he is when he's taking pictures— completely absorbed. We waited at the hotel for a while, then figured they'd come along eventually." He glanced around at the rest of us and asked nervously, "We did the right thing, didn't we?"

"You always do the right thing," Jillian cooed. She gave his outfit a final tweaking, then grabbed Bertie's hand and pulled him across to where I sat. "Bertie McManus, this is my little cousin Abby," she said as I rose to meet him.

I winced at the word *little*. She'd pay for that remark. She knew I had height issues.

"A pleasure to meet you," Bertie said with a big smile and an Irish lilt.

We shook hands. "Dublin?" I asked.

"County Clare, to tell the truth, not that I always do. Will you tell me where you got that lovely dark red hair that poor Jillian missed?"

I gave her a smug smile and turned my full attention to my new friend. I liked Bertie right off. He didn't put on the affectations the Osbornes did. He had a pleasant face, wore ordinary khakis and a short-sleeve shirt, and had a modest job with a small advertising agency in Manhattan. He was my kind of people.

Jillian handed out more martinis—I took a pass, opting for white wine—and we waited another half hour for the missing boys, making small talk until my eyes glazed over. The only thing that kept me from nodding off was Claymore's anxious pacing. He was a walking mass of nerve ends. Finally, Aunt Corrine came out, conferred with Jillian, then waved us all into their lower-level family room, where a buffet had been set up.

We had just finished loading our plates with an assortment of delectable finger foods and were perched on leather sofas and chairs around the spacious room when a muscular, jock-type guy ambled into the room. He had short, thick brown hair, the tips dyed blond, a square jaw, and a gold punching-bag earring dangling from one earlobe. His face was flushed, as if he'd just run a mile, and his clothes looked like they'd been put on in a hurry. I noticed Onora scrutinizing him from the other side of the room, but I couldn't tell what she thought behind that emotionless expression she wore.

"Punch!" Jillian cried, causing Claymore to drop his quesadilla. "Where have you been?"

"I went to the lake and lost track of the time." The way he'd spit that out, he'd obviously practiced it.

"Where's Flip?" Sabina asked, watching the doorway.

Punch glanced around. "Isn't he here?"

"We thought he was vith you," Ursula said, a little of her Germanic accent coming through.

"Did something happen to Flip?" Sabina asked, starting to look distraught.

"Have a drink and unwind," Pryce said to Punch. "You look like you could use it."

Punch took the glass, then caught sight of me sitting on a sofa between Jillian and Bertie. He sauntered over, his small, beady eyes assessing my boobs. "You must be the flower girl." He leaned over to say with a leer, "You be sure to let me know if your *blooms* need fertilizing."

"You must be Paulin Chumley," I said, ice dripping from each word. "Chump, isn't it?"

He grimaced, then turned to Pryce. "You were right about those thorns, man. Know what I would have done if I'd been engaged to a broad like her?"

"That's enough, Punch," Bertie said in a quiet but firm voice.

Punch swung around to face him, puffing out his chest in true bully fashion. "What are you gonna do, Mr. Small-time Ad Man? Write a nasty advertisement about me?"

"Wouldn't do much good," Bertie said evenly. "You couldn't read it anyway."

Punch's nostrils flared and his huge, meaty hands curled into fists. Anticipating an ugly scene, I was about to jump up and say something brilliant, such as, *"Hey, we're not five years old, are we?"* when suddenly a glass shattered across the room.

I looked around Punch's thick body to see Pryce grab a handful of paper napkins and bend down in front of Onora's chair, where her empty martini glass lay in pieces. Onora sat like a stone statue, her face utterly composed, but her eyes were on Punch and they were livid. Obviously, she had dropped the glass to break up the confrontation. Also obvious was that she was not going to forgive Punch for dumping her anytime soon.

"Didn't I tell you Punch was obnoxious?" Jillian hissed in my ear before jumping up to help Pryce.

I wish I could have said the evening got better, but it merely got hotter, and that applied to tempers as well as the temperature, as we sat around on the patio, torches burning to ward off mosquitoes, waiting for Flip to arrive. The general consensus was that he had gotten a flat tire, otherwise nothing would have prevented him from being there. Apparently he was extremely conscientious when it came to his friends.

The only dissenting opinion was Punch's. He had a few choice comments about Flip being self-centered, moody, and sullen, but I chalked that up to Punch's contentious nature. Nevertheless, it made the others testy and they were quick to rush to Flip's defense.

At ten o'clock, unable to stifle any more yawns, I rose.

"Leaving us already?" Sabina chirped cheerily. She was on her fourth martini and feeling no pain. Thankfully, Pryce had agreed to drive the girls back to their hotel. He was always the designated driver because he never allowed himself more than one drink. He also applied that rule to friends.

I said my good-byes and escaped into the coolness of the house, followed by my cousin, who grabbed my arm and pulled me to a stop before I could make the stairs. "Aren't you going to talk to Pryce?"

"Oh, right." I paused to think. "Tell him your mother has a question and wants to see him upstairs."

I waited in the kitchen, and when Pryce appeared, I said, "Jillian wanted me to have a word with you."

He gave me a wary look. "About what?"

"About your brother. Why don't you walk me to my car?"

"Sorry. Jillian's mother needs my expert legal advice."

"That was just a ploy to get you away from the group."

Watching his ego deflate was always a rewarding experience, even if my ploy did backfire. As we headed for the Vette, I caught my aunt peering from an upstairs window. Within minutes I knew she'd be on the phone with my mother, telling her she'd seen us leaving together. I didn't even want to think about all the explaining I was going to have to do.

"What's the problem with my brother?" Pryce asked, crossing his arms and frowning down at me as I leaned against the door of my Vette.

"No problem, just a request from Jillian. She wants you to be the best man." I slapped my arm, hoping I'd nailed the mosquito that had just bit me. The neighborhood didn't have streetlights, only decorative lamps at the end of each driveway, which didn't make much of a dent on the darkness.

"It's not my decision," Pryce said. "It's Clay's."

"Wrong. It's yours, because if Punch is best man, Onora will *not* be maid of honor, and if Onora backs out, Jillian will call off the wedding, and if Jillian calls off the wedding, she will keep that three-carat diamond ring Claymore probably went into hock to buy her, and if she keeps the ring, Claymore will hate you forever."

He glared at me. "I'll talk to Clay."

"I thought you'd see the wisdom of it."

I slid into my car as Pryce strode back to the house. I had just inserted my key into the ignition when Punch came out of the house. Pretending not to see me, he jogged over to a dark SUV, got in, and sped away. The moment he turned the corner, Onora glided out, got into another car, and left. Not that I really cared, but it seemed pretty obvious she was tailing him.

I started the ignition, turned on my radio, and drove off in the opposite direction, glad to be leaving that bunch behind. I still had to get through the shower, the rehearsal dinner, the wedding, and the reception, but that was only four events. I could handle four events.

Simon's wet nose pushing against my chin woke me up minutes before my alarm went off the next morning. He had an inner clock that never failed. I snuggled with him a few moments, then hit the alarm's Off button and got up to dress for my walk at the track. The phone rang just before I left, and I grabbed it so it wouldn't wake Nikki, snoring soundly across the hall.

"Abby?" Jillian's voice—panicky, on the verge of tears. Nothing unusual about that, only that she was awake so early. "Claymore just called. Flip didn't come home last night. Something must have happened to him."

"It's still early," I said, trying to think what to do. "Don't let fear override your common sense." Common sense? Jillian? What was I saying?

"This is the worst thing that's ever happened to me!" Jillian wailed in my ear.

"No, it's not. Vomiting on your high school gym teacher because she wanted you to climb the rope was the worst thing that ever happened to you."

"I'd just had my nails done. Who could blame me? Oh, Abby, what if Flip is lying dead in a ditch somewhere? Do you know what this will do to my wedding?"

I rolled my eyes, but only Simon was there to witness it, and he was busy cleaning his ear with one paw. I took the phone to the living room and sat on the sofa. "What was Flip driving?

"A rental car—a Ford Taurus or something."

"Is it in the hotel parking lot?"

"No, it's gone, too."

"Has anyone called the police?"

"I don't know. I can't think. You've got to help me, Abby. You always know what to do."

"I'm on my way to the track. Can't Claymore handle it?"

"Claymore? You're joking, right? You know how high-strung he is. His parents gave him a sedative and put him to bed."

"How about Pryce? He doesn't have nerves."

"He's taking depositions all week."

"Flip's parents?"

"Cruising down the Nile. Please, Abby! I need you desperately."

"Okay," I said with a sigh. "I'll see what I can find out."

Nikki emerged from her bedroom in her crumpled pink

pj's, her short dishwater-blond hair sticking up all over. Nikki was tall and lanky and completely believed that there was a prince out there waiting for her to kiss him. Her latest frog was a male nurse named Scott, a very decent sort and, more important, unmarried. I knew this because I'd checked him out. Nikki had been hurt too many times by guys who'd hid their wedding rings from her.

She dropped onto the sofa, yawning. "Who called so early?"

"Jillian. One of her groomsmen is missing—a guy called Flip."

"No kidding! Where is he?"

"Nik, if we knew that, he wouldn't be missing."

"It's too early for logic." She clumped into the kitchen in furry purple slippers in search of orange juice. "What happened last night? Did you talk to Pryce?"

I followed her into the kitchen and gave her the complete rundown on the soiree and ended with Jillian's latest plea for help.

"You can't very well turn her down," Nikki pointed out. "She might ban you from the wedding, and then what would you do with that hideous bridesmaid dress?" She aimed her gaze at the photo clipped to the refrigerator. Jillian had cut it out of a bridal magazine for me. On the other bridesmaids the dresses would look elegant, like a watercolor of tall white tulips swaying gracefully against an aquamarine sky. Give me a red rubber nose and oversized shoes and I could get a job with the circus.

"Omigod!" I grabbed the calendar off the fridge. "I have to go for my fitting tonight."

Nikki downed the juice and put the glass in the sink. "I'm going back to bed. Good luck finding Flick."

It wasn't until I had dialed the police station that I realized what she'd said. "It's Flip," I called, but she was already in her room and might even have been asleep.

The police dispatcher switched me to a grumpy cop who insisted no one had been in a serious or fatal car accident in the previous twelve hours, and who the hell had connected me to his line anyway? He suggested I call lockup, so I did, and gave them Flip's real name and description. No luck there, either. I called the hospital next. Again, no luck, which was actually very good news.

Then where was Flip?

CHAPTER FOUR

"He's not in the hospital, the morgue, or the jail," I reported to Jillian via cell phone as I walked the track. "So maybe he met someone and spent the night at her house."

"Flip isn't like that. He's very shy with women."

"You're just going to have to wait until he shows up, then."

She moaned loud and long. "I knew something would go wrong with this wedding. Why did I ever propose to Claymore?"

"You're such a pessimist. Give Flip a few more hours and he'll show up."

I was wrong. At noon there was still no word on Flip's whereabouts, and even I was starting to be concerned, so I took a stroll down the block to pick Marco's brain.

The Down the Hatch Bar and Grill was teeming with judges and attorneys from the courthouse across the street, in for a hearty lunch together before returning to battle the injustices of the world as well as each other. According to

Lottie, the bar hadn't changed in fifty years, and shouldn't, since it was a piece of local history.

My opinion was slightly different. If a town's history could be represented by a fake carp, a bright blue plastic anchor, a big brass bell, and a fisherman's net hanging from the ceiling, then the town had a major image problem.

Now that Marco had taken the helm there was hope for change. And if the rehab he'd done on his office was any indication, the residents of New Chapel were in for a surprise. The office was sleek and modern, with dove gray walls, silver miniblinds, and black steel and leather furniture. His desk was black and chrome, and that's where I found him, hunched over ledgers, working industriously while the black TV mounted in a corner opposite him was tuned to CNN Headline News—muted, of course. It was a spare, masculine room and it fit Marco to a T.

"What's the problem?" he asked without looking up.

"How do you know there's a problem?" I plunked down in one of the leather director's chairs opposite his desk.

"Because you never come here unless you need my help."

How awful. Was that true? "That's not true!"

He raised his head and fixed me with that penetrating, brown-eyed gaze that could melt a girl's mules. I played it safe and slipped mine off. I couldn't afford a new pair.

"Isn't it?" he asked.

"If you will remember, the first time I ever came here I was delivering flowers."

He got up and came around the desk, all five-foot-ten hunky man of him. He leaned against an edge and folded his arms across his chest. "And you were delivering flowers because . . . ?"

"I don't remember." We both knew I remembered.

"Because *you*," he said, grabbing the end of my nose,

which he once told me was pert, "asked me to find a hit-and-run driver, so we traded favors—twelve of your finest roses for my expert help."

I batted his hand away. "The next time I come here, it will *not* be for your help, expert or otherwise. I promise." I meant it, too.

"Want to put your money where your mouth is?" He smiled a Marco smile, which was a slight upward hitch of one corner of his mouth. He didn't do big emotions; I was sure this was due to his special operations training with the Army Rangers. But his little emotions said a lot.

I gave him a sultry lift of one brow and lowered my voice to husky. "What did you have in mind?" I knew what I had in mind.

"If I win, you have to provide a fresh rose for every one of my tables every night for a week."

Not what I had in mind. "Could you pick something a little less costly?"

There was that adorable little twitch of his mouth again. "What's the point of making a bet if it doesn't cost you?"

"Fine. A rose for every table for a week." Which meant I had to win because I couldn't afford to lose. "And if *I* win?"

He sauntered to his chair, leaned back in it, and folded his arms behind his head. "You won't."

"Arrogant bastard."

"I hope so."

I had to laugh at him. Marco was the only guy I knew who could be arrogant and cool at the same time. "Okay, if I win I want you to make dinner for me. A real dinner, too, not carryout from the bar and grill."

"Deal. So what are you meddling in today?"

"I'd like to remind you once again that I do not meddle. I solve problems. You know this wedding of my cousin's I mentioned? Well, one of the groomsmen is missing in action and Jillian asked me to find him. He was last seen yesterday afternoon at the hotel where the wedding party is staying. I called the police, the jail, and the hospital with no luck. Since you're the professional PI, I thought you might advise me as to what to do next."

"Why isn't the groom looking?"

"His nerves can't take it. And the missing man's parents are in Egypt. I already asked." I smiled at him expectantly.

Marco scrutinized me for a long moment, probably trying to decide if it was worth the effort to argue me out of it. Finally he said, "Okay, here's what I'd do. I'd start by notifying the police he's MIA, then I'd interview his friends to find out his interests and where he likes to hang out. That should give you a clue where to look. It's probably nothing more than the guy got drunk and is sleeping it off somewhere, but you don't want to take any chances."

"I'm sure he'll turn up before then. If not, I'll be seeing the other bridesmaids tonight. I'll start my questioning with them."

At three o'clock that afternoon I drove into a ritzy neighborhood near my aunt's, parked in front of Trudee DeWitt's sprawling pink brick home, gathered my purse and notebook, and got out of the car. Trudee was standing in the doorway arguing with a teenaged girl with pink spiked hair and dangle earrings made of beer caps.

"You'd better be home at six o'clock on the dot, young lady, or—hi, Abby, I'll be with you in a minute—you'll be grounded for a month! Heather? Do you hear me?"

"Whatever."

"Don't give me *whatever*. I hate that word."

"Could you yell it any louder, Mother? My eardrums are already bleeding."

"You think *that's* loud? I'll show you loud. Go on inside, Abby. I'll be right there."

As the argument raged on, I let myself into the house through huge, double doors, where I gaped at the immense space around me. The home had only one floor, but the ceiling rose a full two stories high, a vast, oak-beamed structure with big skylights and hanging fans. I couldn't begin to imagine what their heating bill was like.

Trudee's husband, Don, was a self-made multimillionaire who had started his career selling bottled water. Trudee had been a savvy hair stylist who knew how to spot potential. She'd convinced Don to shave off his full beard, ditch the farmer's overalls, and hire her as his accountant.

Now they jointly owned the water bottling plant, a fleet of trucks, and a vacation home in the Bahamas, where she'd developed a penchant for the tropics. She had decorated her New Chapel house accordingly, with lots of wicker and rattan, sisal rugs over Mexican quarry tile floors, an indoor waterfall, and ceiling fans with fake palm leaves for blades.

"Teens!" Trudee exclaimed, shutting the doors behind her. "What was I thinking?"

Trudee was built like a centerfold from the forties—hourglass shape, gorgeous gams, and an affinity for high heels, short shorts, and sleeveless shirts tied under her bust. Her hair color was different every time I saw her. Today it was a shiny auburn, long and full of big curls. It had to kill her to see her daughter sporting hair by Kool-Aid.

"Let's go back to the kitchen. I've got beer cooling in the fridge."

I passed on the beer and took a glass of lemonade instead, settling on a bamboo stool at the granite-topped island. "So when is the party?" I asked, trying not to pucker. Clearly, someone had skimped on the sugar. I did a quick scan of the kitchen, looking for signs of a sugar bowl.

"On the Fourth of July."

That was a problem. How was I going to decorate this huge house in addition to all I had to do for Jillian's wedding? I pushed the lemonade aside and walked through the house, doing mental calculations. If I could pull it off, Trudee's party would pay for the ugly bridesmaid dress *and* a gift for the bride and groom. "What time is your party?"

"Six o'clock for a barbeque. I've got my caterer lined up already. All I need is for you to come in and decorate."

If I decorated Trudee's house in the morning and the reception hall in the afternoon, I should still have time to shower, dress, and be back for the wedding. "Okay. It's doable. Let's talk theme."

Trudee strutted around the room, making large arm gestures as she described her *vision,* as she called it. I probably would have said *hallucination,* but I wasn't a psychologist. I took notes and drew sketches, then told her I'd run up an estimate and get back with her in a few days.

When I got home, Simon was waiting for me at the door, a straw at his feet and an expectant look on his face. I tossed the straw, and when he went to fetch it, I played the message waiting on the machine.

"Abby, it's Jillian. Flip still isn't back and I'm worried sick." Then, in a breezy tone, "I'll see you at the bridal boutique at seven thirty. Don't forget to bring heels."

Heels? To make that dress work I'd need stilts.

Betty's Bridal Shop was in an old, Victorian-style house three blocks north of the courthouse, a typical style for shops that weren't on the square. According to a study done at New Chapel University, people were more likely to open their wallets in old, comfortable surroundings, such as a Victorian house. My hunch was that the study was funded by a local contractor.

When I arrived, the other bridesmaids were waiting in the front parlor. Onora was seated on a red tufted settee, picking off her nail polish, a sulky look on her face; Sabina was rummaging through the dresses hanging on a wall rack; and Ursula, seated beside Onora, was flipping through a bridal magazine. Sabina saw me and bounced over to say hi. Ursula held up a hand and smiled. Onora lifted her index finger and dropped it again, obviously sapped of energy.

"Jillian isn't here yet," Sabina informed me. "She had to wait for Claymore and she wasn't happy about it."

"Claymore is coming?" I asked.

"He vants to be involfed," Ursula remarked from across the room. "He was feeling left out."

"He's a nervous wreck," Sabina added. "I think he just wants to keep his mind off Flip."

Speaking of whom, now was the perfect time to start delving. "How long have you known Flip?" I asked her.

Sabina glanced at Onora, as if asking for permission to talk, but Onora studiously ignored her. "I met him my senior year of college." She leaned closer to whisper, "I dated Punch briefly, and Flip was always hanging around us. That's how I got to know him."

"Why are you whispering?" I whispered.

"Because Onora doesn't like to be reminded that there were other women in Punch's life. She's very jealous." Then, in a normal voice Sabina continued, "Flip is a really private person, always keeps to himself. He owns a rare and used bookstore in Chelsea. He wasn't one to participate in clubs in college. He took photos, read literary stuff. Kind of a loner."

"He has issues," Onora muttered, her gaze never leaving her nails.

"Issues?"

She shrugged. If she knew more, she wasn't telling.

Jillian breezed in and she was in a stew. "Sorry for the delay."

"Where's Claymore?" Sabina asked.

"He's parking the car. Shall we get started?" Jillian signaled the saleswoman who had been hovering nearby, guarding the dresses Sabina had been fingering.

Sabina volunteered to go first, bouncing into the curtained dressing room to don the gown, after which she stood on a low stool in front of us, before a three-way mirror, so the seamstress could pin the hem. I took one look at her waspish waist and trim hips and made a quick decision to go last, hoping the others would leave before it was my turn to be embarrassed from three angles.

Claymore strode in looking pinched and pale. He saw Jillian perched on the end of the settee and went to stand beside her. Jillian turned her head away. Time to show him who was boss.

While Sabina was being pinned, I wandered over to the dress rack on the pretense of looking through it. Seeing so many pretty, solid-color dresses, I wanted to choke Jillian for having such deplorable taste, but since my main objective was speaking to the man standing behind her, biting his nails down to stubs, I suppressed my killer instincts and homed in on the fiancé.

"How's it going, Claymore?" I said casually.

He stopped biting and looked around as if surprised to find me there. "Not well. Not well at all."

"Which is why you should be home in bed," Jillian said through clenched teeth.

"Still no word, huh?" I said.

"Nothing." He looked faint. I thought I caught a twitch in his right eye.

"Did Flip ever go off by himself at school?"

"Sometimes he'd drive to the coast on his own. He loved

to walk the beaches with his camera. He's quite the pho-tographer, you know."

"He wrote poems there, too," Sabina added brightly.

"Did he ever stay away more than a day?" I asked Clay-more.

"Sure. He'd be gone for the entire weekend. His family always went to the ocean in the summer, so it was kind of his thing."

"Then maybe he's at the dunes now," I suggested.

Jillian scoffed at the idea. "He doesn't even know how to get there."

Hearing that, Claymore started to hyperventilate. Jillian instantly pushed him down on the settee and fanned his face with a magazine. "What is it, precious?" she asked, sud-denly concerned for his well-being.

"He knows the way. I took him there. To the dunes. Flip wanted to see the bird blind Pryce and I had made when we were kids. We all went out there."

Bird blind. Right. Make-out spot was more like it. "Is that blind still there?" I asked.

Claymore nodded miserably.

As Jillian cooed over him I said, "But even if Flip did go there on his own, he wouldn't have stayed the night, would he? It gets chilly up there at night."

No one had an answer.

"Next," the seamstress called. Ursula unfolded her long legs and glided off.

"Does Flip have any hobbies other than photography and writing poems?" I asked.

"That's it," Jillian said, still fanning. "He's obsessed with nature photos. He'll spend hours waiting for a perfect shot of a silly bird."

"They aren't silly, Jillian," Sabina said, looking per-turbed. "They're beautiful." To me she said, "He's an excellent photographer. His work was always on display at the university."

I paused to suck in my breath as Ursula came out. No way was I going to expose my abbreviated torso to these women. "Does Flip go to bars?" I asked Claymore.

He pushed the magazine out of his face. "Not that I know of. In college we took him a few times, but he didn't enjoy it."

"He knows a lot about wine, though," Jillian said to Claymore. "I saw him admiring your father's wine collection."

"Next," the seamstress announced. I pretended not to hear her, so Onora raised herself from the settee with a resigned sigh and drifted off. She was back within two minutes. The clothes must have just slid off her body.

"Does Flip have friends other than you, Bertie, and Punch?" I asked Claymore, as Onora took her place in front of the mirrors.

"I don't know. Talk to Punch. They were friends before college, maybe as far back as elementary school."

"Next." The seamstress aimed a "gotcha" smile at me.

I sidled up to Jillian and said quietly, "Since everyone else is finished, why don't you take the gang back to the Osbornes' house and I'll meet up with you later?" Like I would ever set foot in *that* house again.

She looked shocked. "And leave you here alone?" She put an arm around my shoulders. "I can't ditch my little cousin."

"Sure you can." I put my arm around her waist and gave her a discreet pinch for calling me little. "In fact, I insist."

"Ouch! Okay, fine. Come on, everyone. Let's go back to Claymore's house."

I watched them file out and only then did I march resolutely into the dressing room to do battle with the garment.

As I stood in front of the mirror peering at my reflection through eyes scrunched halfway shut—a secret I discovered that makes me look taller and thinner—my cell phone rang.

"Excuse me," I said, holding up the partially pinned hem as I stepped off the stool. "I have to get this." Ignoring the woman's disgruntled glare, I grabbed the phone from my purse.

"Abby?" Jillian said excitedly. "We just got a call from Punch. He found Flip's car at the dunes parking lot, but there's no sign of Flip. We're going there now to search for him."

"I'll meet you there." I closed the phone, tossed it in my purse and dashed to the dressing room. "I'll have to come back tomorrow," I called to the seamstress from behind the curtain as I unzipped the outfit and shimmied out of it. "It's something of an emergency. Ouch!"

"Be careful of the pins," she called dryly.

Twenty minutes later I pulled into the Indiana Dunes State Park main entrance and drove up to the guard station where I was informed the park would close in fifteen minutes. I had to fork over the entry fee anyway.

In the nearly deserted parking lot I spotted four vehicles: one old VW Beetle off in a far corner by itself, its body spray painted in various colors to look like it had been tie-dyed; and three new vehicles, side-by-side. One was a navy Taurus, another I recognized as the big SUV Punch had driven the night before, and the other was Claymore's silver Lexus sedan. I pulled up beside the Lexus and got out. Bertie was standing at the open trunk handing out flashlights.

"No word yet on Flip's whereabouts?" I asked Jillian, as Sabina and Ursula sprayed each other with insect repellant. I declined the bug spray, sparing my sensitive skin the effects of the poison. I had on chinos anyway, so my legs were covered.

"Nothing." Jillian shined a flashlight at the Taurus. "But that's his rental car."

The windows were open, so I stuck my head through on the driver's side to look around.

"I already looked," Bertie told me. "Nothing there."

I turned around and did a quick head count. Punch, Onora, and Pryce were missing. "You're three short."

"We think Punch went ahead to search," Bertie said, handing me a flashlight.

"Pryce had to prepare for a deposition tomorrow," Claymore reported.

Gee. What a shame. "How about Onora?"

"She didn't come back to the Osbornes' with us," Jillian answered. "She wasn't feeling well."

"She gets migraines," Ursula explained.

"I tried to reach her on her cell phone after Punch called me," Jillian said, "but she didn't answer, so I left a message, not that it will do any good. She'd never find her way here. She has a terrible sense of direction."

"That's vat you said about Flip," Ursula reminded her.

"This way," Claymore called, heading across the parking lot.

"Where are we going?" Jillian asked, hurrying to keep up with him.

"To the bird blind. Punch said Flip's camera was missing from the hotel room, so my hunch is that he went there to do some photography."

"If something happened to him, I'm sure the park rangers would have found him," I said. "They check these trails regularly."

"They'd never spot him in the blind," Bertie said in his

charming lilt, falling into step with me, "unless they knew to look there."

"You've been to the blind?"

"With Clay and Flip."

We passed a ranger station and crossed a sandy beach area where a lone couple lay on a blanket, necking. Six people tramped past them and they never broke lip-lock. Now that's concentration.

We followed the signs for trail number three and headed into the woods single file—Claymore first, then Bertie, me, Ursula, Jillian, and Sabina—our flashlight beams throwing circles of light in front of us so we could avoid low-hanging branches and the occasional gopher hole, not to mention snakes that might be slithering across the path. Ten minutes into the walk, Claymore turned off the trail and pushed through heavy brush to the left. Like a unit of soldiers we dutifully followed, fighting the thorn-covered branches that snagged our hair and tore at our clothing.

"Punch!" he called, his hands cupped around his mouth. "Flip! Can you hear me?"

I hoped they were the *only* ones who could hear him. Anyone else would think he was calling out acrobatic exercises.

We all began to call, following Claymore up a scrubby dune to the top, where through the tree branches I could just make out the glittering surface of the lake as the moon reflected silver on the ripples. It was a beautiful spot, well hidden and filled with the heavy fragrance of jasmine. It was a perfect meeting place for lovers.

"The blind is over here," Claymore said, shining his light on a semicircle of thick shrubby plants in front of him. He circled around behind it and came to a sudden stop, staring down with mouth agape.

Bertie stepped up for a look and crossed himself.

I pushed between them. In front of me lay a man sprawled in the sand, his face turned toward the ground as if he'd fallen straight forward. The back of his head and the sides of his face were covered in blood, as was a blanket next to him, where he'd obviously bled out.

As Bertie crouched down to check the wrist for a pulse, I reached for my cell phone to call an ambulance.

"He's dead," Bertie said, looking up at us in disbelief.

"Who's dead?" Sabina asked, coming up from behind, her voice rising steadily toward hysteria.

"Is it Flip?" Ursula asked, peering over my shoulder for a look.

"I knew something terrible had happened to Flip," Jillian cried. "I knew it!"

Bertie moved the beam up to the face. "It's not Flip," he said. "It's Punch."

CHAPTER FIVE

"That can't be Punch," Jillian said adamantly as I opened my cell phone and dialed 911. She shined her light on the man's bloody right ear, where a hole in the lobe was visible. "See? No punching-bag earring."

"Oh, God! Someone bashed in his skull," Claymore said, then clutched his stomach and staggered to a bush about two yards away, where I could hear him retching.

"Maybe it's someone who looks like Punch," Sabina offered hopefully.

"It's him," Bertie said. "Take a look at his hands."

Five beams focused on his hands, thick meaty slabs with heavy fingers, three of which wore heavy gold rings that could very well have served as brass knuckles. "It's Punch," several voices said together.

"I'd like to report a murder," I said to the dispatcher, turning away from the gruesome sight. I gave directions, then turned back to find Bertie poking around in the tall sedge several feet from the scene.

"I found the murder weapon," he called.

We gathered around as he parted the thin reedy grass for

a better look. The light glimmered off a rectangular, silvery object, one corner coated in blood, pieces of scalp, and short strands of two-toned hair.

"Is it a gun?" Ursula asked.

Bertie crouched down for a better look. "It's Flip's camera. I'd know that fancy strap anywhere."

"Flip is strong enough to kill Punch vith his camera?" Ursula asked. "I don't think so."

"Is the camera strong enough?" I asked.

"It's a professional photographer's camera," Bertie explained and reached toward it.

"Don't touch it," I warned him, causing him to jerk his hand back. "The police will want to check it for fingerprints."

Sabina began to sob, and Jillian dug for her phone.

"Let's move away from here so we don't disturb things more than we already have," I suggested. "We'll go back the way we came, single file, and wait for the police in the clearing back there."

"What about Flip?" Bertie asked. "Shouldn't we keep looking for him?"

"Maybe he's dead, too," Ursula said, which made Sabina cry harder.

Jillian shut her phone with a snap. "Onora still isn't answering. She must have taken a sleeping pill."

"Maybe she's not there," I said.

"Of course she's there," Jillian replied, but she didn't sound totally convinced. "Where else would she be?"

We gathered about ten yards down from the blind. Claymore paced, jingling coins in his pocket. Bertie kept watch, in case the killer was still in the area. Sabina wept, and the rest of us whispered together, still trying to absorb the shock of finding Punch's body. In the distance sirens wailed.

"I killed him," Claymore said in a hoarse voice, coming to a stop beside Jillian.

As we all turned to stare at him, Jillian said, "Clay, don't be silly. You wouldn't harm a fly." She shifted several inches away, just to play it safe.

"Claymore," I said, "do *not* say that to the police unless you actually did kill him. They tend to take statements like that seriously."

"Well, I'm the one who showed him the blind."

"Come on, Clay," Bertie said. "Go easy on yourself, boyo. You didn't know someone wanted Punch dead."

"Are you serious?" Jillian asked. "I know a lot of people who wanted Punch—"

I stuck my hand over her mouth. "Now is not the time to be snide, Jill."

"I suppose it could have been accidental," Sabina said, wiping her eyes.

Jillian peeled my fingers off her mouth. "I'll bet it was Punch's new girlfriend. She probably conked him when he got rough with her."

"We don't know that he had a girlfriend," Sabina reminded her.

"Then where did he go every night?" Jillian retorted. "And why did he strut around, acting like he had this big secret?"

No one had a better answer.

"The problem with Jill's theory," I said, "is that Punch was hit on the back of the head," I patted my skull to demonstrate, "and fell face forward, which indicates to me that someone hit him from behind when he wasn't expecting it. If he and this mystery woman were engaged in sex play, rough or not, how did she get behind him to hit him with that much force?"

"Are you saying she couldn't have been behind him?" Jillian argued, unsheathing her claws.

"Just that it's not likely. But for argument's sake, let's say this mystery woman *was* behind Punch and slugged him with Flip's camera. How did she get Flip's camera?"

Jillian glowered at me. She hated having her theories disputed. "Maybe Punch brought his mystery girlfriend out here, and Flip was already here taking his silly bird photos—"

"They're not silly," Sabina protested. "Stop saying that."

"Maybe Flip vas upset when they interrupted him, and he left vithout his camera," Ursula finished for Jill.

Bertie scoffed at that idea. "First of all, Flip wouldn't leave an expensive camera behind, and second, Punch couldn't take photos in the dark."

"So you're saying it vas Flip?" Ursula asked Bertie, seemingly intrigued by his opinion.

"He shouldn't be ruled out."

"Let's think about this carefully," I said. "Jillian called me at eight thirty, and it was nearly dark then. She told me Punch had found Flip's car but not Flip. Right, Jill?"

"I guess." She was pouting.

"If Punch had come across Flip at the blind sometime after eight thirty, it would have been dark, and without the right equipment, I doubt anyone would have been doing any photographing at that point. And like Bertie said, Flip wouldn't walk away from a good camera just because he was interrupted."

"Perhaps Flip was already gone when Punch was murdered," Claymore offered, still looking a little green.

"Then why was his camera still here?" Bertie asked.

"Maybe Punch borrowed it earlier to take photos of his girlfriend," Jillian offered, her arms folded defensively, as if daring me to contradict her again.

"In that case, Punch would have found Flip here," I said. "Wouldn't he have called you back to tell you? He knew everyone was worried."

"Perhaps he was attacked before he could make the call," Claymore said.

"We need to find Flip," Jillian said. "He'll know if there's a mystery woman."

"Maybe we should get the film out of the camera," Bertie said, rising to his feet. "It might show us who was here."

"Not a good idea," I told him. "The police dislike evidence tampering."

"Should I call Pryce?" Claymore asked, rubbing his temples. "In case we need a lawyer?"

"Why would we need a lawyer?" Sabina asked instantly.

Bertie paced in the sand behind us. "I suppose we'll be considered suspects."

"Why?" Sabina asked, screwing up her face in preparation for another sobbing session. "It was Flip's camera."

"Any of us could have borrowed it," Bertie reminded her. "You were in our hotel room yesterday, too."

"But we were all together this evening," Sabina protested.

"Not true," I said. "All of the women were together."

"And Claymore," Jillian added, rubbing his shoulder comfortingly.

"By the way," I said, "*did* any of you borrow the camera?"

They looked around at each other and each one said no. It would be interesting to see what was on the film, not to mention whose prints were on the case.

"Maybe Onora killed Punch," Ursula said to me, with the cock of an eyebrow, as if she were enjoying the prospect. "She did leave to go back to her room alone."

"Do you think she's capable of it?"

Jillian sniffed, as if the whole idea were ridiculous. "Onora can barely lift a camera, let alone heave it at someone hard enough to kill him."

"She's stronger than she looks," Sabina said. "At school, when she heard that I went out with Punch, she picked up my desk chair and threw it across the dorm room."

"Sounds like she has a temper," I said, and Sabina nodded emphatically.

"This is just wonderful," Jillian snapped. "My wedding party is turning on each other. Isn't it like Punch to pull something like this?"

Claymore turned his head to stare at her.

"What?" she asked.

"I doubt he purposely got himself murdered, Jill," I said quietly.

"At least this solves the best-man situation," she said morosely.

Across from me, Sabina started to weep again, and Bertie put an arm around her. The rest of us stared at Jillian in disbelief.

"What?" my clueless cousin asked again.

"I'm sure of one thing," Claymore said. "Flip isn't a murderer."

"Then where is he?" Bertie asked.

There was a rustling behind us, and I looked around, hoping to see the missing Flip. Instead I found myself staring straight into the beams of powerful flashlights.

"Abby Knight?" one of the voices behind the light called out.

I shaded my eyes with my hand. "That's me."

Three cops came forward. I recognized one of them immediately—Officer Sean Reilly. He was a good-looking man in his early forties, well trained, physically fit, and as

far as I could tell, honest. He and Marco had worked together to aid in my rescue less than a week earlier.

"How's it going?" I asked him.

"I was actually having a quiet evening—until now." He
shined his light on the others. "Is anyone here injured?"

"No," I answered, since the group was staring at the cops
like a herd of deer caught in the headlights. "Not unless you
consider recently dead an injury." I pointed toward the
blind. "The body is up there, and so is the murder weapon."

"You found the murder weapon?"

"Bertie did, actually," I said, and Bertie lifted his hand to
identify himself. "He found it in the reeds about one yard
west of the body. None of us touched it, by the way."

"A gun?"

"A camera."

Reilly turned to the two cops. "Let's secure this area and
call the coroner." As they moved into action, he pulled a
small notebook and stubby pencil out of his chest pocket. "I
need some preliminary information. Was the victim dead
when you got here?"

When no one spoke up, I decided I'd better say something or Reilly was going to get testy. "Yes," I said, and the
others nodded in agreement.

"Was anyone with him?"

"No."

"Did you see anyone leave the vicinity?"

"No."

"Was the victim a friend of yours?"

"Of theirs," I said, hitching a thumb toward the gang of
mutes.

"And you're here because you like to meddle?"

My turn to get testy. "I do not meddle; that is a vicious
rumor undoubtedly started by Marco. I'm only here because my cousin Jillian—raise your hand, Jill—asked me

to come help her look for her groomsman, who's been missing for two days, by the way."

"So the victim has been missing for two days," he said, writing.

"No, that's a different groomsman."

He looked at me from under skeptical eyebrows. "You've got a missing groomsman and a *dead* groomsman?" He shook his head as he jotted the information in his notebook. "Sounds like a fun wedding."

"Tell me about it," Jillian said.

"Jillian is the bride," I explained, after he gave her a glance. "Flip is the one who's missing."

Reilly paused, his pencil in the air. "Flip?"

"You know, I had that same reaction." I smiled, but Reilly's icy look killed it. "As it turns out," I continued with a straight face, "Flip is his nickname. His real name is Phillip Whitcomb."

"Whitcomb with a *b*," Jillian added. "Everyone forgets the *b* because it's silent."

"Just like Flip," Sabina said with a sniffle.

"And the victim's name?" Reilly asked, ignoring the dramatics.

"Punch," I replied. "Again, a nickname. Real name Paulin Chumley—so you can understand the need for a nickname. I don't know what his parents were thinking. Punch came out here looking for Flip and spotted Flip's car in the parking lot. Then he called Claymore." I hitched my thumb in his direction. "He's the groom, and that's his real name. And then Jillian called me, and here I am."

Reilly gave me a look that said, *Another calamity, eh, Jane?* "Am I to understand, then, that the victim's car is in the parking lot?"

"It was there when we arrived. We haven't checked lately."

"What about the missing person's car?"

"It was there, too."

"Anyone have a phone number for the victim's parents?"

"I can get it for you," Claymore said.

Reilly glanced over his notes, then closed the notebook. "That's enough for now. I'm getting a headache. Everyone have a seat." He started toward the blind and I followed.

"That means you, too," he called over his shoulder.

Of course it did. I U-turned and went back to the group.

Several more cops joined the party, along with two park rangers, a coroner, and a two-person crime scene investigative team. After receiving orders from Reilly, the cops began doing interviews, taking each one of us some distance away so we couldn't hear what anyone else was saying, although I did catch the sounds of Sabina's noisy sobs.

Reilly conducted my interview, and behind him I could see the bright flash of cameras as the investigators did their work. I wasn't much help with personal information about Punch, but I did give him good time references. Reilly seemed most interested in what I knew about the three absentees, especially Flip, since his camera appeared to be the instrument of death. Other than providing information about Pryce, I wasn't much help in that area. Although I would have loved nothing more than to see my ex-fiancé put under a hot lamp and grilled like a leg of mutton, I did concede that he was a busy lawyer, and it was very likely that his excuse for not joining us was legitimate.

In truth, I told Reilly, Pryce wasn't really a part of their inner circle, and had only been included in the wedding party because he and Claymore shared the same dysfunctional but highly elite gene pool. Reilly didn't think that last line was funny, which was fine because I hadn't meant it to be.

He tapped the end of his pencil on his notepad as he

glanced through his scribbles. "Who among those here would you say the victim was closest to?"

I paused to look back at the group. Certainly not Jillian, or Sabina. Ursula didn't seem particularly close to any of them. Bertie hadn't exactly sung Punch's praises. Claymore had apparently only asked him out of duty, and Pryce didn't know him that well, since he'd graduated two years before. That left Onora and Flip, I told Reilly. I didn't dish the dirt about Onora because what I knew about her being angry with Punch for dumping her was pure hearsay. But I did start to wonder what her alibi would be.

"You'll be able to get prints off the camera, right?" I asked. "That should tell you a lot."

"Depends on how many people used it. Right now that and the film are our best shots."

"What about footprints?"

"Since all of you trampled the sand around the body I doubt we'll find much there."

"Sorry. If I'd known I was going to find a body I would have been more careful. One thing I forgot to mention, and I don't know if it's significant or not, but Jillian noticed that Punch's gold earring is missing. Apparently he wears it— wore it—all the time."

Reilly wrote it down, though he didn't seem very impressed.

"And one other thing," I said, catching him before he walked away, "I know it looks bad right now, but I truly don't believe Flip—Phillip—is your murderer."

"And yet you told me," he paused to check his notes, "you don't know him. In fact, you've never met him."

I bent to scratch the top of my sandaled foot, which had started to itch ferociously. "I don't understand it myself, but it's this strong gut feeling I get about things. I mean, look at the evidence—a bloody camera owned by a missing groomsman—it's just a bit too obvious, don't you think? Like those TV shows where you think it's the first guy— the jealous co-worker— and then it turns out to be the victim's barber who'd been stiffed a tip one time too many?"

Reilly put his notebook and pencil away. "But this *isn't* TV, remember? When we find strong evidence pointing to one perp, as a rule we've got our man."

"Okay, you said as a rule," I countered, "which means it could be that—"

"Thank you, Ms. Knight," Reilly said. "That will be all for now."

A flashbulb went off near our faces, temporarily blinding me. I glanced around to find a seedy-looking man with two cameras hanging around his neck getting ready to shoot a picture of Jillian and the gang. Another man came scurrying toward us, notepad in hand, causing Reilly to mutter, "Just what I needed to cap my evening, a nosy reporter."

By midnight, the scene of the crime had been cordoned off with yellow police tape, the photographers had packed up their equipment, the coroner was preparing to move the body, police and park rangers were conducting a search for Flip, and we had all been interviewed and fingerprinted. I was the only one of the group, however, who had been targeted as food by sand fleas. The little buggers had crawled under the legs of my chinos for a bedtime snack. So much for the protection of pants. I had broken my own rule about using insect repellent and now I would pay for it.

"You should have sprayed," Jillian scolded, as I raked the skin around my ankles.

"I know that, Jill."

She put her hands on her hips and gave me a glare. "Don't get snippy with me. You're always the one preaching about using bug spray."

"I don't preach."

"Yes, you do."

Reilly came over to where we stood facing off like mortal combatants, our teeth chattering slightly in the cool night air. "Okay, ladies and gentlemen, time to go home. Just make sure you don't leave the county. And I want to know the minute any of you hear from your friend Phillip."

"Don't you think you'll find him?" Sabina asked, her eyes still bloodshot from crying. "His car is here. He *has* to be here. You'll keep looking, won't you?"

"Come on, Sabina," Bertie said, looping an arm through hers. "Let's let the police do their work."

"What if he's hurt, Bertie?" she whined. "What if he's staggering around in the woods in the dark, dripping blood? What if a cougar smells blood and attacks him?"

"We don't have cougars," I told her. "Just squirrels, raccoons, deer, and a few coyotes."

I shouldn't have mentioned the coyotes. As we headed back down the trail, Claymore again in the lead, Sabina clung to us fearfully, muttering to herself about bloodthirsty coyotes. When we got down to the parking lot, the old VW Beetle was gone, but Flip's rental car was still there. We had checked the inside earlier, but no one had opened the trunk. Now I thought it might be a good idea just in case Flip had been bound and gagged and thrown inside.

"You probably shouldn't touch that," Claymore said as I approached the driver's side. "Fingerprints, and all."

"I know that, Claymore. Jill, do you have a pen handy?"

"You should probably call the police," Claymore added nervously.

"Do you want to run back up and get them?" I asked him. "And waste valuable time?"

Jillian pulled a sterling silver pen from her purse and handed it to me.

"Not the *Montblanc,*" Claymore cried.

"I'm not going to chisel my way into the trunk with it."
I walked up to the driver's window, leaned in, and used it
to press the trunk release.

Everyone hurried around to take a look, five flashlight
beams aimed inside. I edged between Jillian and Bertie and
peered into the hollow, but that's what it was, hollow. Not
a clue to Flip's whereabouts to be found.

"What are you looking at?" said a soft-spoken male
voice behind us.

I glanced around to see a tall, slender man in hiking
shoes and khaki shorts, a brown T-shirt with a World
Wildlife Fund logo on it, pale skin, and fine, brown hair
swept to one side, holding a hand over his eyes as six bright
circles of light swept over him.

"Flip!" Sabina cried joyfully and stretched out her arms
to welcome him.

CHAPTER SIX

He was covered in nasty red bites, had sand stuck to his arms and legs, and looked disoriented.

"Where have you been?" Bertie asked as everyone crowded around.

Flip turned to point down toward the lake with one hand. The other hand he kept on his forehead. "Down there, somewhere."

"Didn't you hear us calling?" Jillian asked crossly. "Do you have any idea what you've put us through?"

"Take it easy, Jillian," I said, squeezing her arm. "Flip, are you feeling all right?"

He looked at me and said in childlike wonderment, "Who are you?"

"I'm Abby, Jillian's cousin. Does your head hurt?"

"My head?" He stared at his hand as if he hadn't realized it had been on his head. Then his knees sagged and he grasped Bertie's shoulder to keep from collapsing.

"Let's get him on the ground," I said. Claymore and Bertie helped him sit, his back against the car. He promptly leaned his head back and closed his eyes.

"Did you hit your head?" I asked him.

He said in a faint voice, "I don't remember."

"What's your name?"

"Phillip."

"Do you know what day it is?"

He opened his eyes and looked at the faces staring at him. "Why are you asking me these questions?"

Ursula moved in, kneeling beside him and sweeping away his hair to examine his head. "He has a huge bump. He may haf a concussion."

"Flip, do you know what happened to Punch?" Jillian asked.

He looked at her with something like fear. "Why? Isn't he okay?"

"He's dead, Flip," she said with her usual tact. "Someone murdered him."

It took a moment for the news to register, then Flip clutched his head with both hands and began to rock back and forth, crying, "No! No! No!" Then he covered his face and broke out in loud, heavy sobs.

"Nice going, Jillian," Sabina snapped, and got down beside Flip and wrapped her arms around him, murmuring soothing words until he stopped rocking and collapsed against her.

I crouched in front of him. "Flip, did you see Punch this evening?"

In between sobs, he nodded.

"Was he alone?"

Another nod.

"Are you sure he didn't have a girl with him?" Jillian asked.

"I'm s-sure."

Bertie knelt beside me and asked, "Flip, did you and Punch have words?"

He nodded and the sobs got stronger. " Bu-but I di-didn't kill—kill him. I only thr-threw my camera at—at him."

"Did the camera hit his head?"

He scrubbed his eyes to gaze at us. "I—I don't kn-know. I r-ran. Oh, God, he can't be d-dead!" The sobs started again.

"Hey!" I heard from behind. I looked around to see Reilly and another cop come striding toward us. "What the hell is going on here?"

I got up and brushed the sand off my knees. "We found our missing groomsman."

Reilly's eyes got wide, and I motioned for him to step off to one side so I could explain. "Flip came walking up from the direction of the lake five minutes ago. He's disoriented from a knock on the forehead. I don't know how serious it is, so go easy on him, okay?"

Reilly gave me a look that said he didn't appreciate being told what to do. "All right, everyone back away from the car." He pointed at Flip and said, "Except for him. He stays." And after the group took three giant steps backward, Reilly crouched in front of Flip and tried to make eye contact.

"Son? Are you ill?"

Flip sniffled, his shoulders still shaking from the hard sobs. "I don't know."

"Did you get into a fight tonight?"

I could tell where Reilly's questions were leading and decided to put an end to it. "Not that I don't trust you, Reilly, but he should have a lawyer present for anymore questioning."

He gave me that exasperated look again, then said to his companion, "Let's get an ambulance out here." He got to his feet and turned to look at the wedding party, or what was left of them, all milling around like lost sheep. "Would you please go home." He didn't pose it as a question.

"I'd like to come with him in the ambulance," Bertie said, which was quick thinking on his part. No sense giving the cops the opportunity to interrogate Flip alone.

"Unless you're family, I'm afraid I can't allow that."

"Will a cousin do?"

Reilly looked at him askance. "You're his cousin?"

"On my mother's side."

"All right. You can ride with him."

When Reilly looked away, Bertie winked at us.

"Claymore," I said, "call Pryce and have him meet the ambulance at the hospital."

Jillian handed him her phone, and Claymore turned away to make the call.

"Let's go back to my house," Jillian said to the rest of us. "We need to talk about this."

"I have a better idea," I said, scratching mercilessly at the bites on my legs. "Let's go see if Onora is in her hotel room."

The lobby of the New Chapel Inn and Suites was typical for a moderately priced hotel—designed to make a person feel like he was in more expensive lodgings without worrying that his money was being sucked from his wallet. To the right of the revolving doors were groups of upholstered bucket chairs in soft green tones nestled around cube-shaped coffee tables, beige Berber carpeting, fake palm trees, and vinyl wallpaper in a muted print. To the left was a maple reception counter topped in a pale green cultured marble. Beyond that was the elevator vestibule.

All five of us strode straight past the counter to the elevators. The clerk, a man in his late twenties, was sitting behind the counter reading a paperback and never looked up.

It must have been quite a book. We took an elevator to the fourth floor, walked down the hall to room 412, and Sabina opened the door with her key.

The suite was narrow and deep, starting with a small sitting room outfitted with an upholstered chair, convertible sofa, and TV, followed by a kitchenette, a generous bathroom, and a bedroom beyond it. The door to the bedroom was locked, so Sabina knocked and called, "Onora? Are you in there?"

It took Jillian and Sabina both pounding and calling to rouse Onora, and then she opened the door and peered at us through heavy-lidded eyes. I couldn't help but notice her outfit. No cotton pj's for this siren. She had on a long, sleek, bloodred satin gown with a vine of black flowers embroidered down one side, with a thigh-high split over her right leg. It was something I might wear to a New Year's Eve party—if I were built like Nicole Kidman— but not to bed to toss around in all night. Looking at Onora's perfect hair, however, I doubted she tossed, or even moved.

"I'm trying to sleep off my headache," she said crossly. "What do you want?"

"Where did you get that nightgown? It's gorgeous!" Jillian exclaimed. Leave it to my cousin to zero in on the important matters.

"Didn't you hear the phone?" Sabina asked. "We tried to reach you all evening."

"I took a sleeping pill. Now go away." She glided back to the bed, eased herself down onto it, and draped a folded washcloth over her eyes.

Everyone but Claymore followed her into the room, which was quite spacious, with two queen-sized beds covered in bland bedspreads that matched the wallpaper, and a long, low bureau with a TV on top. In front of the heavily draped window were two more bucket chairs identical to the ones in the lobby.

"Don't you want to know why we were trying to reach you?" Ursula asked. I was beginning to think she was quite an instigator.

"No!" Onora snapped.

I knew Jill was on the verge of telling her, so I trained my eyes on Onora's face to catch her reaction.

"Punch is dead," Jillian said, right on cue.

Onora was good, if she was acting. Pulling off the cloth, she sat up and looked at each one of us in turn, as if trying to verify the information. "You're kidding, right?"

"For God's sake," Claymore said from the doorway, "why would we kid about that?"

For a long moment Onora sat there, frozen. Then she got up and went to the window, parted the drapes, and stared down at the parking lot. The only sound in the room was my scratching.

"Who killed him?" she asked in a monotone, her back to us.

My ears perked up. No one had said he was murdered, only that he was dead.

"That's what everyone wants to know," Jillian said.

Onora turned to look at me, then Sabina, then Ursula. "Do you think I did it? Is that why you're here? Oh, my God, it is! You think I killed Punch!" Her voice became shrill and her fingers curled into her palms. "Have you all lost your minds? Why would you think that about me? I loved Punch!"

"We're not accusing you, Onora," Sabina said. "We came because we were concerned about you."

"She's right," Jillian added. "I mean, who knows what we could have found here? You might have been murdered, too."

I could always count on Jill to make a bad situation worse. "Time to go," I said to my obtuse cousin. I hooked her arm and dragged her out of the room. It was pointless to stay anyway. If Onora had killed Punch, she wasn't going to admit it to us.

It was after one o'clock in the morning when Claymore, Jillian, Ursula, Sabina, and I huddled in the lower family room at my Aunt Corrine's house. We had left Onora behind at her insistence. She'd wanted to be alone to grieve for the not-so-dearly departed Punch. But the rest of us needed to talk about what had happened. After seeing such a gruesome sight, none of us felt much like sleeping.

While Jillian went to find an ointment for my bites, I sat on the carpet, stripped off my sandals, and rolled up my chinos to take a look at the damage the little fleas had wrought. Ursula and Sabina curled up on opposite ends of the leather sofa behind me, and Claymore poured orange juice from a pitcher and handed out glasses.

"Who could possibly have done such a terrible thing?" Sabina asked, her lower lip starting to tremble, threatening a new wave of tears.

"Let's look at our possible suspects," I said. "So far we have Flip, Onora, and the mystery woman. Anyone else?"

"Bertie," Ursula said. At my surprised look she said, "He hated Punch. He vas fired from a big Manhattan ad agency because of Punch."

"But he says he's happier in his new job," Sabina argued.

As I recalled, Bertie had also told me he didn't always tell the truth. "Did he have the opportunity?" I asked Claymore, who had taken a seat in the oversized leather chair.

He sipped the juice, thinking. "When I took the guys to the dunes the other day, Bertie spotted a bar just off the highway called the Luck o' the Irish. That's where he went this evening. It's a ten minute walk from there to the dunes, five minutes by car."

"Are you positive he was at the bar?" I asked him.

"Most assuredly. After Punch called us, we phoned Bertie, and he asked us to pick him up there on our way to the park, which we did."

"He could have walked back to the bar before ve arrived," Ursula reasoned.

"Then we have to put Bertie on the list." I was reluctant to do it because I liked him. "What about Onora. What would her motive be?"

"Revenge," Ursula said. "Onora gets angry, then she gets even."

"Did she have the opportunity?"

"She could have slipped out of the hotel without anyone seeing her," Claymore said. "We got in without being noticed."

"How would she have found her way to the dunes?" I asked.

"She could have asked for directions, or taken a cab," Ursula said.

I dug my nails into a particularly nasty bite on my ankle. "We're assuming she knew Punch was there."

"Which means it would have been premeditated." Claymore held the cool juice glass to his forehead, looking faint again.

"She couldn't have known where Punch was," Sabina said. "We dropped her off at the hotel before Jillian got Punch's call."

"Maybe Punch called Onora first," Ursula said.

"The timing would be tight," I told them. "After receiving Punch's call, Onora would have had to speed to the dunes—a good twenty-minute drive from the hotel—find Punch, strike him, then leave before you got there."

"Unless she didn't have to wait for his call," Ursula suggested. "Maybe she followed him there in her rental car."

"Would she have been able to find her way home again?" I asked.

No one wanted to speculate on that, but neither did they say a word in Onora's defense. Even I had to admit that the theory was plausible, especially since I was pretty sure she had followed Punch after Jillian's soiree. "Let's move on to Flip," I said. "He had the means and the opportunity. What about a motive?"

"Flip was probably the only one who liked Punch," Jillian said as she walked into the room. She handed me a bottle of calamine lotion, which I immediately applied to my bites. She'd been gone so long I had begun to think she'd fallen asleep while rooting through a medicine cabinet.

"For argument's sake," Claymore said, sounding like he would much rather have been in bed, curled up in fetal position, "do you honestly believe Flip could have thrown the camera hard enough to kill him?"

"At close range it's possible," I said. "He could have struck him hard enough to cause him to black out, and then he could have bled to death."

"But Flip told us he didn't know if he'd hit him," Jillian replied. "If Flip had been standing close to Punch, he'd know that, wouldn't he? There would be a *thunk,* or Punch would cry out or Flip would hear him fall—something."

"Unless Flip lied to us," I said.

They all started arguing with me at once, none of them believing he would lie.

"If the police consider him a suspect, we have to, as

well," I reminded them. "Let's go back to the scene. From the way Punch fell, he would have been on his knees facing away from his attacker."

"Maybe Punch vas folding up the blanket," Ursula suggested. "Flip got angry and walked away, then came back, threw the camera, and ran."

"I'll bet they argued about Punch's mystery girlfriend," Jillian said. She just wouldn't let the idea go.

"If there is a mystery girlfriend," I said, "what is it about her that would make Flip so angry he'd hurl a camera at his friend's head?"

"He probably resented Punch spending time with her and not us," Jillian offered.

"Resented it enough to hurt him?" I asked.

"Ask Jillian about the time she chucked a plate at my head," Claymore said, throwing my cousin an accusing glance.

"You were flirting with a waitress," Jillian said coolly, and I could see the claws begin to emerge.

"The difference," I said to Claymore, before they got into a spitting match, "is that Flip is Punch's friend. A friend wouldn't behave like that."

"But a fiancée would?" Claymore asked.

"*Your* fiancée would." I dodged Jillian's hand as she tried to jab me with her fingernail.

"So vould a girlfriend," Ursula tossed out.

"Shut up, Ursula," Sabina said quietly.

Ursula lifted an eyebrow at me, as if she knew a secret, then she unfolded her long legs and headed across the room to get a refill of juice, leaving me to wonder what she had meant.

"Let's say that Punch's mystery girlfriend hit him with the camera," I posed. "Then we're assuming, first of all, that there *is* a girlfriend. Second, that she was there with

Punch. And third, that Flip lied about being alone with him."

That started a new round of protests as they again jumped to Flip's defense.

"Unless," I added, holding up my hand to get their attention, "someone came later, after Flip had thrown the camera and left."

"That makes more sense," Claymore said.

"It has to be the mystery woman," Jillian said. "You have to find her, Abby."

"Me? Uh-uh. No way. That's police work. I don't do police work. I do flowers." I finished my juice and rose. "And if I want to continue to do flowers, I need to get some sleep so I can make it to work tomorrow. Good night."

By the time I got back to the apartment I was in an itching frenzy. I opened the door and slipped quietly inside so I wouldn't wake Nikki. In the darkness I failed to notice Simon sitting at his bowl just inside the kitchen doorway. As I tiptoed past I caught the end of his tail under my sandal, prompting Simon to let out a screech that must have set off earthquake sensors in San Francisco. Startled, I jumped back and hit the front door with a bang.

Of course, Nikki woke up.

Lights went on and she came flying out of her bedroom wailing like a banshee, brandishing a can of hair spray. Obviously she was prepared to not only shock the intruder so his hair stood on end, but also to make sure it stayed that way.

"It's me!" I said, waving my arms at her. "Don't spray!"

She came to a stop, panting and staring at me with a bewildered look. I could tell I'd awakened her from a very deep sleep, so I turned her around and guided her back to her doorway. "Go to bed. I'll talk to you in the morning."

"Why are your ankles covered in red welts?"

"It's a long story."

"You'd better put something on them."

"I'm too tired for that. Good night."

I took a cool shower, then crawled into bed and immediately dropped into an exhausted sleep, only to wake an hour later in total agony, my legs from toes to knee one massive hive of torture. I stumbled to the bathroom, dug through the jumble of ointments Nikki kept in a shoe box under the sink, found some anti-itch cream, and slathered it on. I waited a few minutes for it to soak in, then shut my bedroom door to keep Simon out and lay on an old beach towel on top of my bed so I wouldn't stain the sheets.

Anti-itch medication, I discovered, works for about fifteen minutes. So I slept in fits and starts and, in between bouts of scratching and slathering on more cream, I dreamed about dead bodies, bloody cameras, and murderous barbers.

"Abby?"

Someone shook my shoulder. I peeled back scratchy eyelids to squint at Nikki. "What?"

"Don't you have to go to the flower shop?"

"In the morning, Nikki."

"It *is* morning. Eight thirty, to be exact. Did you get any sleep last night?"

"Maybe an hour," I muttered and closed my eyes again. Then I opened them. "Did you say eight thirty?"

I was always at the shop by eight o'clock. It was my rule. In a panic I sat up and slid off the bed, a simple maneuver, as it turned out, with an inch-thick coating of goo on my legs. "Pour juice for me, Nik," I said, starting for the bathroom. "I'm going into emergency mode."

"I'm on it. Omigod, Abby, look at your legs! You've scratched them raw."

I stopped to look down at the itchy limbs protruding from my short pj's. Blood had oozed through the salve and run down my ankles. "Sand fleas," I told her and went to drown myself in the shower.

As I stood over the kitchen sink gobbling a bowl of wheat flakes that Nikki had hastily assembled for me, I gave her a condensed version of the prior evening's tragic events.

"Weird," Nikki concluded, tossing a plastic straw for Simon to chase. "Especially since you know the suspects. You've got to stop scratching, Abby. You'll infect the sores."

"I wish I could stop." I had put on a green print cotton skirt with a white T-shirt. Slacks, even capris, only caused more itching.

"Slap the bites."

"My legs will be black and blue."

"Better that than pus green."

"You have a point."

As I ate the last of my cereal, Simon decided to rub against my legs, which set off a whole new round of torture, not to mention that all his loose white fur stuck to the ointment.

"Simon!" I shrieked, causing him to shoot out of the kitchen and collide with Nikki's legs as she came in holding two tablets in her palm. He dodged her and scrambled down the hallway, fur flying.

"Great," I said, trying to pick spikes of white hair out of the goo. "I look like I'm morphing into the abominable snowman."

"Take these tablets. They're antihistamines. They should give you some relief."

"I'm willing to try anything short of amputation. Maybe that, too, if the itching doesn't stop."

"What's going to happen with Flip now?"

"They probably questioned and released him last night. I'll call Jillian later this morning and get the scoop." I swallowed the pills and glanced at the clock. "If Grace calls here looking for me, tell her why I overslept. It'll save me a lot of explaining later."

The phone rang. "There she is," I said, and dashed for the bathroom, only to hear Nikki say, "Yes, she's here. Hold on." A minute later she appeared in the bathroom doorway with the phone in her hand.

"I thought you were going to talk to her," I whispered.

"It's not Grace. It's Jillian."

"Abby," my cousin wailed in my ear. "Flip's been arrested for murder!"

CHAPTER SEVEN

"Why did they arrest Flip? Did he confess?" I asked Jillian, slapping my left leg.

"No." I could hear her gulping something. "His prints were on the camera, and he didn't have a good alibi. That was enough for the cops." She gulped again. "Abby, this is a nightmare."

"What are you drinking?"

"Coffee with brandy. Ursula made it to steady my nerves."

"Caffeine and alcohol? Wouldn't those ingredients work against each other?"

"At this moment I don't really care."

From the corner of my eye I caught sight of Simon peeking around the corner. Seeing that I was preoccupied, he came in to try the leg rub again, but I crouched down before he could make contact, holding the phone between my ear and shoulder so I could keep him at arm's length. Always a sucker for a good chin scratching, he sat on his haunches and began to purr.

"Pryce says the cops aren't investigating any other leads

now because they have their suspect," Jillian said. "You've got to help, Abby. You've got to prove Flip didn't do it. Claymore says we can't get married if there's a cloud hanging over the wedding."

"Let me guess. It wouldn't be seemly."

"His very words."

Pryce's words, too, when he'd called off our wedding. For that reason alone I wanted to help, although I knew I'd be in for a stern lecture from Grace. My parents wouldn't be a picnic either. I didn't even want to think about what Marco would say.

"Just to play devil's advocate, what if I find that, say, Onora did it?" I posed. "Is the wedding still doomed?"

"You're kidding, right? Do you actually believe the Osbornes would let Claymore marry a woman who associates with murderesses?"

I was surprised they were letting him marry a woman who associated with *me,* but I wasn't about to say so and give her something else to fret over.

"Besides," Jillian added, "Onora's prints weren't on the camera."

She could have worn gloves, but I decided to keep that thought to myself, too.

"Please, Abby," Jillian wailed. "You've got to find this mystery woman and prove she did it."

Fortunately for Jill, there were several factors working in her favor: 1) If Claymore called off the wedding, I was stuck paying for an ugly dress I wouldn't wear to a costume party; 2) I had lots of bills to pay; and 3) The police should not have stopped investigating other leads just because Flip's prints were on the camera. Why wouldn't they be on the camera? He owned it.

"Where is Flip now?" I asked.

"Sitting in that horrid jail. Pryce says they don't grant

bail for people charged with murder. Will you help, Abby? Pretty please?"

"If I say yes, you'll have to promise not to tell anyone. I'd rather work behind the scenes—undercover, so to speak."

"I promise. So is that a yes?"

I sighed loudly, just so she wouldn't think I was happy about it. "I suppose."

"I wub you, Abs," Jillian cooed and hung up.

"Yeah, I wub you, too."

Simon looked at me in disdain and marched off, tail twitching. He wasn't one for baby talk.

But I had more to worry about than Simon's disdain. First and foremost, I needed Marco's advice on where to start my investigation. He'd bet me that I would only pay him a call when I needed his help, so unless I wanted to provide him with seven big bundles of roses, I had to make it seem otherwise.

"So you're going to investigate," Nikki said, settling on a counter stool with a cup of tea.

I shrugged. "Looks like it."

"You're loving it, aren't you?"

"I wouldn't go *that* far."

"Yes, you would. Just so you know, I'm here if you need my help."

I gave her a hug and reached for my toothbrush, planning how to explain my decision to Grace. If I handled it right I might escape a lecture.

"Trust me. I didn't go looking for this. It just found me." Too passive, and she wouldn't buy it anyway.

"I can't let my cousin down and have her suffer the same horrible embarrassment I did when Pryce called off our engagement." No good. Grace knew Jillian had been the one

to cancel her prior engagements, and besides that, Jillian wasn't easily embarrassed.

"You want me to trust the police to solve this?" Better than the first two, but still debatable.

"This wedding must go on, Grace. I need the money." She couldn't argue with the truth. Well, yes, knowing Grace, she probably could.

How about I don't tell her?

There you go.

"Hey, Nikki?" I called from the bathroom doorway. "Don't mention anything about my part in the murder investigation when you talk to Grace, okay? I don't want her to know."

"Afraid of getting a lecture?"

"You betcha."

I was on my way out the door when the phone rang again. Nikki waved me off, and as I pulled the door shut behind me, I heard her say, "I'm sorry, Grace, she just left, but let me tell you what happened last night."

Let's hear it for Nikki.

Nikki did her job well. By the time I arrived at Bloomers Grace had heard the whole complicated story and had passed it along to Lottie. Both were waiting with coffee and sympathy, especially when they saw my pathetic-looking legs. Neither mentioned my role in the investigation, which meant Nikki had followed my instructions.

"Sweetie, why didn't you wear slacks?" Lottie asked. "People will see your bites in that skirt."

"Anything touching my skin makes the itch even worse."

"Is that why you're wearing flip-flops?"

"Yes, and I can barely stand *them*."

"Why not try an oatmeal bath?" Grace said.

The thought of soaking in a bathtub made me shudder. I like *clean* water on my skin, not used water. But if I told her that, she'd pull up some old quote about a bath being a curative, or some such thing. So instead I said, "Sure. I'll give it a try. Any messages?"

"Two from your mother."

"Let me guess. Dinner at the club tomorrow night. You didn't mention anything to her about me being at the murder scene, did you? You know how she frets."

Grace assumed her statesman's pose. "As René Descartes once said, 'It is not enough to have a good mind; the main thing is to use it well.'"

That meant no. Lottie and I gave her a round of applause.

"Sweetie," Lottie said, following me through the curtain to the workroom, "I hate to spoil the mood, but your mother knows."

"How?"

"You didn't see the morning paper, did you?" She handed me the front section. In big bold letters the headlines stated: MURDER AT THE DUNES. Underneath were two black-and-white yearbook photos, one of Punch and one of Flip. In the article's second paragraph it announced that both men had come to town for the wedding of Jillian Knight and Claymore Osborne.

"I don't see the problem."

"Turn the page."

There it was, on page two: a photo of me talking to Reilly, with Jillian and company standing just behind us. "Now I see the problem."

Oh, yes. My mother knew. But as long as Jillian kept her mouth shut, my mother wouldn't know I had agreed to look for the killer.

Lottie glanced at her watch. "I'd say you have about five minutes before she calls again. Got any errands to run?"

"Do I have time?"

"Plenty. Only two orders came in over the wire last night."

Even more reason for me to make sure that wedding went off as planned. "I'll be back shortly." I opened the cooler, took a handful of brightly hued daisies, and started for the curtain.

"Sweetie?" Lottie said, as she climbed a step stool to reach a pot on a high shelf. "Are you sure you want to get involved?"

"Involved in what? I'm just going down to the bar and grill."

"You know what I mean."

I peered through the curtain to make sure Grace wasn't hovering nearby. "Did Nikki tell you?"

"She didn't have to. I know you too well." Lottie snagged the pot she wanted and brought it to the table.

"Jillian asked me to help, Lottie. I didn't want to say anything because I know how everyone will worry. Do you think Grace suspects?"

"If she suspected, she'd say something."

"A lot of somethings. It would be in my best interests if word of this doesn't get out."

Lottie began to cut green foam to put in the pot. "She won't hear it from me."

That was exactly what I'd been hoping to hear. I gave her a hug. "Thanks, Lottie."

Flowers clutched in one hand, I hurried up the sidewalk to the Down the Hatch, rehearsing what I was going to say to Marco. Bringing him a bouquet wasn't the best excuse for stopping by, but it was the only one I could come up with on ten seconds' notice.

I cupped one hand around my eyes and peered in the glass door, rapping lightly when I saw people inside. The bar and grill didn't officially open until eleven o'clock, but since the staff knew me, they always let me in.

"Marco's on the roof," a scrawny, middle-aged waitress named Gert told me, her voice deep and rough from too many cigarettes. "Last time it rained water got in and worked its way down to the kitchen. This morning we found an ugly brown stain on the back wall. Marco didn't think the health department would like that, so he went up to fix the problem."

"I'll bet that didn't put him in the best of moods."

She coughed for about five minutes before she could say, "You got it."

"I'll come back later."

"Good idea."

I thrust the flowers at her. "For you. And take care of that cough so I don't have to send the next bunch to the funeral parlor."

I walked back to Bloomers still pondering a way to pick Marco's brain without him catching on. I stopped to glance up at the top of his building, which, like mine, was three stories high with a flat, tar-papered roof. It had to be hot up there. Perhaps I could drop by later to take him a cold drink. Or a picnic basket for a surprise lunch.

That was it! I'd pick up deli sandwiches and a bottle of chilled chardonnay and throw him a picnic. Once he'd filled up on food and wine, I'd casually ask what I needed to know.

Way to go, Abby!

As I stepped inside Bloomers, Lottie hung up the phone

at the front counter. "You just missed a call from your parents. I told them you were just fine."

"Timing is everything."

"Don't get too excited," Lottie said, heading for the workroom. "Your mother will be here in half an hour."

"She's not bringing another one of her sculptures, is she?"

"Lordy, I hope not. I'm still recovering from the last one."

We both glanced at the multiarmed object in the far corner. Yep. Still there.

I spent the half hour before my mother's arrival drawing up plans for Trudee DeWitt's Fourth of July party. Thanks to Nikki's antihistamine I had stopped scratching, but for some reason I had a hard time keeping my eyes open. I chalked it up to a lack of sleep.

The next half hour was spent assuring my mother that I hadn't been in any danger at the dunes and that I certainly wasn't going to get West Nile Virus from sand fleas. She hadn't mentioned a word about my part in the investigation, which meant Jillian had kept her promise.

We were sitting on stools at one end of the worktable, both of us with cups of coffee provided by Grace. At the other end, Lottie was putting together an arrangement of her own creation called the Red Hot Mama Bouquet—cherry red carnations, vivid orange Gerbera daisies, a fiery explosion of blooms from the firecracker plant, and green button mums.

"Your aunt Corrine is absolutely beside herself with worry that the wedding will be canceled," my mother told me. "You know how much she wants Jillian to get married." She sighed wistfully, leaning her chin on her hand. "Isn't that every mother's dream—to watch her daughter

march down the aisle into the arms of a financially respon-
sible male, then turn her bedroom into an exercise area?"

"You didn't wait for *me* to get married before turning my
room into your exercise area."

My mother patted my hand and smiled obliquely. "Abigail, by the time that happens I'll be too old to climb onto
the treadmill."

"I'm not the one who called off the wedding," I reminded her, mentally sharpening my dueling sword.

Sensing a brewing storm, Lottie decided to make herself
scarce and nearly collided with Grace at the curtain. She
stepped back, and Grace whisked in with a thermal pot in
her hand. "More coffee?" she offered with a smile. Grace
had the uncanny ability to step in at just the right moment.
I think it came from her habit of eavesdropping.

"Yes, thank you," my mother said, sliding her cup forward. She stirred in cream and sugar and took a sip. "It's
wonderful. Thank you, Grace. Now, Abigail," she said as
Grace left the room, "about this groomsman the police have
charged—Fonzie—Flipper—what was his name?"

My hands went cold. Had Jillian blabbed? I glanced
around to be sure Grace was gone. "His name is Flip."

"What an odd name. Anyway, your aunt Corrine said
you'd offered to find—"

"Will you look at the time!" I exclaimed, tapping my
watch. " I'd love to chat longer, Mom, but I have so much
to do."

"But I haven't finished my coffee yet."

I jumped off the stool, grabbed my purse, and threw it
over a shoulder. "I'll walk you to your car. I'm heading that
way, anyway."

She took a quick slurp and set the cup down with a clat-
ter. "I don't understand your hurry. Are you that busy?"

I hooked my hand through her arm and nearly dragged

her through the curtain, telling her all about Trudee De-Witt's party to distract her. We zipped past Grace and were at the door when my mother interrupted my chatter to say, "For heaven's sake, if you're busy why on earth did you offer to help find the murderer? The success of the entire wedding is now resting on your shoulders."

Silence frosted the air behind me. I imagined long, fragile icicles dangling from floral arrangements, thin sheets of ice glazing the wooden floor, unsuspecting customers windmilling their arms as they slid across the room. It wasn't a pretty picture.

With a wedding on my shoulders and a pair of disapproving eyeballs on my back I made my exit, fairly pushing my mother out the door ahead of me. It wasn't that I was trying to escape from Grace's inevitable lecture, but—well, yes it was.

"I didn't want you to say anything in front of Grace," I explained as I tucked my mother into her van. "She has this crazy idea that I'm a meddler."

"You get that from me," she said proudly.

I assured her I would show up for dinner at the club the next day, then I took off for the deli, where I had two honey-baked ham and baby Swiss cheese sandwiches prepared. No cold chardonnay in stock so I grabbed a bottle of pinot grigio and a bag of chips. Then, armed with my excuse for dropping by, I headed for Marco's bar.

"He's still on the roof," Gert told me.

I carried my bundle past the bar that was now buzzing with patrons downing burgers and beer and watching golf on the overhead television and stowed it in Marco's office. I managed to snag a tablecloth, two wineglasses, and a spare votive candle from a supply cabinet, then I unfurled the checkered square on the light gray carpet, set out the food picnic-style, and lit the candle for effect.

Now to find my prey.

To get to the roof, I had to exit the building and climb a fire-escape pull-down ladder on the alley side. I had no problem grabbing the wrought-iron ladder and tugging it down to my level, but I ran into problems climbing the rungs in a short skirt. Luckily, the alley was deserted, or someone would have had a daring view.

Marco was standing near the front edge of the roof, a shovel in his hands, examining the results of his handiwork when I stepped onto the hot black surface and shifted my skirt back into place. He was the only man I knew who could look sexy in denim bib overalls. Wearing a sleeveless T-shirt underneath that showed off his great biceps didn't hurt any either.

"Do you hire out?" I called.

He turned and gave me that half grin that drove my insides into an Irish jig. "Depends on the job." He held up a bucket filled with black goo. "Need anyone tarred and feathered?"

"I'll give you a list."

He watched me approach, his eyes smoldering with what I imagined to be burning desire, but when I got up close I saw that his gaze was instead brimming with laughter. "What the hell did you do to your legs?"

"Long story. Too warm up here to tell it," I said, fanning my face. My legs had started to itch from the heat but I didn't want him to know. I walked over to the front edge and gazed down at the square. "Cool view."

"Not if you're working with tar. Then it's a hot view." Marco came to stand beside me and we gazed together.

"What are you doing for lunch?" I turned to look at him and my head started to spin, maybe from the antihistamine, or maybe from the smell of hot tar. Whatever the cause, the effect was instant dizziness. I gasped as I swayed toward the edge, where I had a quick view of the roofs of the cars parked alongside the curb below. A hand clamped around my arm and yanked me back from the brink of death.

"What did you have in mind?" he asked, as though nothing had happened.

What I had in mind at that moment was breathing again. Once that started up, I felt an overwhelming gratitude for Marco's quick reflexes. My first instinct was to throw my arms around his neck and shower him with grateful kisses. But since I was already pressed against his hot body, gazing up into those sexy brown eyes, I wet my lips and said, "How about a picnic?"

"Here?"

"Come with me." I led him across the roof to the ladder. And that's where I had to stop, because there were now people in the alley below who appeared to be digging through a trash bin. If I went first, those people would have a view I wasn't particularly inclined to share. If Marco went first and I backed down after him—I still wasn't inclined to share the view. Some things are better left for the dim light of a candle.

"What's the problem?" he asked, peering over the side.

"I'm not dressed for descending a ladder with people below."

"I'll go first."

"Wait." I grabbed his arm before he could start backing down. "Let me go first."

"But you just said—"

"Pay no attention to me. I'm high on antihistamines." And not only that, but I didn't know the people digging through the trash, so what did I care if they saw my pasty white thighs?

I made my way down the ladder, feeling for each rung with one foot, then the other, until I hit bottom. I stepped

out of Marco's way, shifted my skirt into place, and turned
to gaze into the stunned faces of the assistant pastor of my
church and his wife.

"Hello, Reverend McCrory," I said sheepishly, feeling
my entire head turn red with mortification.

"I thought that was you, Abby," he said.

He had recognized my thighs? I tugged my skirt lower
and introduced the couple to Marco. Then, being female, I
had to ask, "Why are you digging through the trash bin?"

"We're looking for our daughter's retainer," the pastor
explained. "She wrapped it in her napkin and didn't remember it until after we'd left the restaurant. Naturally, by
the time we returned, the table had been cleaned."

"I'll get someone out here to help you," Marco promised, and went into the bar through the back door, leaving
me to stand there with my bitten legs and red face, making
small—actually minuscule—talk until a busboy came out
to assist.

"Nice to see you," I called, and darted through the door
before it closed.

Marco was talking to someone at the bar, and when he
saw me, he signaled that he'd be right there. I went ahead
to his office to light the candle.

Standing in his doorway, staring at my little feast, he
said, "You weren't kidding about the picnic."

I held up the pinot grigio. "I even brought wine."

Sitting on his carpet with my knees tucked beneath me,
gritting my teeth against the carpet fibers that rubbed my
itchy skin, I divided the food and poured the wine. Marco
practically inhaled his sandwich and in between swallows
muttered things like how he'd worked up quite an appetite
on the roof, and how thoughtful I was to bring food, and
how sorry he was that my legs were in such a state, making

me feel almost guilty for my subterfuge. Almost, but not enough to prevent me from doing it.

He polished off his second glass of wine and the rest of the chips, then leaned against the wall with a satisfied sigh and a glimmer of curiosity. "Are you going to tell me where you got those bites or am I supposed to guess?"

I laughed lightly and waved him away. "You'll never guess, but give it a whirl."

"You were at the dunes last night and the sand fleas got you."

My smile turned wary. "That's right."

Marco placed his fingers against his temples and shut his eyes, as though he were a fortune-teller. "I see you with a guy—in the sand."

"It's not what you think."

"I'm getting another picture now—sand dunes, water, blood—wait, it's a *murder* scene, with witnesses and police and—who is that young woman elbowing her way to the front? Why, it's Abby Knight, of all people. What could she be doing there? Could she be meddling?"

"You talked to Reilly, didn't you? Listen, Marco, Jillian asked for my help. The police arrested her groomsman based on flimsy evidence, and if he isn't cleared soon, the wedding is off. *Off,* Marco! That means I'm out a load of money that I desperately need to pay my bills."

He held up a palm. "I'm getting something else . . . kind of fuzzy . . . A ruse designed to trick me into helping you with the case. Now, what could that ruse be? Could it be a picnic?"

He opened his eyes and fixed me with a knowing look. The jig was up, but I wasn't about to admit it. I hadn't lost the bet yet.

"You're completely off base," I said with dignity, then got up on my knees to gather the goods, at which point

Marco tackled me and we landed in a heap on the carpet, with him braced on his hands above me.

"Who bet me that the next time she came here it would *not* be to ask for help?"

"Have I asked?"

"Were you going to?"

I pushed against his shoulders. "Let me up, you oaf."

He lowered his head so that I was staring straight up into those sexy eyes. "Fess up, sunshine, and I'll consider it."

His male scent wrapped around my sensibilities, raising my pulse rate and making me go soft and gooey in the center. Instead of thinking about a witty comeback, I started thinking about what I could do to make him kiss me. "And if I don't confess?" I said in a suggestive manner.

His mouth curved, his lips dangerously near mine. "You don't want to know."

"Maybe I do," I replied, and then, instead of waiting for his comeback, I said, "Oh, hell," and grabbed his head and pulled his mouth down to meet mine.

We kissed hard, lips moving against lips, fingers threaded through hair, eyes closed. His mouth tasted like grapes and his body felt like iron. I'd never been that intimate with Marco. I'd never even dreamed about it. But if I had, it couldn't have done that kiss justice. He had the technique down pat.

We kept it up for several long, glorious minutes, making me start to wonder where it would go from there. Would this change our relationship? For better or for worse?

Suddenly, someone knocked on the door staccatolike, and Marco was on his feet before I could blink, muttering oaths under his breath.

CHAPTER EIGHT

"Who is it?" Marco barked as the rapping continued.

"Jillian Knight. Is Abby in there?"

"Oh, for heaven's sake!" I whispered, as Marco pulled me up by the hand. "Tell her I'm not here."

"Abby?" Jillian called, beating the door with the palm of her hand. "Is that you whispering? Are you in there?"

"She's here," Marco replied testily, and flung open the door as I hastily smoothed my hair and clothing.

Jillian stood in the doorway in a gauzy mint green summer outfit that looked like it had come straight from the runways of Paris, her hair a shimmering copper waterfall, her skin glowing with just the right amount of color, and not a bite on her anywhere. She took a look at the mess on the floor and turned to give me an innocent stare. "Am I interrupting something?"

"Take a wild guess," I said in a lethal tone, tempted to inflict at least one bite on her perfect skin.

"Were you asking Marco what to do about Flip?"

Marco took a seat behind his desk. "She was just getting to that."

"No, I wasn't. We were having lunch, Jill. That's all. Just lunch." I glowered at her.

Jillian heaved a sharp sigh. "Well, when *are* you going to ask him? I don't have forever, you know. My wedding is less than three weeks away."

"What makes you think I'm going to ask Marco anything?" I countered, while the subject of our discussion leaned back, folded his arms, and put his feet on the desk.

"I win," he said smugly.

"No, you don't. I didn't ask you for help. Jillian did."

"I didn't ask Marco," Jillian shot back. "I asked *you.*"

"Have a seat, ladies, and let's get on with it," Marco said with a resigned sigh. "I don't have forever, either."

"How did you know I was here?" I asked Jillian, flopping into one of the black leather chairs.

Jillian sat down carefully, so as not to wrinkle her outfit. "Jingles told me."

"The window washer knew where I was?"

"Jingles knows everything that happens on the square," Marco commented blandly.

"How did you know to ask Jingles?" I asked my cousin.

"Grace said he'd know."

"How did Grace . . . ?"

"Ladies?" Marco said, swinging his feet to the floor. "I have a business to run. What do you need to know?"

I opened my mouth and Jillian spoke. "My groomsman has been charged with murder, and I need to get him uncharged so I can get married."

I rolled my eyes at Marco. "She went to Harvard. I thought I should point that out."

Jillian eyed me with disdain."What's wrong with you?"

"You can't *uncharge* a person. You have to clear him."

"I uncharge my credit cards all the time."

"Sorry. No such word."

She swiveled to face me, her fists planted on the slim belt around her waist. "The people at Nordstrom's don't have a problem understanding me, Miss Law School Reject. If you can charge, you can uncharge."

Law School Reject? Jill was playing dirty now, just like she did when we were kids. And I was always the one who got in trouble afterward. But that was usually because I had decked her. "Listen, Miss Flunked College English Twice—"

A drawer slammed shut, making us both jump. We looked over at Marco, who checked his watch, held up an index finger, and said, "I'm giving you exactly five minutes to explain—starting now." The finger came down; the clock was ticking. "What evidence do the police have, and make it quick."

"The murder weapon—a camera—with Flip's fingerprints on it," Jillian said.

"It's his camera," I added, "but he has a weak alibi."

Marco grabbed a piece of paper and started to write. "Do you think he did it?"

"Absolutely not," Jillian said. " He's just a sweet, harmless guy." At Marco's skeptical look she said, "No, really! Flip wouldn't harm a fly."

"You'd be surprised how often the police hear that remark."

"We have other suspects," I told Marco. "A bridesmaid who's been carrying a grudge against the victim. Another groomsman who had his career kicked in the groin by the deceased. And possibly someone the victim has been bragging about seeing, but we don't know who she is, or if she even exists."

"She's our mystery woman," Jillian put in.

"Are you sure it's a woman?" Marco asked her, still making notes.

Jillian looked taken aback. "Well, yes. Of course."

"How do you know?" Marco retorted.

"Because I know Punch."

"But not well enough to know who he was seeing."

Jillian blinked at him.

Marco asked a few more questions, looked over his notes, then fixed his gaze on me. "Is there any way I can stop you from getting involved?"

I glanced at Jillian, who gave me an imploring look. Her next ploy would be to start with the baby talk, so I told Marco no before she embarrassed us both.

"I didn't think so." He drummed his fingers on the table, studying me. Finally he said, "If this were my case I'd start with the girlfriend. Find out if she exists or if it was just a case of male posturing. Remember what I told you about the missing groomsman? Apply it to Punch. Learn his interests. It'll give you a clue where to look. Then I'd find out if the reclusive bridesmaid left the hotel any time last evening, and if she did, where she went. Start with the hotel staff. It could be that this bridesmaid is the one Punch was bragging about."

"Not a chance," Jillian said.

"Anything else?" I asked, making notes in my appointment book.

"Yes. Don't tell anyone that you're investigating."

"So I can catch the murderer with his guard down?"

"So he doesn't catch you with yours down."

"Who has what down?" Jillian asked.

"No one has anything down," I told her, tucking away my notes, "and it will stay that way as long as you don't breathe another word about it. I know you've already blabbed to your mother because my mother knows, but that's it, right? You haven't told anyone else?"

"Does Claymore count?"

"Yes," Marco said.

"What about Pryce?"

"He counts, too."

"Bertie?"

I grabbed her arm. "*Everyone* counts, Jill."

She sucked in air through her teeth. "Then we have a slight problem."

"How many people did you tell?" Marco asked, and I could see his jaw grinding.

"Just three . . ." She paused to count on her fingers. "Six."

Marco muttered an oath and shoved back his chair. "That's it, Abby. You're out of it."

"I can't be out of it unless I want to be out of money. Jill, let's start with Punch's hobbies. What did he like to do?"

"Work out. Lift weights. Hit a punching bag."

"Then I should check with the gyms first. He might have purchased a guest pass." I glanced at Marco. "Am I right?"

"Don't look at me. I'm not going to encourage something that might get you hurt."

"Fine. Come on," I said to Jill. "This is your idea. You can go with me."

She checked the slender gold watch on her wrist. "Can't. Sorry. I have to meet the girls for a shopping trip. My bridal shower is this Sunday and I need something to wear."

"Heaven forbid I mess up your priorities."

Marco took each of us by the elbow and guided us to his door.

"What about the picnic?" I asked, pointing to the abandoned heap on the floor. He firmly assured me he'd take care of it. Anything to get us out of his office.

"Don't forget," he said, just before he shut his door. "You owe me roses—for a week."

"Oh, no, you don't," I said, pounding on the wood. "You didn't win. I never asked for your help. Not once."

There was silence on the other side of the door.

"I'm leaving," Jill said, and started up the hall.

"Don't burn up your credit card."

I waited until she was gone, then I raised my fist to knock again, but the door opened suddenly. "You're right," Marco said. "I owe you dinner. How's Saturday night?"

Something was fishy. He gave in too fast. "Saturday night is fine. What's the catch?"

"Your apartment."

"Why my apartment?"

"Take it or leave it."

"Nikki might be there."

"Get her a date."

I liked the way he thought.

When I entered Bloomers, Lottie was waiting on a middle-aged woman buying a miniature, six-paned black window frame I had whitewashed with lime and decorated with sheet moss, green silk ivy, and pink tea roses. As the woman counted bills from her wallet, she kept giving my mother's coatrack wary glances, as if afraid the green palms were going to pluck the money right out of her fingers.

"What *is* that?" she asked, clutching her purchase to her chest.

"A coatrack"—I patted one of the palms to show it meant her no harm—"made by a local artist of some note."

She felt for the doorknob with one hand. "How nice," she said and backed out in a hurry.

"We need to get rid of it," I told Lottie. "It's scaring the customers."

"Down to the basement?"

The basement was our place of last resort, the graveyard of unsold Maureen Knight creations. But I hated to bury the tree without giving it a proper mourning period, so, after studying it from two angles I said, "Let's give it a few more days. If it hasn't sold by next Wednesday, down it goes." Sometimes one had to show no mercy.

"On a positive note, four funeral orders came in," Lottie told me. She had long ago come to terms with someone else's tragedy paying her bills. I was still learning to deal with it. "We need to get them down to the Happy Dreams Funeral Home by five o'clock. And I saw on your calendar that you have a manicure at one."

My manicure! In the chaos from the previous evening I'd forgotten all about the Emperor's Spa. I glanced at my watch and saw that it was nearly twelve thirty. "I was supposed to trade lunch hours with Grace. Now she has another reason to hate me."

"She doesn't hate you," Lottie called, heading back to the workroom. "But she's miffed that you felt the need to hide this investigation from her. I heard her muttering some quote about deception."

"On a scale of one to ten, how miffed did she sound?"

Lottie emerged with her bright pink vinyl purse. "Where would you rank disappointment?"

"Eleven." Miffed I could handle, but I hated to disappoint Grace. It was like wounding Mother Theresa. What I needed was a quote in my own defense. I'd have to put my father on it. That was exactly the kind of task he liked to do. "This is Grace's fault," I told Lottie. "If she wouldn't keep insisting that I'm meddling, I wouldn't have to hide anything from her."

"You keep right on shifting that blame, sweetie." Lottie patted my shoulder. "Have to dash. I promised Herman I'd meet him at the deli for a sandwich."

Herman was Lottie's teddy bear of a husband. He'd had major heart surgery over a year ago and had racked up huge medical bills, which was why Lottie'd had to sell

Bloomers. With Herman unable to go back to his job at the steel mill, Lottie hadn't been able to afford to pay his bills, keep the shop running, and buy health insurance for both of them.

"How is Herman?" I asked.

She paused at the door. "Lately he gets so winded he can barely get around. It makes me worry, you know? I don't know what I'd do if I lost him." Her chin was trembling and she was getting teary eyed just talking about it. Lottie came off as an outspoken, tough-as-nails woman, but underneath she was pink cotton candy. She loved her husband of thirty-two years with an intensity of which most men only dream.

"Never mind me," she said, sniffling and trying to smile at the same time.

"Herman is tough. He'll be fine." I truly hoped so, anyway.

As soon as Lottie was gone, I called my father, who spent much of his day at his computer doing genealogy research about the Knights for a book he planned to write someday.

"Hey, Dad, how fast can you find a quote about not being totally forthcoming with the truth?"

"You mean lying?"

I winced. "More like withholding information."

"Time me," he said. "And for the record, I'm not in favor of this murder investigation."

"Ticktock," I reminded him.

Within three minutes he had one. "Here it is," he said. "A quote by Margaret Thatcher. 'You don't tell deliberate lies, but sometimes you have to be evasive.'"

"Perfect. And from a Brit to boot. You're amazing, Dad." I made smooching noises and hung up. Nothing like fighting fire with fire. Blame shifter, indeed.

While I waited for Grace to return and/or a customer to

walk through the door, I cut Punch's and Flip's photos from the newspaper and tucked them into my purse. They would come in handy for questioning potential witnesses. Then I flipped through the phone book looking for local gyms. I phoned two, but neither had any record of a man fitting Punch's description registering as a guest.

At the third gym, the young man who answered wasn't sure whether he should give me that information, so I asked to speak with someone who was sure and was put on hold. A woman picked up at last, and after I told her what I was looking for, I could almost hear her shudder.

"Oh, yes. I remember him. Please don't tell me he's a friend of yours."

"Not a problem."

"That's good news. What an abusive jackass he was. I left orders he was not to be issued a guest pass again. I refuse to have my female staffers treated with such disrespect."

"I doubt he'll be coming back. He was murdered yesterday."

There was a long pause and then she said somberly, "You know, I hate to say this about any living being, but I'm not sorry."

"It seems not many people are. Did he come in or leave with anyone?"

"No, but he did go on and on about this hot date who just couldn't keep her hands off him. Kept calling her his little passion flower. Made me want to puke. Who are you, by the way?"

"A private investigator." Which was not a lie. I *was* investigating privately.

The bell over the door jingled, and Grace walked in. "Thanks for your time," I said quickly and hung up, bracing myself for a lecture on deception.

"Sorry I forgot about switching lunch hours," I said sheepishly as she took off her straw hat and tucked her bag under the counter.

"I understand, dear," she said. "It's a difficult task, isn't it?"

I knew I was stepping into it, but I had to ask, "What's a difficult task?"

"Keeping your stories straight."

And the batter steps up to the plate.

Grace peered into a silver-framed mirror on one wall to adjust the collar of her blouse. "I want you to know, dear, that you need never feel obligated to discuss your decisions with me. Whether I approve of your meddling or not is beside the point."

"It's not meddling, but thank you anyway," I said, relieved to have gotten off so lightly.

"The point is, rather," she said, turning to fix me with her wise gaze, "to have integrity."

Grace swings and hits.

"And one cannot help but consider Sir Walter Scott's infamous words, 'Oh, what a tangled web we weave, when first we practice to deceive.'"

It's a grand slam!

Okay, Abby, show her what you're made of. Drive it home, baby.

I cleared my throat, Margaret Thatcher's words on the tip of my tongue. And that's where they stayed, because I couldn't force them out. I had already disappointed Grace. Could I steal her glory, too?

"I just want you to know," I said, slinging my purse over my shoulder, "I'm helping Jillian for very good reasons and not because I want to meddle in her affairs. In fact, Jillian's affairs are the last place I'd want to meddle."

"As I said, there's no need to justify your decision. It's

enough that you're no longer trying to cover it up. I would hope if any lesson came out of Washington D.C. in recent years, it would be that a cover-up rarely works. Actually, I believe you've done the right thing in agreeing to help your cousin."

"I have?"

"She's family, after all, and family members should always be there for each other."

I hadn't thought of that reason. But as long as Grace had, I was in the clear and looking pretty good.

"But that scratching simply must stop or those bites will leave scars. Promise me you'll try an oatmeal bath tonight."

"Promise," I said and started for the door, late for my manicure.

"And don't forget the other promise you made."

"I made another promise?"

"To Marco," she said, "about not meddling at the Emperor's Spa. You do remember making that promise, don't you?"

I was trying my best not to. When curiosity takes the reins, it's nearly impossible to get that horse to stop.

I pulled the Vette into the lot of the First Impressions Hair Salon and parked in a space facing the Emperor's Spa lot. As before, there were no cars in front, the spa's windows were covered, yet there was an OPEN sign propped in a window. At the rear of the old house was what appeared to be a newly completed room addition. The siding on that section was much whiter, and there were piles of dark gray roof shingles waiting to be installed. It made me think that, despite the house's shabby outward appearance, business was booming on the inside.

I walked into the beauty salon and looked around for the manicurist's table. Along the long, side wall opposite the door were five stylists' stations decorated in black and white with red accents. At the back of the shop were four red sinks, and in the front was a big picture window trimmed in red. Directly before me was a semicircular counter with a red Formica top staffed by a tall, pretty brunette with a perfect haircut. "Can I help you?" she asked.

I held up my hands, displaying the flat, unpolished nails. "You tell me."

"Carrie," she called over her shoulder, "this one's yours."

A friendly blonde bobbed over and smiled at me. We were the same height so I felt an instant bond with her. "Hi. I'm Carrie. Come on over by the window and have a seat." She led me to a manicure station near the picture window and seated me at a narrow table. "You own Bloomers, don't you?" she asked, putting my nails to soak.

"Mainly just a window and part of the front door. The bank owns the rest."

"I know the feeling. This is my shop—or so I like to pretend." She dried off my fingers and began filing the squares into ovals, looking up as a man darted past the window. She shook her head, sighed, and went back to her work.

"What was that?" I asked.

"Another horny male sneaking over to the massage parlor next door. I post PARKING FOR CUSTOMERS ONLY signs, but they ignore them. Really frosts me when my clients don't have space for their cars."

Playing dumb I asked, "Why don't they park in the spa's lot?"

"If you only knew," she said, rolling her eyes. Then she proceeded to make sure I did.

It was obvious to her that the spa was a place for prostitution. One of her clients had tried to get in for a facial and was refused. They bluntly told her they catered to men only. And according to one of her unsuspecting male customers, the spa offered massages and much more. Top-of-the-line treatment was a two-hundred-dollar special called "The Big Finish."

"Yuck," I said at that remark.

The men who frequented the spa, Carrie said, parked everywhere but there. The worst times were lunch hours and after work. Carrie had talked to patrons of the restaurant/bar across the street who said it went on into the wee hours of the morning.

"Lunch hours, huh?" I commented. "So their unsuspecting wives think they're at McDonald's having a burger, and instead they're at the Emperor's Spa having dessert?"

"You got it. The masseuses come here to buy shampoo and conditioner and they *always* pay in cash—with a roll of bills taken from a wad stuffed in their bras. They won't talk to us. They point to what they want, and then throw the money at us and leave."

"What do they wear?"

"Bright, tight silk dresses."

"Spike heels?"

"Four-inchers."

I watched as Carrie painted on a clear coat of polish. "Have you seen the inside of the spa?" I asked.

"I tried to deliver an order but I couldn't get past the front door. An odd-looking Oriental man peered at me through a window, then opened the door, grabbed the bag, and slammed the door in my face. We've nicknamed him 'the guard' because he seems to watch over the girls. They all live together in an apartment over the realty building down the street. We've seen him walking them back and forth, snapping at them in some Asian tongue."

"Do you think the girls are being held against their will?"

Carrie shrugged. "Could be, but they don't act like it. I mean, they come over here to buy shampoo and things. They could ask us for help. Instead they throw money at us."

"Not very hospitable, are they?"

She scoffed as she stuck my nails under a dryer. "If I were a man they'd be hospitable. Did you see the addition they're putting on the back of the building? We heard rumors that it was built for a sunken hot tub, and from the sound of it, the *hot* part doesn't have anything to do with the water temperature, if you catch my drift."

"Have you complained to the police?"

"You bet I have. I've even put in a phone call to the police chief and written letters to the mayor. I haven't gotten one single response. It's like they're ignoring the situation. Who knows? Maybe they're being paid off."

A woman being permed at the next station snickered at that remark and added, "Yeah, in massages."

Carrie indicated the woman at the reception counter. "Sometimes when Judy sees one of the men sneak across our lot, she'll stand outside our door and glare at them. Not that it does any good. It just disgusts us that this is going on right here in New Chapel. We don't want our children growing up in a town that turns a blind eye to prostitution. It's even worse when it's in the guise of a legitimate business. But without the mayor's cooperation, how do we stop it?"

Hearing the word *how,* my brain began to hum with ideas. It wasn't something I could control. It just happened.

Carrie checked my nails and said, "Do you want to chose a color?"

"What? Oh. Actually, I like them colorless." Plus, I

didn't have the extra cash to pay for a full manicure. It was a luxury I couldn't afford.

"You don't want French tips or anything?"

"Thanks, this will do."

"Okay," she said, as though washing her hands of a hopeless case.

"Have you considered getting a group of women to picket the spa?" I suggested. "Or better yet, take photos of the guys sneaking across your lot and give them to the police."

"You know what the cops will say? 'So what if they're going for a massage? It's a spa. Call a tow truck if they park in your lot.' Besides, I'm afraid of what might happen to my salon if the people next door found out I'd complained. They're not what you'd call neighborly, especially the weird-looking old man. If he retaliated, I couldn't afford to put in another insurance claim. I've already had storm damage twice this spring."

Nothing got my blood flowing like a challenge. Ideally, going in undercover would be the best way to find out what was going on, but Marco had tried it and hadn't seen any Chinese women, so obviously they'd been wary of him. And short of dressing up as a man, I couldn't get in anyway. Besides, there was my promise to Marco hanging over my head.

"What if someone were to take a few photos from across the street and send them to the newspapers?" I asked.

"I tried calling the newspapers to tell them what was going on. No one was interested."

"Maybe with photos they would be. I even know a reporter you can call."

His name was Bill Bretton. He'd done several human-interest stories on my father after he'd been shot, and I'd been impressed with Bill's accuracy. He'd also written up a nice piece about Bloomers when I took over. He was a thirty-five-year-old journalist who had aspirations of being a columnist for the *Chicago Tribune*. I hoped that would make him hungry enough to go after a juicy exposé.

"Would *you* take the pictures?" she asked. "They might spot me, but they wouldn't know you."

I hesitated, picturing Marco and Grace glowering.

"I'll throw in this manicure and two free haircuts," Carrie promised.

The two haircuts alone were worth eighty bucks. Besides, it wasn't like I had suggested it myself, so it really couldn't be considered meddling. The glowering faces started to fade. "I'll do it. Where's your camera?"

Carrie pulled the camera out from beneath the front counter, an instant print kind used to take photos of clients' hairdos. She showed me how to use it, then I walked across the street to the Jumpin' Joe's Restaurant and Bar parking lot, picked a spot on the grassy berm next to a utility pole, and waited for the next horny male to arrive.

Within ten minutes a rusty, older model Chevy pulled into the restaurant lot, and a man got out, looked both ways, and headed across the street to the spa. He was a big guy, construction-worker type. He had on a navy baseball cap with a dirty-blond tail of hair poking through the hole in the back, a light brown goatee, faded green T-shirt, blue jeans worn thin at the knees, and yellow workboots. I snapped two photos of him, then, once he'd gone inside the spa, I walked over to his car and took a picture of it from the side and from the rear, catching the license plate.

I placed the photos on the grass to dry, then looked up to see a man in brown coveralls walk across the street from the direction of an auto parts store. I took his picture and one of his vehicle—a county van. Our tax dollars hard at work.

Next a silver Audi pulled into Carrie's lot, and a guy in a suit got out. When he started toward the spa, I focused the lens on his face and snapped. He glanced my way, saw what I was doing, changed direction, and darted across the street toward the auto parts store.

Like I believed that one.

Half an hour and two additional men later, I tucked the stack of photos into my purse, returned the camera to Carrie, and promised I'd call her as soon as I had information from my reporter friend. I also put her number in my cell phone's memory for quick reference.

Outside the salon, I got the newspaper's number from information, then dialed and asked for the features desk. Bill answered, and I explained the situation to him.

"Sounds interesting," he said in a noncommittal way. "I'm going out on an interview, so I'll drive by the place, take a look, and get back to you."

As I closed the phone I had the weirdest feeling I was being watched. I slid into the Vette and very casually glanced at the spa but I couldn't see anyone. I started the engine, put the car in Reverse, and was about to back out when I caught a slight movement in one of the windows. A corner of the paper had been curled back and a wrinkled Asian face was glaring at me with an expression that sent a chill up my spine.

At once, fragments from one of Grace's sayings came to mind, something about being able to kill with a look.

If that saying was true, from the look I was getting now, I'd be a goner.

CHAPTER NINE

Back at Bloomers, I sat at my desk studying the photos. If the newspaper printed them, the men would be easily identified and, hopefully, highly embarrassed, not to mention in big trouble with their wives. That ought to put a damper on the spa's business. No one would risk going there if he thought he might be caught on film and exposed in the newspaper.

I tucked the photos into the top drawer of my desk, then spent the remainder of the afternoon helping Lottie finish the funeral arrangements so we could get them down to our friends Maxwell and Delilah Dove at the Happy Dreams Funeral Home before five o'clock. Grace was busy with customers in the parlor all afternoon, which was good because it kept her from questioning me about my trip to the hair salon. I didn't offer any information either, not to deceive her, but because I hadn't yet figured out how to tell her. One lecture a day was enough. Besides, I was still of the opinion that what she didn't know wouldn't hurt her.

* * *

"You're going to dress up as a man and sneak into the spa?" Nikki asked. She was eating Chunky Monkey ice cream and watching an old Grace Kelly movie on television. She had come home from work at fifteen minutes after midnight and made a beeline to the freezer for her favorite dessert, then plunked down on the end of the sofa where I lay with a fan blowing on me to dry the oozing bites on my legs—the very same bites that were keeping me up past my bedtime.

"You're not listening. I said that was my *last* resort. How do you eat that stuff and not gain weight? I can feel my thighs expanding just by being close to the carton."

"It's genetic." She sniffed the air. "I smell waffles. Did you make waffles for dinner? I'll bet you didn't save me any. And why do you have dried paste on your legs?"

"For your information this isn't paste, it's oatmeal. Grace recommended an oatmeal bath to stop the itching. Since I couldn't sleep and hate baths, I decided to mix a package of oatmeal with a little water and apply it like a salve."

"You can't use the instant maple-flavored kind, Ab," Nikki said, trying not to laugh. "It has to be plain."

"Maybe that's why Simon kept trying to lick my ankles. He's locked in your bedroom, by the way. He wouldn't leave me alone."

Over her peals of laughter I asked, "Want to hear what I did today?"

"Is it as good as smearing maple-flavored oatmeal on your legs?"

"Depends on whether you consider a juicy item *good*."

Nikki hit the Off button on the remote and gave me her full attention. I filled her in on my visit to the hair salon and the pictures I'd taken, then, after she'd shown the appropriate amount of disgust, I told her about my phone call to the health club to ask about Punch.

"His little *passion flower*?" was Nikki's first reaction. "From what you've told me about him, he doesn't sound like the type to give his girlfriend such a romantic nickname."

"Maybe there was a side to Punch no one knew."

"Didn't you say Flip had known him since grade school? He'd be the likeliest one to ask." Nikki licked more ice cream off her spoon. "Did Marco give you any tips?"

"He gave me more than that," I said, wiggling my eyebrow.

Nikki set the ice cream aside and tucked her legs beneath her, turning to face me. This was her *I'm all ears* pose. "You saved the best for last. Tell me everything."

"First of all, I came up with a plan to get on his good side, a private picnic—"

"You and Marco had a *picnic*?"

I nodded. "—with sandwiches and wine from the deli, and a tablecloth and candle from the restaurant. I spread everything out on the floor in his office—"

"In his *office*?" she squealed.

"Nikki, are you going to repeat everything I say?"

"Sorry. Continue."

"Where was I? Oh yes. We finished eating"—I paused, waiting for her to repeat, but she was behaving, so I went on—"then he kissed me."

Nikki bounced on the cushion like she was sixteen again. "He *kissed* you?"

"Well, actually, it was the other way around. But he did kiss back."

She let out a shriek of delight that started Simon howling for his freedom. "Tell me everything," she commanded.

"Okay. Close your eyes. Now imagine the sexiest movie

star you've ever seen, give him nice, firm lips, a hard body, muscular hands running up and down your back . . ." I let out a wistful sigh.

Nikki's eyes flew open. "And?"

"Jillian arrived."

Seeing that Nikki was about to repeat me, I held up a hand. "Yes, Jillian, and yes, that was the end of the picnic and the kiss. But the story doesn't end unhappily. I did get advice from Marco on where to start investigating, without losing my bet. In fact, he's going to make dinner for me here Saturday night, so you have to find something to do."

Nikki stared at me in surprise. "You're kicking me out?"

"Please, Nikki? I'll buy you a new carton of Chunky Monkey."

"You're kicking me out of my own apartment and for that I get one lousy container of ice cream?"

"A month's supply then."

She picked up the carton and her spoon and dug in once again. "Okay," she said with a mouthful. "I have a date with Scott on Saturday night anyway."

She dodged the pillow I threw at her, so I grabbed her spoon and ate the mound of calories on it.

"I deserved that," she said. "So what did the fabulous kisser say to do first?"

"Find Punch's mystery girlfriend."

I fell asleep that night out of sheer exhaustion and made it through with only one interruption, when Simon decided to sleep next to my legs, which only made them itch more from the tickle of his fur. I decided against locking him out—he'd only sit outside and meow, and that would be harder to ignore than a tickle.

Although the heat and humidity that had moved in overnight were murder on my raw skin, I kept to my routine of an early-morning walk at the track. Not only did it energize me, but it also gave me a chance to form a rough game plan for the murder investigation.

First, I needed to talk to the night clerk at the New Chapel Inn to see what information he might have about the mystery girlfriend. I also wanted to get over to the health club to see if anyone working out had seen Punch with his hothouse flower, or heard him mention her real name. Then on Saturday, hopefully, I could get over to the jail to talk to Flip. And Monday I would call Greg Morgan and set up a lunch date to get even more information.

After a cool shower and a slathering of anti-itch lotion, I put on another lightweight short skirt with a top and my flip-flops and scooted off to work.

"Good morning, dear," Grace called from the parlor. She walked out, took a look at my legs, and said, "Did you try the oatmeal bath?"

No way was I going to admit my mistake. It just wasn't the kind of thing you wanted a person who said "bawth" to know.

"Yes, thanks, I did try the oatmeal, and the itching isn't as bad." That was the absolute truth.

"Marvelous. Here are your messages and your coffee. We had an early delivery of freesias, and you'll be pleased to know they're in tip-top shape. The deliveryman got rather surly with me when I told him to wait while I checked the flowers for brown spots. Nevertheless, he waited. The flowers have been cut and put in hydrating solution."

"You're a marvel, Grace. I'm amazed you were able to get the guy to wait. I usually have to threaten to call his boss."

"There's nothing like a good, hard rap on the head with an umbrella handle."

I blinked at her several times. "You hit him?"

"Shall I give Dave Hammond a call to see if your insurance premium has been paid?"

"Great idea." I took the slips of paper in one hand, the cup and saucer in the other, and headed for my desk in the workroom. "Where's Lottie?"

"Herman wasn't feeling well this morning so Lottie took him to the doctor. She was quite worried. Shall we think good thoughts for Herman?"

"We shall." I sipped the coffee and discarded the first three messages, all from my mother reminding me about the dinner that night. Like we hadn't been doing it for the past four years. The fourth message was from Greg Morgan. I placed that one next to the phone. The fifth was from Trudee DeWitt, who had a new idea for her party.

I checked to see if any orders had come in over the wire and found six, two of them needing to go out by early afternoon. I put them on the worktable, checked our flower supplies, then picked up the phone and called the prosecutor's office.

"Greg Morgan, please," I said briskly to the nasal-toned secretary. "Abby Knight calling."

"Are you an attorney?"

She knew darn well I wasn't. She and I had tangled before. "I'm the florist."

"Hold, please."

I sat there for at least three minutes, the phone against my ear, listening to an FM radio station play a harpsichord piece, imagining the secretary sitting in front of her phone, filing her nails and smiling while I cooled my heels. I got so bored that I pulled out the spa photos and glanced through them. Five men, five different walks of life, all after one thing. Disgusting.

After that, I arranged the paper clips in my tray from

small to large, then did the same with the rubber bands. I wouldn't have endured another second of the *plinkety plink* sound of the harpsichord if it weren't for Morgan's having access to information that could help send Jillian cruising down that aisle. Luckily, Morgan got on the line before the musician had harped his last chord.

"Abby! I'm surprised you called back so quickly."

I grabbed Grace's message and checked the time. The call had come in a mere ten minutes ago, which made me look pathetically eager to talk to him, or maybe just pathetic. Either way, it wasn't the image I wanted.

I'd had a total of three dates with Morgan since he'd rediscovered me, and if I'd had to rank them on a scale of one to ten, they wouldn't have made the long climb up to two. Somehow I had to make it clear that I was neither eager nor pathetic, yet still arrange a meeting as soon as possible.

My father always said the best defense was a good offense, so I replied pleasantly, "Did you call?"

"Well, yes. Isn't that why you called?"

"Isn't that odd?" I said with a light laugh. "I was responding to the suggestion you made—when was that . . . way back on Monday?—that we set up a lunch date."

He laughed, too. "Great minds think alike."

Not in a million years, buster. "So how does your calendar look for next Monday?"

I heard him flipping a page. "I've got a full day. How does Tuesday work for you?"

It would work, but I didn't want to waste a single day. "Not as good as Monday."

There was a pause and then he said, "Tell you what. For you, Abby Knight, I will switch appointments around, as long as we can make it for one o'clock at Rosie's."

Rosie's was a diner around the corner from the courthouse. It wasn't known for great food, but it was quiet and slow, both of which worked for my purposes. "That's good. See you then." I crumpled his message and tossed it in the trash can. One chore out of the way.

Next on my list was a call to my father, asking him to use his connections to get me inside the jail. He promised to phone as soon as he had the okay. Within the hour I had the third chore marked off as well—a plan and estimate for Trudee DeWitt's party. I phoned her and got her pink-haired daughter.

"Hi, this is Abby Knight. Is your mother at home?"

"Who's calling." No tone to her voice, not even a question mark.

"Abby Knight, as I just said."

"Would you spell that?"

"Sure, but let's take one question at a time, the first one being, is your mother *home*?"

"I guess so."

She was purposely trying my patience, but having had a few psychology classes in college, I knew just how to handle her—with sympathy and a firm hand. "Look, I understand that it's difficult being a teenager because I was there a few years ago, and I also know that you know whether your mother is home or not. You can't guess about those things. So, may I please speak with her? Now?"

There was a pause and then she said, "I'll call her." Half a second later my eardrum shattered when she yelled "Mo-o-o-om! Are you ho-o-o-me?"

She put down the phone and walked away.

"Hello?" I called, after several minutes passed. Then louder, "HELLO?"

I heard footsteps, then the atonal voice came on the line. "I *guess* she's not here."

Checkmate.

"Would you tell her to call me, please?"

"Who's calling."

Forget the child psychology, this girl needed a good smack upside the head. I was just about to tell her so when I heard the sharp click of high heels, then a loudly whispered argument, then the sound of a struggle, after which Trudee said, "Hello?"

"Trudee, it's Abby Knight."

"Abby, I'm so sorry. Hold on." She put the phone away from her mouth and yelled, "You're grounded for a week, young lady. No, make that a month!"

In the background I heard a door slam.

"Two months!" she shouted. Then to me, "Is the army recruiting office open?"

"Probably, but you can't sign her up."

"Her? Hell, I'm talking about me. The problem is that if I enlist, my husband will, too, in self-defense, and then my kids will destroy the house. So it looks like I'm stuck. How are you with flags?"

"Excuse me?"

"I had this great idea for my party," she said. "A big U.S. flag done in flowers."

"How big are we talking?"

"Thirty-six by seventy-two."

"About the size of a kitchen table?"

"About the size of my backyard. I'm talking feet, not inches."

I tore up the estimate and dropped the pieces in the trash can. "I need to look at the lawn. How is Monday morning at ten o'clock?"

"Great. I'll see you then."

My second line rang and I answered it to find my father on the other end. "You've got a visit set up for Sunday morning at eleven o'clock."

"Sunday?"

"One day is the same as another in jail. Ask for Patty. She'll process you through." Patty was a jail matron my dad had known for years. I thanked him profusely and hung up.

I heard the bell jingle in the front so I went out to lend Grace a hand. She was busy at the counter with a customer, so I greeted the two arrivals from the courthouse who had come in for their afternoon break, and showed them to a table in the parlor.

"Mocha latte," one of the girls said.

"Same for me," the other one said. "Heavy on the mocha."

I took one look at the latte machine and knew I was in trouble. "Your drinks will be right up," I promised, and slipped out of the room to find Grace.

"You've got to teach me how to run that machine," I told her as soon as her customer had gone.

"I have taught you, dear. You've simply forgotten." She gave me an encouraging pat on the back. "You've got a lot on your mind with your cousin's dilemma. It's perfectly understandable."

Under the force of her compassion I felt like a real heel. There was only one recourse: I had to come clean about the Emperor's Spa investigation.

At that moment, Lottie breezed in, all smiles. "Herman's okay; he's just got a touch of asthma. It's not his heart after all."

We hugged her, and everyone was happy, so I decided to live with my secret a little while longer.

The parlor got very busy over the noon hour, so I ended up serving coffee, tea, and scones well into the afternoon. I stepped out once to take a call from Jillian, who wanted to know if I had solved the murder yet. Time was running out, she reminded me. Then I reminded her that I did have a struggling business to run, and that I was doing the best I could.

Sensing my irritation she lapsed into baby talk. "I'm sowwy, Abs. I still wub you."

Wub wasn't exactly what I was feeling for her at that moment. *Stwess* was more like it.

Around two thirty that afternoon, as I was pouring refills of vanilla-flavored coffee for a table of chattering ladies, I happened to glance out the bay window and see a slender boy standing beside my Vette. He appeared to be in his early teens and was dressed in gray sweatpants and hooded sweatshirt, the hood pulled up, an odd choice for a hot summer day.

I watched closely as he leaned in for a closer look, as if he were checking out the dash. It was something people often did when they saw a snazzy convertible. I'd done it myself. It was one of the drawbacks of leaving the top down. But when I saw him reach inside, I put down the coffeepot, slipped out of the parlor, and dashed for the door. Looking is fine, but no one touches my Vette.

"Hey!" I called from the sidewalk. "Get away from my car!"

I figured he'd jump back and look around in guilty surprise. Instead, he calmly put his hand down by his side and walked quickly toward the courthouse, keeping his back toward me. I hurried across the street to check out my yellow baby, but there was no apparent damage.

Because I'd once had my fuel line cut by a deranged male, I got down on my bare knees, placed my palms on the paved street, and peered underneath the car. Fortunately, nothing appeared to be cut or leaking. Maybe I was just being paranoid.

I got back to the shop just as two rush orders came in. One was particularly challenging, a floor arrangement in a seaside theme. Lottie and I brainstormed that one and finally came up with an idea. We filled an aquarium with sand and seashells, then I drove up to the lake and cut a selection of ornamental dune grasses that grew along the roads, added blue bachelor's buttons to represent the sky, bright anemone for the sea, and tufts of goldenrod and wild yellow daisies for the sun, and voilà! Our masterpiece was finished.

By four o'clock business had slowed to a crawl and the square looked like a ghost town, probably due to the soaring temperature and high humidity. New Chapel residents didn't cope well with extreme temperatures. If tumbleweed grew in our area, even it would stay home.

At four forty-five I called it quits, sent the ladies home, and was just about to lock up when I again had that odd sensation of being watched. Instantly I turned, scanning the cars in the street and the people around the square, but didn't see anyone paying particular attention to me.

Suddenly, someone called, "Wait! Oh, please, wait!"

I glanced to my left and saw a well-dressed, thirtysomething woman hurrying up the sidewalk carrying a child-sized, green wooden wheelbarrow. "I'm having a dinner party tonight on my deck and I need an outdoorsy decoration," she said, wiping her damp forehead with the back of her hand. "Would you whip up something for me and put it in this?"

It was a great antique barrow and I could imagine all kinds of fun things to do with it, but I didn't dare walk into the country club late, not with Pryce and family there to cluck their tongues at me. "I'm really sorry, but I have a dinner date."

"I'll pay you twice what it's worth. Just please help me."

Double payment. Sweet. It would pay for a pair of sexy heels to offset the horrid bridesmaid dress.

I invited her back to the workroom to get her opinion on what I had in mind—wild daisies, pink dianthus, and blue forget-me-nots, with sprigs of mountain grass drooping like a waterfall and green ivy spiraling down the sides. She thought it sounded perfect, so I set to work.

Her name was Elizabeth Bentley, I soon discovered. She and her husband had moved to town a year ago to teach at the university. She was throwing the dinner for other profs and their wives, which was a great opportunity for me to promote my work. And because I was being accommodating, she decided on the spot to permanently switch her business to Bloomers.

"It's marvelous!" Elizabeth gushed when I'd finished. "I can't thank you enough. How much do I owe you?"

If there were any exclamations better than those three, I didn't know about them. I did a quick calculation and named my price. She paid in cash and didn't even flinch as she counted out the bills. I wrapped floral paper around the barrow and carried it to the door for her.

"Thanks again, Abby," she said. "I'll tell everyone I know to come here."

Okay, there was an exclamation better than the first three, and it was music to my ears. But now I had only one hour to drive home, make myself presentable, and get to the club.

Quickly, I cleaned the mess on the worktable, grabbed my purse, set the alarm, and locked the door. As I turned to go to my car, I caught a sudden movement in my peripheral vision. I turned my head and scanned the sidewalk to my right, but all I saw was a piece of newspaper being carried along by a hot breeze. I crossed the street and was about to open my car door when my cell phone rang. I dug in my purse and flipped open the phone.

"Abby, this is Bill Bretton. Just wanted to let you know

I took a look at the Emperor's Spa this afternoon, and I have to agree with you. It doesn't look legitimate."

I leaned against the Vette and put one finger in my ear to block out a particularly noisy truck rumbling past. "What do you think about doing an exposé?" I asked loud enough for him to hear me.

"I'll have to check with my boss first, but I'd sure love to poke around a bit and see what's going on there. You say you have photos? Can I stop by the shop on Monday and have a look at them?"

"Absolutely. If I'm not there, ask for Lottie—only Lottie. The photos are in my top desk drawer."

I called the salon's number and gave Carrie the news.

"That's terrific, Abby. I really appreciate your help. But please be careful. I get really bad vibes from next door."

"Don't worry," I told her. "They don't know where I live."

I glanced at my shop across the street and saw the hooded youth I had seen earlier staring into one of Bloomer's bay windows. Just before another truck rumbled by he turned to gaze straight at me, as if he knew I was watching. But it wasn't a boy's face. It was a wrinkled old man's face, the same one I had seen peering at me from the window of the Emperor's Spa. As before, under the intensity of his hostile glare, a chill slithered up my spine.

When the big vehicle had passed, the old man was gone, not a trace of him anywhere.

"Don't worry," I assured myself again as I climbed into the Vette. "He doesn't know where I live."

CHAPTER TEN

D inner at the country club was at seven o'clock, as usual, but instead of it being just my family—a group that normally included my two brothers Jonathan and Jordan, their wives Portia and Kathy, occasionally my niece Tara, my parents, and me—I also had the Osbornes to contend with, a number that now included Jillian, who already considered herself an Osborne. She had even gone so far as to have her Ralph Lauren towels monogrammed with big satin O's. In fact, Jillian had had so many towels personalized over the last five years that she was on a first-name basis with the ladies at the Bloomingdale's monogram counter.

Because I was not up to any more questions about my legs, I had put on the lightest pair of slacks I owned, a beige linen that I rarely wore only because I looked crumpled enough without purposely trying. I had lucked out to find a clean, short-sleeved navy sweater in my closet, and after hastily applying a lip and cheek stain—there was no covering those freckles anyway, so why bother trying?—and running a comb through my hair, I was off in my Vette, top down, radio tuned to light jazz because I was in that kind of mood.

I arrived at the last minute, hoping to avoid seeing Pryce and his family for as long as possible. I had armed myself with antihistamines so I wouldn't scratch, anti-itch lotion in case the antihistamines failed, and the knowledge that no matter how bad things got, being married to Pryce would have been worse.

As I walked across the parking lot I saw my mother pull her van into a handicapped spot near the front door, so I veered left to greet my parents. My father opened his door and a platform automatically slid forward to lower his wheelchair to the pavement.

"Here's my baby," he said cheerily. I bent to hug him, in-haling that familiar Old Spice scent that always made me feel safe. I got a peck on the cheek and an outfit inspection from my mother. She didn't remark on it, which meant I had passed. But she couldn't resist straightening the charm dangling from a skinny silver chain around my neck. At least she hadn't licked her palm to smooth my hair.

"Have your brothers arrived?" she asked.

I pointed out their Jags and then spotted Pryce's BMW just pulling into the lot. "Hey, let's get inside," I said, start-ing toward the door. "There's a storm coming."

My parents tilted their heads upward, searching the crystal blue sky for that dark cloud, when it was actually stepping out of the Beemer that very moment.

"Coming?" I called, waving them toward me like a po-liceman directing traffic.

Too late. They spotted him.

"Oh, look, here comes Pryce!" my mother said excitedly, forming a reception line.

Gritting my teeth, I walked back to stand dutifully be-side my father as Pryce played the role of gentleman-of-the-year. He was dressed in his usual preppy mode: brown tasseled loafers, gray flannel slacks, white shirt with button-down collar, and despite the heat, a marine blue sweater draped with studied casualness over his shoulders. It was a dated look. Or maybe it was Pryce who was dated. I hung on to that thought.

"Good to see you both," he said, putting on a smarmy smile. "You're looking well, Mr. Knight. Mrs. Knight, you're as beautiful as ever. What about those Cubs? Think they'll take the division this year?"

He nodded in my direction once, but other than that, politely ignored me. When his parents pulled in, he went to meet them, and I hustled my parents inside before I had to endure more of the same from them.

"You're always rushing me," my mother complained.

My father reached back to pat my hand as I pushed his wheelchair into the restaurant. "Maureen, it's painful for Abby to be around Pryce. Imagine how you would have felt if I had dropped *you* two months before we were married."

"If you had dropped me," my mother said, an impish twinkle in her eye, "*you* would be the one feeling the pain."

As we crossed to the window side of the room, I was surprised to see Onora there, since this was a family-only event. She was sitting across from Jillian at the long table listening to my cousin rattle on nonstop. Like Jillian, she wore a chic black outfit and, to look at her, one would think she was her normal, bored self. But her left hand was doubled into a fist on the table and her right hand was wrapped around her knife so tightly that her knuckles were white. I wouldn't have been surprised to see a trickle of blood run down her wrist. If anyone was in pain *that* night, it was Onora. But was it from grief, or guilt?

I managed to snag a chair on Jillian's left, not that I had a burning desire to sit beside my cousin, but so that I could quietly question her about Onora's behavior since Wednesday night. I was relieved to see Pryce take the chair on the other side of Claymore, on Jillian's right, and his parents sit at the far end. My brothers and their wives filled the opposite side of the table, with pale Portia ending up next to the bloodless Onora. It was a good match.

My niece Tara had a babysitting job, lucky her, and had escaped the weekly ordeal. My mother sat on my left, with my father at the end of the table to accommodate his wheelchair.

The meal started with a toast to the soon-to-be-wed couple, made, of course, by Pryce, who thought himself a witty orator and proved to everyone that he was wrong. It was the highlight of my evening.

"To my brother and his lovely fiancée," he began, holding his wineglass high, "two people about to embark on the high seas of life, captain and first mate—"

I assumed he knew that Jillian would be captaining that ship.

"—sailing through troughs and tempests, births and deaths—"

At the word *death* Onora paled and several others sucked in their breaths hard enough to cause the tablecloth to shudder. But did that stop Pryce?

"—cruising starboard to port to that final sunset on the distant horizon . . ."

He stopped, his words hanging in midair, apparently having run out of sailing references. It took a moment for people to realize he was done—or for them to wake up— then everyone took a sip and sat back with sighs of relief. Onora tilted her head back and drained her glass. At that rate, she wouldn't be in pain for long.

As the bread baskets were passed, I whispered to Jill, "How is Onora?"

"Quiet."

"She's always quiet."

"Deathly quiet."

"Poor choice of words, Jill." Stifling a sudden urge to yawn, I took a slice of crusty bread, passed the basket to my mother, then turned back to Jillian. "Has Onora said anything about the murder?"

"Nothing."

"Why is she here, exactly?"

"Because I can't get rid of her," Jill whispered back. "She's sticking to me like glue. It's driving me absolutely crazy. I took an hour-long bath today just to have time to myself."

"You hate baths."

"Do you see my desperation? After dinner I'm meeting up with the girls at my house, tomorrow we're all going to the outlet mall, and Sunday is my bridal shower. It's become like a twenty-four-hour, seven-days-a-week TV station. All Onora all the time."

I poured olive oil on my bread dish and passed the cruet along. "What's her problem?"

"Depression, I suppose. She was crazy-in-love with Punch."

Crazy enough to kill him? I shot a glance in Onora's direction. She was picking at the crust of her bread, appearing to be oblivious to what was going on around her. I wondered how much of that was an act.

"How's Flip doing?" I asked Jill, dipping a hunk of bread in the oil.

"He's miserable. Clay got in to the jail to see him today. He said he's never seen him so overwrought. It's a good thing they took away his shoelaces or—" She made a gesture that was supposed to look like someone tightening a noose around her neck. I saw Onora's eyes flick over to us briefly, then shift away. She wasn't oblivious.

"Has Flip said anything about Wednesday night?" I whispered.

"I'll ask." Jillian elbowed her fiancé, interrupting his conversation with Pryce to ask my question. You just couldn't hide good breeding.

Claymore took the interruption calmly, then leaned behind Jillian to say to me, "Flip is so upset that I didn't have the heart to mention it, and he didn't volunteer anything. He might have said something to Pryce, but, naturally, that's confidential."

"Have funeral arrangements been made?"

"As soon as the autopsy is completed Punch's body will be flown back east. The sad thing is that none of us can leave to attend the funeral. I think that's bothering Flip more than anything else."

I let it go at that and contented myself with observing Onora, who had given up the knife in favor of the wineglass stem. Her hand shook as she lifted the glass to her mouth, and then she met my gaze over the rim of her glass and practically shot daggers at me.

What had I done?

I decided to abandon that pursuit in favor of a new one: trying to stay awake. My drowsiness was easy to explain, given the ridiculously dull conversation going on around me, possibly because everyone was being careful not to speak of the murder in front of the bride-and-groom-to-be. I was so overcome with the urge to put my head down and take a snooze that at one point during dinner I got a discreet poke from my mother, who claimed I had begun to snore.

"You're not on drugs, are you?" she whispered loud enough for my father to hear.

"Who's on drugs?" he said, leaning toward us.

"No one is on drugs," I whispered back, although at that point there wasn't much use in whispering since word was quickly spreading to the other end of the table. I could just imagine Pryce's mother muttering to her husband, "I knew there was something wrong with her. Thank goodness Pryce dumped her when he did."

"I am not on drugs," I said loud enough to clear it up in everyone's mind, even the busboy cleaning up the table behind us. "I took an antihistamine. One lousy antihistamine."

"Antihistamines cause drowsiness," my brother Jordan felt compelled to point out. And that prompted Jonathan to remind me that I should always read the side effects printed on the package.

My mother rose to my defense. "If I read about all the things that could go wrong, I'd never take so much as an aspirin."

Her remark caused all sorts of debate about the pharmaceutical industry—a much better subject for discussion than my potential drug habit—but it did little to keep me awake. That was until my sister-in-law Portia, known around town as the albino babe in the burgundy Bentley, leaned across the table toward Jillian and said bluntly, "That's a shame about your groomsman being murdered. Have you found a replacement for him yet?"

Apparently, it hadn't occurred to Portia that finding a stand-in for a body not yet buried wasn't Jillian's top priority at the moment. And by the horrified expression on Jillian's face, it was only now occurring to her that she needed one.

There was still another repercussion to Portia's thoughtless comment. Onora threw down her napkin, stood abruptly, nearly tipping over her chair, and sailed full speed from the room.

I shot my brother Jonathan a look that said, *What the hell was Portia thinking?* Then he leaned in to whisper something in his wife's ear, after which they had a private—and none too friendly—moment of conversation. To cover the awkward silence that followed, my father immediately began a discussion about the White Sox.

"Abby," Jillian said, pulling at my arm just as I was about to take my last bite of mashed sweet potato.

"I know, Jill," I said quietly. "That was a horrible thing for Portia to say, and I apologize for her."

"Never mind about that," she said in a rising panic. "Who can I get on short notice? The tuxes have already been ordered."

I chewed my food and swallowed. "Aren't the groomsmen part of Claymore's responsibilities? Let him pick someone."

"Are you serious? It was hard enough getting him to pick the first time."

"How does Claymore function, Jill? How does he decide what socks to put on in the morning?"

"Are you helping the situation?" she countered tersely.

"Point taken. What about Claymore's childhood friends?"

"Moved away."

"All of them?"

"You say that like he had more than one."

Jillian was right. I'd forgotten about the lengthy screening process the Osbornes used to weed out undesirable playmates. Most kids either flunked the initial genealogy requirement or grew up before completing the battery of tests. "How about a good client?"

Jillian conferred with Claymore, then turned back, happy once again. "Clay knows just the guy. He's two years older than us, but Clay plays tennis with him every Saturday. You might know him. He's a deputy prosecutor."

"Don't tell me you're talking about Greg Morgan."

"You do know him!" Jillian squeezed my arm. "Great, because that's who you're partnered with."

Check, please.

As soon as the dessert tray was brought out I muttered a hasty good-bye and made my escape. The conversation had been so dull that if I'd stayed any longer I'd have fallen asleep in the sorbet. Since it was only eight thirty, and since I didn't want to sit at home trying not to think about what being partnered with Morgan while wearing a clown outfit would do to my psyche, I decided to pay a visit to the New Chapel Inn to talk to the night clerk.

The clerk was once again sitting on a stool behind the reception counter reading a paperback, oblivious to my presence even though I had been boring a two-inch hole in his forehead with my eyes for at least three minutes. He was the same clerk I had seen Wednesday evening—a few years older than me, with short brown hair and ultralong sideburns. Looking at him up close, I also noticed a bristly growth under his lower lip that he must have thought made him fashionable. The brass name tag on his shirt said TODD.

"Excuse me," I said pleasantly.

"Are you checking in?"

He didn't look up, he didn't even bat an eye. If there's one thing I hate it's a clerk who treats me as if I'm invisible. Trying to maintain a pleasant tone I asked, "Would you stop reading that book if I said yes?"

He glanced up and blinked rapidly, possibly trying to fire up his brain cells. "Huh?"

I knew right then I'd have to keep it simple. "Would you mind if I asked you a few questions, Todd, such as whether you were on duty Wednesday night?"

"Why? Are you a cop?"

"Actually, I have this really annoying cousin who has to get married in less than three weeks and I'm trying to help that process along by finding a killer. So, were you on duty Wednesday night?"

He glanced at his computer screen, hit the Tab button a few times, then said, "Yeah, I was here."

"Good. Next question. There are three girls staying in room four twelve. Tall, gorgeous, long-haired . . . Do you know who I'm talking about?"

He perked up suddenly. "Yeah. They're babes."

"On Wednesday night, around eight o'clock, one of these—um—babes came back here alone—the dark-haired one. Do you remember that?"

He scratched the little strip of fuzz below his lip. "No."

Which meant either that Todd hadn't been paying attention (no surprise there), or that Onora hadn't gone directly to the hotel after her fitting at the bridal salon. "Okay, now think hard, Todd. This is important. At any time after eight o'clock that evening, did you see this black-haired babe enter or leave the hotel?"

He shook his head.

It had been worth a try.

"But I *did* see her in the parking lot."

It was my turn to perk up. "What time?"

He thought for a moment. "Nine o'clock."

If Todd was correct, that was an hour not accounted for. "You're sure of the time?"

"It was my break." He hitched a thumb toward the brass chiming clock on the wall behind his right shoulder, next to a doorway. "I always duck out the back for a smoke at nine. I was standing out there when she drove in."

"And you're absolutely positive it was the dark-haired girl?"

"Hey, you don't forget a body like that." He looked at *my* body and turned beet red. "Sorry."

"So am I, Todd."

"It's just that she had on these long, shiny black gloves and this really hot red outfit with a slit up to her—"

I didn't want to know which body part he was about to name, so I cut him off with, "Could that red outfit have been a negligee?"

"A what, now?"

"Nightgown."

He scratched the fuzz, looking perplexed. "I guess. But why would she wear her nightgown to go out?"

Good question. And why the black gloves? Was she worried about fingerprints? "You're absolutely sure you saw her Wednesday night?"

"Yeah, because it was Maria's last night here—she was the housekeeper on the late shift." He snickered. "Maria walked in on some naked chick and got reamed out so bad she gave notice. Nice lady, but she's got a short fuse."

I pondered the nightgown problem. Onora had been wearing it when we came to check on her, so at some point after she left the bridal salon, before Todd saw her in the parking lot, she had put it on.

Todd shook his head ruefully, still musing about the housekeeper incident. "*Man,* I wish I'd seen that. A naked Chinese chick. Can you believe my luck?"

My brain snapped to attention at the word *Chinese.* "Back up a minute, Todd. Is this Chinese woman staying here?"

"If she is, I sure haven't seen her."

I knew I ought to stick to one subject at a time, but now my curiosity was aroused. If this Chinese woman wasn't a registered guest, then she must have been visiting someone. That brought two questions to mind: 1) Could she be an employee of the Emperor's Spa; and 2) were hotel visits part of their services?

"Did you see this woman leave the hotel after her encounter with Maria?"

"No. But she could have left while I was outside."

"You were outside only that one time?"

"Right. Oh, wait. Make that twice. Some weird old dude was hanging around the parking lot. I saw him through the window and went outside to chase him off."

"In what room did this reaming-out take place?"

He shrugged. "You'd have to ask Maria."

"I'd like to do that. How do I find her?"

Todd punched in something on his keyboard, wrote down an address, and handed it to me.

Maria Mendoza, I read. I'd have to add a visit to Maria's house to my Saturday to-do list. "Just out of curiosity, what does a housekeeper do on the late shift?"

He hunched a shoulder. "It's more of an emergency thing, like someone runs out of tissues or clean towels, or pukes all over the bathroom floor and needs a cleanup."

I made a mental note to never take a job as a night housekeeper. "One more question, Todd. What time did this reaming-out happen?"

"Like an hour before my break. Maria usually covers the desk for me, but since she had just quit," he looked over his shoulder, then leaned toward me to whisper, "I had to leave it unattended."

I found myself glancing around, too, as I leaned toward him. "Why are we whispering?"

"I don't want anyone to know."

"Is your manager around?"

"No. He leaves at six."

I looked around at the empty lobby. "There's no one here but us, Todd, so we don't really need to whisper." But I did need to take a look at the guest register to see if an Asian woman was registered. I pulled out a five-dollar bill and placed it on the counter. "It's about time for your break, isn't it?"

He eyed the money. "Yeah."

I shoved the bill toward him. "Tell you what. I'll watch the counter for you while you run outside for a quick smoke." I shuddered on the last word, sure I'd be struck by lightning for encouraging him to light up.

Todd reached for the money, then drew his hand back. "I don't know. If my manager finds out, he'll fire me in a second."

I took out another five and laid it on top of the first. "I promise I won't tell."

"Sweet." He snatched the bills and ducked through the doorway behind him.

I darted around to the other side of the counter, perched on the vacated stool, and stared at his computer screen, wondering how to get to the guest list. I found an icon in the shape of an open book, double clicked, and a register popped up. I typed in Wednesday's date, checked the list, and worked backward from there, searching for an obviously Asian first or last name.

I had gone back three weeks when the phone rang. Since Todd was nowhere in sight I grabbed the handset and blurted, "New Chapel Inn and Suites. Will you hold, please?" I pushed the Hold button, went to the doorway, and called for Todd, then went back to the computer to continue my search.

But Todd didn't return, and the Hold button kept flashing. Knowing how irritating it is to be left waiting, I punched it again, picked up the handset, and said, "Someone will be right with you."

"Who is this?" a male voice on the other end snarled.

Like I would give up my name to an anonymous caller who could potentially be an ax murderer. "Who is *this*?" I countered.

"Sergeant Reilly of the New Chapel Police Department."

Oops.

CHAPTER ELEVEN

My finger went instinctively to the Hold button—purely as a matter of self-preservation. I was fairly certain Reilly was working on the murder investigation, and I knew he wouldn't take it well if he found out I was poking around in his case. But then I thought, *What the heck, might as well see what I can learn from him.*

"Can I help you?" I asked sweetly.

"Do I know you?" Reilly barked. "You sound familiar."

Scratch that plan. "I have one of those familiar voices. Please hold for the night clerk." I punched the button and ran to get Todd.

"Here's another five," I told him, slapping a bill in his hand as we jogged toward the front desk. "Forget I was ever here."

"Sweet."

Since I had exhausted my list of questions anyway, I decided it would be easier on Todd's conscience if I actually did leave, so I slipped out the revolving door and headed for the Vette. It had been an expensive trip, but I had uncovered a valuable bit of information: Onora had lied about being in her hotel room all evening. I wasn't sure what to do with the information about the Chinese woman, so I tucked that away for another day.

Setting up a time frame in my mind, I decided it would have been possible for Onora to leave the bridal salon, drive out to the Dunes National Park, slug Punch with the camera, and return by nine. But that begged the questions of what had prompted her costume change and why she had gone to the dunes. Had Punch called her first, as someone else had suggested? Or had she gone back to the hotel parking lot, spotted him driving away, and decided to follow him?

I should have asked Todd what he knew about Punch.

I glanced through the hotel's big picture window. Todd was on the stool reading again, which meant his conversation with Reilly was over, leaving it safe for me to go in. A quick peek in my wallet showed another five and three ones, enough for a little more information.

"Hello again," I said cheerily, striding toward the counter.

"Hey," he said tonelessly and turned the page.

"I have one more question for you, Todd. Do you remember seeing a hulking brute of a guy wearing a gold earring that looked like a punching bag?"

He looked up at me in surprise. "You mean Punch? Yeah. He was cool. He taught me some boxing moves." Todd got into a sparring stance and threw a few jabs my direction before sobering again. "I can't believe someone offed him."

"Did you see Punch Wednesday evening, the night he was—offed?" It was a stupid term—would saving someone be *onning* them?—but I figured he'd relate better if I used his lingo.

Todd scratched his lip fuzz again, contemplating my

question. "Punch came in a little after I started my shift at six o'clock. We talked about boxing for a while, then he said he had to get ready because he had a big night ahead. He shook my hand and told me to wish him luck."

"Wish him luck? Did he say about what?"

"He just said, 'Wish me luck, dude.' "

"You didn't see him after that?"

"Nope."

I dug a business card out of my purse and handed it to him. "Here's my name and phone number. If you remember anything else about that evening, something Punch might have said, anything out of the usual, give me a call."

"Cool."

Headlights shone through the window. I turned for a look and saw a squad car pull up to the front. "That policeman on the phone, Todd, did he say he was coming over to talk to you about the murder?"

"Yeah. That's probably him now."

I handed Todd my last five and said in a rush, "Hide that business card. I'm going to leave through the back."

"And I'm supposed to forget you were here again, right?"

"You got it." I dashed through the doorway just as the revolving door started to spit out blue shirts.

The effects of the antihistamine wore off ten minutes after I'd crawled into bed, ready to settle into a much needed slumber. Simon was stretched out beside me, the air conditioner wasn't groaning as much as it usually did, and the itchy bites were starting to dry up, leaving me ripe for dreamland. Then my eyes popped wide-open and I lay there staring at a ceiling patterned by shadows from the streetlights shining through the slits in my miniblinds.

I started thinking about the murder, sorting through the

sketchy details I'd gleaned from Todd the night clerk. Clearly, Punch had been about to do something he thought was daring and felt he needed some luck. I had a hard time believing it involved picking up a date, since he'd apparently never had a problem attracting women.

Then what had he been up to? A job interview? Not likely late in the evening. A boxing match? He would have bragged about it to Todd. Other than weddings, for what other occasions were people wished good luck? Gambling? A big poker game? Kind of odd to ask a hotel clerk for luck with that.

Unable to put my finger on that answer, I turned my attention to the person who was fast becoming my prime suspect: Onora. Where had she gone that she couldn't tell us, especially in that slinky red outfit?

Outside my window, someone blew their car horn— once, twice, three times—jarring me further awake and sending Simon scurrying under the bed. When the noise continued, I got out of bed and peered through the blinds to see what idiot was causing the ruckus.

The idiot was me. Or rather, my car, whose lights were flashing and horn was blaring. Someone had set off my alarm, and the first suspect that popped into my head was the wrinkled old man. I scanned the parking lot from my window, but didn't see anyone in the area, so I threw on a sweater, slipped into my flip-flops, grabbed my car keys from the kitchen counter, and raced down the stairs and out the door to the parking lot before the entire apartment complex turned out to boo at me. The bad thing about having an alarm system installed on a car that wasn't designed for it is that it doesn't take much to set it off.

I aimed the keyless remote at the car and everything shut off, leaving the lot eerily silent. I glanced up at the apartment building windows and saw faces scowling down at me. "Sorry," I mouthed and gave a friendly wave. Blinds dropped back into place, and suddenly I was alone.

I kept one eye on the surrounding area as I inspected the car, just in case someone should be lurking, but the Vette didn't appear to have been bothered. Casting repeated glances over both shoulders, I headed back to the building and met Mrs. Sample at the door. Luckily, Peewee was on a leash. I didn't need more bites on my ankles.

"Did someone try to break into your car?" she asked in her rapid-fire way. "Someone broke into our car once and took our radio—a silly little radio not worth the bother—and caused all kinds of damage, and that car has never been the same. I hope they didn't steal anything."

I knew she had to stop to draw a breath eventually and, as soon as she did, I seized my opportunity. "Nothing," I said forcefully enough to get her attention, "was taken. You can go back to bed. Thanks for checking, though."

"Peewee had to do his duty anyway—you know how dogs are—well, I guess you don't after all, what with a cat and all—"

"Say hi to your husband for me," I said and dashed up the stairs. I hurried to the end of the hall and stopped abruptly. My apartment door was open. Had I left it that way?

No reason to panic. There was a logical explanation. Sure, I had it. Nikki had come home while I was downstairs and . . . *No good. You would have met her on the stairs or seen her in the parking lot.*

How about this? Simon had somehow managed to turn the doorknob. . . . *Now you're really reaching. How about you just ran out and forgot to shut it?*

Of course. I simply forgot to shut it when I ran downstairs. And that's when the ax murderer slipped in.

I considered asking Mrs. Sample if she'd noticed my

door standing open when she came out of her unit across the hall, but the thought of getting her going on that thread was deterrent enough. Instead, I decided to cautiously check it out myself.

I took one step inside and stopped, listening, ready to flee at the slightest sound, but all I heard was the wheezing of the window air conditioner. Or was that Simon snoring? Hearing nothing else, I peered around the corner into the kitchen. Nothing out of place there. Quietly, I slipped my phone off the charger on the kitchen counter, turned it on, and punched in 911. Holding my thumb over the Send button, I crept into the living room for a look around.

Nothing out of place there either. I glanced up the hallway that led to the bedrooms and bathroom and could see that the fire escape window at the end of the hall was tightly shut. Feeling braver, I tiptoed to the bathroom and slowly pushed the door wide open. The tub/shower was to my right, partially hidden behind the door, and the vinyl shower curtain, a dark purple, pink, and blue swirl of color, was pulled closed.

I knew I'd never rest until I looked in the shower, but I couldn't bring myself to actually open the curtain. I'd seen the movie *Psycho* too many times. I came up with another plan instead. I backed out of the room and said in a deep, booming voice, "Okay, men, check the bathroom." Then I stamped my feet on the floor as if there were several of me running up the hall.

Nothing. Not one sound. Even the air conditioner had shut off. Simon must have gone back into hiding.

I stepped into the bathroom, drew a steadying breath, and carefully wrapped my fingers around the edge of the curtain. But before I could yank it open I heard a *thud* somewhere in the apartment—not the guilty thud a cat makes jumping off a table after licking butter from the dish; it was a human thud. Cat owners know the difference.

Having nowhere else to hide, I stepped into the tub, hoping if someone was lurking there, he wouldn't mind sharing space with me. Fortunately, I was the sole occupant.

My heart slammed against my ribs as quiet footsteps moved across the carpet. I looked around for a weapon, but other than a bottle of strawberry-scented shampoo and a bar of soap, all I had was my cell phone. I dared not make a call, afraid whoever was out there would hear me. I eased the phone shut and held it in my sweaty fist, ready to ram it into the trespasser's nose.

Suddenly, the footsteps stopped, then began to move rapidly in the other direction. Moments later I heard three beeps and a whispered voice in the kitchen, "Hello, police?"

It was Nikki.

I jumped out of the tub shouting for her to stop, got tangled in the curtain, and pulled the whole thing, rod and all, down on top of me. In the kitchen, Nikki began screaming into the phone, "My roommate is being murdered!"

"Nikki!" I yelled at the top of my lungs. "Don't call the police! Hang up!"

Suddenly she was in the doorway, her face as white as her uniform, a huge butcher knife raised above her head, looking like a female version of Norman Bates. Thinking she was about to slice into the curtain—and ultimately me— I screamed, which caused her to scream again, until she realized that it was just me and her and the shower curtain, and then she stopped. We looked so ridiculous that I started to laugh, and so did Nikki, until we were rolling on the floor in the hallway, gasping for breath.

"I thought," she said between gasps, "you were being attacked!"

"By a shower curtain!" I cried, and held my ribs as I howled. "You looked like Norman Bates on a bad-hair day."

"*Psycho!*" we both cried together, and flopped back onto the rug, wiping our eyes and laughing until our lungs ached. Simon peered cautiously from Nikki's room, then, deciding we were simply lunatics, he disappeared again.

"Abby? Nikki?" It was Mrs. Sample's voice, followed by loud banging. "Are you girls all right?"

We stopped laughing long enough to consider what we were going to tell her, and that started us laughing again. Five minutes later there was more loud knocking followed by a key in the lock, and then the door banged against the wall as if something heavy had crashed against it.

That put an end to our hilarity. We stared at each other for a moment, then Nikki sprang up and ran out of the bathroom clutching the knife as I untangled myself from the curtain and dashed out after her. I rounded the hallway into the living room and collided with a big solid object that turned out to be a man in a police uniform.

Who turned out to be Reilly.

He grabbed me by the shoulders to keep me from reeling backward, then took a good look at me. "I should have known I'd find you here."

I shrugged sheepishly. "I live here."

"Abby!" Nikki wailed from the kitchen. "I'm in handcuffs! Tell them I'm not a murderer."

"She's not a murderer," I told Reilly. "She's my roommate Nikki Hiduke. I was hiding in the tub, so she thought I was an intruder, and that's why she's wielding a knife."

I spotted our superintendent making his way toward the bathroom to inspect the damage. "Everything is fine, Mr. Bodenhammer. We'll take care of the shower curtain."

"Why do I rent to young people?" he muttered, throwing his hands up in disgust as he stalked away.

Reilly called out to his partner to release Nikki, then he folded his arms and peered down his nose at me, just like my father used to do. "*Why* were you hiding in the tub?"

"Would you like to sit down? It's actually kind of an amusing story."

He made a circling motion with one hand. "Just get on with it."

Nikki came out of the kitchen rubbing her wrists and looking morally wounded. She was followed by a face I recognized: Motorcycle Cop, aka Officer Gordon. He had been the cop to respond to my distress call a few weeks earlier when my Vette was smashed by a hit-and-run driver, and again when my brake lines were cut. What fond memories we shared.

"Not you again," he said with a grimace.

The same thought was running through my head, but I had the tact to keep it to myself. I gave them my story, then Nikki told her side, and the thought of it started us laughing again. But one stern look from Reilly put an end to that.

"Are you sure you didn't leave the door open when you ran out?" Motorcycle Cop asked.

"If I had been sure, believe me, you wouldn't be standing here now."

"Next time," Reilly said with an exasperated sigh, "call us first. We'll check it out for you." He radioed in to let the dispatcher know everything was fine, then he turned to aim his index finger at me. I sat down on the sofa, figuring a lecture was forthcoming.

"You!" he said, then apparently didn't know where to go from there, and finally just gave up, shook his head, and left.

Nikki locked the door behind them, poured two glasses of Merlot, and joined me in the living room. Simon peered around the corner to make sure the coast was clear, then came galloping across the room toward us, his tail curved like a question mark, delighted that we were awake during his playtime. Nikki dug a plastic straw out from between the cushions and played fetch with him, while I gave her a rundown on the country club dinner, my discoveries about Onora at the hotel, and the odd sighting of the Chinese woman.

Nikki thought I should leave further investigation on the spa's activities to Bill Bretton, but she agreed that I should pay a visit to Maria Mendoza to ask about Punch's activities while he was a guest at the hotel. "Only if you take me with you," she added.

"Why do you want to come with me?"

Nikki's eyes sparkled with excitement. "Remember how we used to pretend we were Nancy Drew?"

"That was me, Nikki. I used to pretend to be Nancy Drew. You used to pretend to be her sidekick."

"I still want to go along. I can help with the questioning. I'm good with people. Please?"

How could I say no to Nancy Drew's sidekick?

We finished our wine, rehung the shower curtain, then took ourselves off to our respective rooms to get some sleep. I put on my pj's, stretched out on my bed, and was staring at the patterns on the ceiling, chuckling to myself at the thought of Nikki attacking a shower curtain with a butcher knife when I suddenly realized the patterns had changed. Instead of the straight-lined shadows from the miniblinds, there were crosshatches, tent shapes, squiggles, and other oddities.

I knelt on my pillow at the headboard, stretched my arm across the space between bed and window, and lifted the blind. Painted on the outside of the glass were big black letters. Big black Chinese letters.

They did know where I lived.

CHAPTER TWELVE

"Nikki!" I yelled, letting the blind drop into place. I jumped off the bed and ran for the door. We met in the hallway between our rooms, and I grabbed her by the wrist and pulled her to my window. "Look!"

I pulled up the blind and she gasped. I shut it immediately, afraid that whoever had painted the symbols was watching.

"Call the police," she said, turning pale.

"Nikki—"

She was bouncing up and down on tiptoe, shaking her hands, showing signs of the panic that I was trying very hard to suppress. *"Call the police, damn it!"*

I wrapped my fingers around her arms to steady her. The last thing I needed was for her to lose it, because I would surely follow. "Think, Nikki! The writing is on the outside. No one was in our apartment. We're not in danger. Besides, what will I tell the police? That someone scribbled on my window? Do you know how irritated Reilly will be if I have him come out here for graffiti?"

"Don't you get it?" she cried. "Someone is threatening you! You can't shrug it off as graffiti."

"How do we know it's a threat? Can you read it? Maybe it's a good-luck wish."

"You don't seriously believe that, do you?"

I sat down on the bed in a slump. "No."

"It was that old man," Nikki said, pacing in front of the bed. "The one messing around with your car and peering in your shop window." She glanced around, spotted my cell phone on the bed, and snatched it up.

"What are you doing? You'd better not be calling the police. Do *not* call the police, Nikki!"

She was staring intently at the screen, working the buttons with her thumbs, no doubt going through my phone book.

"Nikki, are you listening to me?"

She hit a speed dial number and put the phone to her ear, then gestured for me to wait. "Hello, Marco? This is Nikki. We have a major problem."

I fell back onto the bed with a loud groan and pulled the pillow over my head to muffle her voice. Marco was going to hit the roof when he found out I'd been nosing around at the Emperor's Spa. The only good thing about Nikki making the call was that it wasn't me asking for his help.

"Abby," she said, tugging at one corner of the pillow, "Marco is on his way."

"Do me a favor," I mumbled through the feathers. "Press down real hard and don't let up until I stop struggling."

"You're an idiot. I'm going to put on a robe and make a pot of tea."

"In the middle of the night?" I tossed the pillow aside, glanced up at the scary patterns still filtering the through the blind, and hit the floor running. Maybe Marco's coming over wasn't such a bad idea after all.

*   *   *

We stood in my bedroom, Marco on the right side of the window, Nikki beside him, and me way back in the doorway, a sheet wrapped around my shivering body, studying the characters on the glass. I wasn't actually cold, so I assumed my shivers were a delayed reaction to the fright of seeing the writing on the window. In fact, I should have been warm, because Marco had shown up wearing very snug navy sweatpants and a sleeveless T-shirt cut off above his belly button, showing some pretty impressive abs.

He'd been working out, he told us. Right. At one thirty in the morning? Working out with *whom* was what I wanted to know.

He hadn't asked me any questions yet, but I could tell by the little downturn of his mouth that they were piling up inside. I watched as he studied the writing, then glanced around my room, spotted a pen and a pad of yellow sticky notes on my nightstand, and began copying the figures.

"Is it a warning?" Nikki asked, making me shiver harder.

"Probably. I'll take it over to the college and have it translated. I'm guessing Abby has been meddling again, and someone doesn't like it." He tossed the pen onto the stand, tucked the yellow square into his pocket, and turned to eye me. "When did you notice the writing?"

"About an hour after the police left. I know it wasn't there earlier."

"What I want to know," Nikki said, "is how the person got up to her window. It's a flat wall. There's nothing to climb or stand on outside the window."

"Have you ever read Edgar Allen Poe's *The Purloined Letter*?" Marco asked. "What's the best way to hide something? In plain sight. The ladder has probably been there awhile, so you've stopped noticing it. When was the last time the windows were washed?"

Nikki and I looked at each other and shrugged.

"Ask your superintendent."

"I think the old Chinese man did it," Nikki-the-squealer said. "He was peering into her car and shop window earlier today."

Marco turned to look at me. "What old Chinese man?"

"Who's ready for tea?" I asked and headed for the kitchen.

I filled three mugs with Nikki's brewed tea. Nikki opened a package of sweetener, I got out the squeeze bottle of honey, and Marco took his straight. We sat in the living room, Nikki and me on the sofa, and Marco in an old, wooden rocking chair I'd unearthed from my parents' basement. Simon appeared from one of his hiding places and jumped onto Marco's lap. He would never have done that to Pryce. *I* wouldn't have done that to Pryce.

"Tell me about this old Chinese man," Marco said, stroking the cat's head as he fixed me with that intense gaze that turned me into a blabbering fool. Being nervous about it anyway, I blabbed, telling him about the various times I'd seen the man around Bloomers and after my stint with the camera.

When I finished, Marco continued to gaze at me, only this time it was in disbelief. "You stood across from Emperor's Spa on a busy street in broad daylight with a camera in your hands, taking photos of men going for a massage?"

"I'll grant that it probably wasn't the smartest thing I've ever done."

He nearly choked on his tea. "The *smartest* thing? That has to rank as one of the *dumbest* things I've ever heard."

"Someone has to do something to stop what's going on there. It's criminal."

"Why does it have to be you?" Marco asked.

"My feelings exactly," Nikki-the-traitor tossed in.

"Because the police aren't doing their job," I replied, ignoring Nikki. "Carrie, the beauty salon owner, complained to the police and the mayor over a month ago. Has anything been done since then? No."

"Maybe they checked it out and didn't find anything," Marco said. "Don't forget my experience there."

"Yeah, yeah. The hairy European woman. Look, Carrie asked me what she should do, I suggested the photos, then she asked me to take them. That's all there was to it."

"Where are the photos?" Marco asked.

"I put them in the top drawer of my desk at the shop. Bill Bretton from the *News* is coming to look at them on Monday."

"You're going to give him the photos, and then you're out of it, right?" Marco asked.

I nodded enthusiastically. "Right." Nikki snickered, and I shot her a dark look.

"Did you tell Bill not to reveal you as the photographer?" Marco asked.

I took my time putting the cup to my mouth, trying to frame an evasive reply. "I still have to do that."

"Damn right you have to do that." Marco put Simon down and walked to the door. I abandoned the sheet and followed him, with Nikki bringing up the rear.

"Listen to me, sunshine," he said, tilting my chin up so he could look me in the eye, "forget about this little grudge you have against the Emperor's Spa. You have enough to do helping your cousin solve her murder without adding another murder to the pot."

"There's been another murder?" I asked stupidly.

"There could be. Yours. If those photos make the newspaper, there will be some extremely angry men who'd love to get their hands on the photographer. Let's just hope none of them got a good look at you." Marco opened the door, then bent to examine the lock. "I see you still haven't put on that dead bolt."

"I've been meaning to get around to it."

"I'll bring one with me tomorrow night when I come to dinner." He walked out shaking his head, muttering, "Females."

"We can put our own lock on the door!" I called.

"Thanks for coming over, Marco," Nikki said over my shoulder. "You're an angel."

She shut the door and leaned on it. "He has the sexiest swagger of any man alive."

"He knows it, too. What an ego on that man."

"I wouldn't have called it an ego, but whatever, you've got to go after him."

"Like I have nothing better to do. Come help me hang a blanket over my window."

Nikki's room was much quieter than my room.

I discovered that at three o'clock in the morning, after I'd gathered my sheet and pillow and sacked out on her floor. Her room faced woods, whereas mine faced the parking lot. But noise really hadn't been the problem. I couldn't fall asleep in there knowing those symbols were peering in at me—even with a blanket taped over the window. I kept wondering what evil they were supposed to inflict. But I slept at last and didn't wake until late in the morning when Nikki tripped on me on her way to the bathroom.

"What are you wearing?" I asked, massaging my bruised leg. "Iron-toed shoes?"

She rubbed her eyes and peered at her alarm. "It's ten o'clock in the morning. Don't you have to be at the shop?"

"Grace and Lottie are working this Saturday because they'll both be out of town next Saturday, which reminds me, what do you have planned for next Saturday?"

"Nothing. I can help you out. Wait. Scratch that. I have to drive up to Chicago. It's my parents' twenty-eighth wedding anniversary. Oh, no! If you work, you'll miss their celebration."

I rolled up my blanket, remembering many days I'd spent as a kid at Nikki's parents' house. The Hidukes had been like a second family to me, and Nikki's mother had been even more bizarre than mine. It was another reason we were compadres.

"I'm sorry, Nik, but that's what happens when you own a business. I'll send a big floral arrangement with you. And that reminds me, it might be a good idea for me to take flowers when I visit Maria this morning, as an icebreaker."

"You might want to give some to Mr. Bodenhammer, too. He's not going to like having to clean black paint off that window."

We were surprised to find the building superintendent working in the basement, since he usually managed to slip in some fishing on the weekends, but it turned out someone had a leaky pipe and he was having a devil of a time repairing it. We told him about the writing, and he said there'd been a ladder propped up against the corner for two weeks. He'd just taken it down that very morning, in fact, and wasn't pleased he'd have to drag it out again. He hoped the graffiti was water soluble or he might have to charge us for it.

Yes, flowers for the super would definitely be a good idea.

We piled into the Vette for the quick trip to Bloomers. The only empty parking space was at the far end of the block, so I pulled into it and we got out. As we headed up the sidewalk toward the shop, I kept looking over my shoulder, expecting to see that hooded, wrinkled face watching me from some recessed doorway.

While I put together a bouquet of pink caspias, white daisies, and lavender in the workroom, Nikki, having nothing better to do, decided to keep Grace and Lottie company in the shop. It wasn't until I was wrapping raffia around the stems of the bouquet that I remembered I hadn't warned Nikki not to mention anything about the Emperor's Spa to Grace.

I quickly tied off the trim, wrapped florist's paper around the flowers, and dashed through the curtain—where Grace was waiting for me. By the expression on her face I knew that I'd been found out. Not by coincidence, Nikki and Lottie were nowhere to be seen, no doubt lying low in the parlor.

"I was going to tell you about it, Grace, honestly, but something always came up."

"I'm not upset with you, dear," she said calmly.

"You're not?"

"I've come to the conclusion that it's in your nature to meddle, and for me to insist otherwise isn't fair to either one of us. So go ahead, dear. Meddle till your heart's content. I shall not try to deter you."

"Thank you, Grace," I said in awe, and gave her a grateful hug.

"You needn't thank me, dear. But there is one thing you can do for me."

"Anything," I said gratefully.

"Have your will drawn up." She pivoted neatly and marched back to the parlor.

Touché.

As Nikki and I put the flowers in the trunk of my car, I noticed that a fresh produce market had been set up on the courthouse lawn. Deciding that we were due for some nutritious food, we crossed the street and strode over to the sellers' tables. I wandered around until I located a fruit stand, then I brown-bagged a few peaches and went looking for Nikki, who was at another table paying for a cantaloupe.

As I waited for her, I glanced toward the street and saw a black Ford Crown Victoria stop just behind the Vette's back bumper. A man in a dark suit scooted to the passenger side, leaned out the window, focused a small camera at the back of the Vette, then slid back to the driver's side and sped away.

"Did you see that?" I asked Nikki, pointing down the street. "Someone just took a picture of my car." I picked up her brown bag and dashed toward the Vette.

"Maybe he's a Corvette enthusiast," Nikki called, hurrying after me.

"Corvette enthusiasts don't do drive-by photo shootings. They get out and study the cars up close."

We stopped to wait for a car to pass, then jogged across the street, coming to a stop behind the Vette. "What do you want to bet it was one of those men you caught on camera yesterday?" Nikki said, panting.

"This was a Crown Victoria, Nikki. None of the men yesterday had that kind of car."

"Maybe he switched cars. Did you recognize his face from the photos?"

"I caught only a glimpse of his profile."

"Why would he take a picture of the back of your Vette?"

We took a step back and studied the bumper.

"Could it be your license plate?" Nikki ventured.

That seemed the most logical assumption. But why would he need a photo of my license plate?

CHAPTER THIRTEEN

aria Mendoza lived in a neighborhood of small tract
houses painted in various pastel colors. The street
and sidewalks were brimming with kids skateboarding, rid-
ing bikes, and playing ball, so I parked the Vette as far away
from the activity as possible, then Nikki and I walked up
the block to a cream-colored house with a blue front door.
A young girl answered my knock then yelled for her
mother. A few moments later a short, frazzled, black-haired
woman stepped to the doorway.

"Are you Maria Mendoza?" I asked.

She eyed us warily. "Why?"

I pulled the bouquet from behind my back and held the
flowers out to her. "If you're Maria, these are for you."

She stepped back in alarm, as if I had something sinister
planted amid the blooms, so I said the first thing that came
to mind. "They're from Todd at the New Chapel Inn."

"Why would Todd send me these? I don't work there no
more. What do you want here?"

"I need to ask you a few questions." She started to shut
the door, so I quickly added, "I don't mean you any harm.

I'm a florist, and the flowers are from me. I own Bloomers, down on the square."

Finally I had said something right. "You're giving away flowers?" she asked, her hostility turning to amazement.

"It's a long story and I'm sure you're not that interested, so I'll sum it up by saying that I'm supposed to do the flowers for my cousin's wedding, but there may not be a wedding if I can't find the person who murdered one of the hotel guests."

Her eyes widened. "I didn't murder no one."

"I know you didn't," I assured her. "But you might have seen something that will help me find the one who did."

"I don't want to get involved. I got kids to think of."

She stepped back, and I knew she was moments away from slamming the door, so I nudged Nikki, who blurted, "Abby wouldn't ask you to do anything that would jeopardize your kids. She's good that way. And see how nice the flowers smell?" She grabbed the bouquet from me and thrust them at Maria, who took them purely out of self-defense.

"Please, Maria. Just a few questions," I said, and hurried to name them before she could argue further. "Do you remember the guest who was killed? His name was Paulin Chumley. Muscular guy, huge hands, short blond hair, wore a gold punching bag in his ear. You might have seen his picture in the newspaper."

She buried her nose in the blooms, took a long whiff, then answered reluctantly, "I remember him."

"Did you ever see him bring a girl to his room?"

"I never saw him with a girl," she said quickly. A little too quickly to convince me she was telling the truth.

"Did you see him last Wednesday evening, the night of the murder?"

There was a long pause, and I could almost hear the de-

bate going on in her head: *Should I tell or shouldn't I?*
"No," she answered at last, but she wouldn't meet my eye.
A child yelled to her from somewhere in the house, and
Maria turned to call back a reply in Spanish.

I glanced at Nikki to see if she had anything to add, but
she merely shrugged, so I said, "Thank you, Maria. My
card is taped to the paper. If you remember anything about
that night, please give me a call."

"Well, that was a bust," Nikki said, as we walked back
to the Vette.

"She lied to us, Nik. She saw Punch that night, and I
have a feeling she saw him with a girl."

"How do you know?"

"Did you see how she fidgeted when I asked her the
questions, and how she wouldn't look me in the eye when
she answered? Those are sure signs."

"Hey, you learned something from your law school
classes after all!"

"Nope. Psychology. Undergrad."

"How are you going to get her to tell the truth?"

"I'm hoping that as she's putting those beautiful flowers
in a vase, she'll feel guilty enough to call me. And if that
doesn't work, you'll think of something."

"Me? You're the one who was Nancy Drew."

"You're the one who claimed to be good with people." I
unlocked the car doors, and we got in. "On to the next problem, the dead bolt. When Marco comes over tonight, he's
going to find a shiny new lock on our door."

"Have you ever installed a dead bolt before? Or any kind
of lock, for that matter?"

"Instructions, Nikki. They always come with instructions."

*   *   *

We stumbled around the hardware store until we found the lock section, then we stood in the aisle for at least ten minutes, reading the backs of the packages, trying to determine the best one for our door. Finally we were rescued by an older man wearing a red vest with an Ace logo on the pocket.

"This is the one you want," he said, pulling a big package off a high hook. "This is the safest dead bolt we sell, and it installs like a dream."

"Sounds like my kind of lock," I said.

"Could you explain how to install it?" Nikki asked, smiling sweetly.

The man proceeded to lay out the steps for us, but when he started talking about drill bits, my mind started to freeze up. When he finished I said, "So all I need is the lock kit and a drill, right?"

"Oh, no," he said with a happy face, reaching for another package. "You'll need this attachment, too. See, it reams out the door so your lock will fit in."

"Okay, so the lock, the drill, and this attachment."

"That should do it. Also a chisel. And a bit. Do you have a hammer, by the way?"

By the time we walked out of the store, I had put ninety-three dollars on my credit card. My self-imposed limit for the month was one hundred dollars, so it was good that the month was almost over.

Back at the apartment, the answering machine was beeping, so Nikki hit it, and we listened. There was a rustling noise, like rough cloth being drawn over the mouthpiece. Then a gravelly male voice spit out, "Stay away from the Emperor's Spa. You don't know who you're up against."

The line went dead, and I went cold. Now they even had my phone number.

Nikki turned big eyes on me. "Did you hear that?"

Of course I heard it. What a silly question. Couldn't she see my hands shaking?

"Stay away from the spa," Nikki repeated, as if that menacing voice wasn't already echoing in every nook and cranny inside my skull. "Isn't that what we've been telling you?"

I sank down onto the sofa, which was about all I could do since my knees seemed to have suddenly become filled with whipped cream. "I think the bigger question here, Nikki, is who left the message."

"A no-brainer, Ab. It's one of those guys you caught on camera. I only hope you're getting *their* message."

"One of the guys I caught on camera. That's your answer for everything lately, Nik, and frankly, it's getting on my nerves."

There was a giant silence in the room, and I had caused it. "I didn't mean that," I said, dropping my head in my hands. "I'm rattled and I shouldn't be taking it out on you."

Nikki sat beside me and threw an arm around my shoulders. "I understand, Abby. The last time there were nasty messages on the machine someone tried to kill you. I'd be rattled, too."

That's why Nikki and I have always gotten along. No matter what stupid things came out of our mouths, we knew that underneath we respected each other's feelings. "Just so you know, Nikki, I *am* getting the message, loud and clear. Something illegal is going on at that spa or my interest in it wouldn't have stirred up such concern."

"Which is why you need to stay away and let your reporter friend take it from here."

"You're one hundred percent right. What do you say we grab a bite of lunch and get this lock installed?"

*　　　*　　　*

That proved to be a lot harder than it sounded. First, Nikki was not mechanically inclined, so me reading the directions and her trying to follow them didn't work. Second, although I was more mechanically inclined than Nikki, I was certainly no "Helpful Hardware Man." Third, when neither one of us understood what we were doing, trying to do it together was a mistake.

"I don't see the little screw they show in this picture," Nikki said at one point.

"I told you, it's *this* one." I held it up for her to see.

"It's *not* that one. That's part F. See right here in the instructions? It has a long tail."

"Screws don't have tails."

"Then what do you call this long thing hanging from the head?"

"Not a tail," I muttered, trying to get the drill bit to stay in the teeth.

An hour later we had managed to drill a hole through the door from front to back. After two hours of struggling to get the lock to fit inside the hole, we gave up.

"I can call Mr. Bodenhammer," Nikki volunteered.

"He just finished cleaning our window. He'll charge us."

"Then we'll have to let Marco do it."

"Marco will never let me forget it."

"What do you suggest we do?" she snapped. Even Nikki ran out of patience once in a while.

I stepped back and studied our handiwork, which basically consisted of an oddly shaped hole in a mutilated black door. "Let's cover it up until we can get more advice from the hardware man."

"Cover it with what? Masking tape? Don't you think Marco will notice?"

I pondered the problem for a few minutes, then came up

with the perfect solution. "Do you still have that black eye shadow you wore at last year's Halloween party?"

While Nikki ran to dig it out of her makeup basket, I packed the hole with a paper towel, then cut strips of masking tape to fit over the circle, just barely overlapping the edges. Onto that I applied her black eye shadow, blending it into the black door until it was barely noticeable.

"I can still see it," Nikki said, crouching down in front of the door knob.

"You won't if the only light source are candles."

We swept up the mess, hid all the lock parts in a paper bag, and shoved it into the small utility closet next to the door. By six forty-five that night the curtains were drawn against the late summer sun, a half dozen candles flickered romantically in the living room, our card table had been dressed with a colorful scarf and set with our bargain basement white plates, and Nikki had gone on her date. I had donned a pair of black mules, black slacks, a yellow V-necked top, black dangle earrings, and finished it with a light peach-vanilla scented perfume. Men seemed to go for pie aromas.

At exactly seven o'clock the doorbell rang. I looked through the peephole, then unlocked the door and opened it with a smile. There stood Marco, dressed in a black polo shirt, light gray slacks, and black mocs, a brown paper grocery sack in his arms. He looked so domestic that I wanted to hug him. Then again, he looked so damn sexy that I wanted to attack him. Simon took care of that for me.

Marco had barely had a chance to step inside when the white fur ball came loping up the hallway, skidded to a stop, and stood on his hind legs to swipe at the sack.

"Must be meat in there," I said. I took advantage of the distraction to shut the door and sweep the sack out of

Marco's arms, trusting that he would follow me to the kitchen, and the hole in the door would go undetected.

But it was Simon who followed, then stood at my feet meowing until I shooed him away.

"Is your electricity out?" Marco asked from the hallway, obviously noticing the abundance of candles.

"What you're looking at is ambiance." I peered into the sack and removed a tall bottle of wine. "An Australian Shiraz. I've been dying to try this. What else did you bring?"

Marco took the bottle from my hands and propelled me from the kitchen, just as I'd hoped he would do. "This is my dinner. Stay out and let the master chef create."

"Don't you want to know where I keep the pans?"

"Sunshine, your kitchen is six feet by twelve feet. I'm betting I can hunt down those rascals in less than two minutes. Where's the light switch?"

He flicked on the kitchen light, which gave me a moment of panic until I saw that the entryway was still in shadow. "Come on, Simon," I said. "We know when we're not wanted."

I hefted the cat over my shoulder and left, plunking us both down on the sofa. I had to chuckle as Marco banged cabinets, rattled pans, and even hummed. He was so busy playing chef that he had completely forgotten about the lock. What a genius I was.

Simon spotted a chewed straw wedged between the sofa cushions and dragged it over to drop in my lap. "I'll play on one condition," I said quietly, holding his little face between my hands, "that you disappear when things start to heat up."

He butted my chin with his cold nose, which was his way of saying, *"I have no idea what you just said, but if you'll toss that straw I'll agree to anything."*

On my twenty-first toss Marco came out of the kitchen

carrying two glasses of wine. He handed me a glass and took a seat beside me. "A little predinner libation."

"Here's to the master chef," I said, lifting my glass to his.

There was a gleam in his eyes that promised good times ahead. My insides tingled expectantly as we sipped, locking gazes over the rims. Suddenly a heavy object hurtled itself into my lap, nearly spilling my wine. "Simon!" I cried, pushing the cat to the floor.

Marco reached down to rub his furry head. "I need to get back to the kitchen anyway."

As soon as he was gone, I shook my finger at the cat. "We had a deal and you blew it. To the bedroom, welcher."

To show me what he thought of my deal, Simon sat on his haunches and began to clean his face. Determined to show him who was boss, I reached down for him, but he dodged my hands and took off up the hallway. I chased him into my room, tossed in his plastic straw toy, and shut the door. A deal was a deal.

The aroma wafting from the kitchen was so intoxicating that I wandered over to stand in the doorway, appreciating the excellent distribution of male muscle as Marco worked.

"When you're done ogling, would you find a platter?" he asked over his shoulder. "The food is ready."

"I wasn't ogling. I was merely standing at the ready." I dug out an oval platter and held it as Marco slid two perfectly sauteed chicken breasts onto it, then scooped up a brown sauce thick with carrot and celery pieces, bits of ham, and thin, golden onion slices. Beside it he put a mound of rice pilaf. I was quite impressed.

"Where did you learn to cook?" I asked as we took our seats.

"From my *mama*."

My fork came to a halt centimeters from my taste buds,

which were drooling in anticipation. "Did you just say *mama* with an Italian accent?"

"Old habit."

I bit into the moist, tasty chicken and sighed as I chewed. "Well, thank your mama for me because this is heavenly. Why didn't you want to make it at your apartment?"

"Because Mama is staying with me temporarily," he said with a grim look.

"I see. You were afraid that after meeting me, she would hound you about getting married."

"No, she's entertaining a gentleman tonight and told me to get lost."

Oh, well. One can always dream. I raised my wineglass and toasted his mother.

As we ate, we talked about the state of the downtown shopping area and debated whether American automakers would ever come out with a car that ran totally on hydrogen. We finished our meal without once discussing either the murder investigation or the spa, which was exactly what I'd planned. I didn't want him lecturing me on staying out of trouble, which might remind him of the lock. Plus I was hoping for a little snuggle time on the sofa, so I wanted to keep him in good humor.

"Since you cooked, I'll clean up," I offered, whisking our plates off the table. "I believe in an equal division of labor."

"Works for me." Marco loaded his arms with bowls and followed me, then returned to the living room with his glass of wine to watch a baseball game on TV.

I was in the middle of scrubbing the last pan when the phone rang.

"Want me to get it?" Marco called.

"Would you, please?"

I heard him say hello, then there was a long silence, then I heard him say, "I'll tell her." Then he hung up.

"Who was it?" I called.

"Bill Bretton. He said he won't be able to make it Monday."

Rats. I'd hoped to get those photos out of my desk and the problem off my shoulders. "When did he say he'd come?"

"He didn't say."

I stopped scrubbing again. Why hadn't Bill made new arrangements? Had he lost interest? I'd have to call him on Monday and find out what was going on.

"Do you know you have a message on your machine?" Marco called.

"I must have been in the shower. Go ahead, play it."

Marco punched a button and suddenly that menacing voice hissed its warning. Damn. I'd forgotten to erase it. I waited a moment, then peeked around the corner. "Oh yeah, I forgot about that message. Want more wine?"

Marco came toward me, glowering. "You forgot about a threat?"

I backed all the way up the hallway to the front door, where I smiled up at him with all the innocence I could muster. "It was probably a prank call."

"A prank call?" He braced an arm on the door. "Sunshine, you are the all-time champion of denial."

Boy, was he wrong, because I sure wasn't going to deny the strong attraction I was experiencing at that moment. The heat from Marco's body was melting my ribs, among other areas, and those sexy dark eyes of his were carving little red hearts in my soul. I put my hands on the front of his shirt, feeling the hardness of his chest beneath my fingers. A pulse throbbed in the smooth skin of his neck. "Are you finding this as much of a turn-on as I am?" I asked him.

His eyes narrowed. "Does it look like I'm turned on?"

"I'm not sure I'd recognize it if you were."

He tilted my chin and gazed into my eyes. "Did you hear what the man said? Stay away from the spa. Do you get the message? If you keep pursuing this, you're putting yourself in danger."

I swallowed. Marco was dead serious. "I get it."

"I want you to promise to stay away."

I stared straight into those pools of dark chocolate. "Okay."

"Say it," he said huskily.

I said it so softly, he could probably feel the words better than hear them. He dipped his head down until his lips were a hair's breadth from mine and said, "Think you've got it now?"

I had it, all right, but if he didn't kiss me that instant I was going to lose it. I curled my toes, closed my eyes, and took the brakes off my pulse, which immediately shot into the stratosphere. *Get ready, Abby.*

At that instant, Simon began to howl from the bedroom. He'd had enough of being a prisoner.

"Ignore him," I said quickly, trying to salvage the moment. "It's Simon's nightly ritual, like a wolf baying at the moon. Simon bays at doors."

I closed my eyes again. *Here it comes. Any second now.*

"What the hell is this?"

I opened my eyes and found Marco studying the fingers and palms of his right hand, which were smeared with black eye shadow. "Whatever it is, I'm sure it'll wash off. Now where were we?"

"Where did it come from?" He hit the light switch in the hallway and began an inspection of the door.

I slid between him and the doorknob. "What do you say we go wash your hand?"

He moved me out of the way and rubbed a finger over my not-so-ingenious cover-up. "What did you do to the door?"

"We didn't have time to finish installing the lock, so I rigged a temporary cover."

"With boot polish?"

"Eye shadow."

"You were trying to hide it from me."

"Why would I try to hide it from you?"

He pulled away the tape, drew out the paper towel, and dangled it before my nose. "Because you don't know what you're doing."

"Sure I do. That's merely step two of the installation process."

Marco handed me the discarded paper and started for the bathroom. "Get out the parts and I'll show you how to do it—if I can get this stuff to come off. You might want to wash your chin, while you're at it."

I scrubbed my chin with the paper towel. What a way to end an evening that had started with such promise.

As soon as Marco returned, hands freshly scrubbed, I thrust the sack of parts at him. "Here. Go for it."

He made short work of it, too, and although he walked me through each step so that I knew exactly what to do if I was ever again called upon to install a lock, I was very glad that he was doing it. The last thing my budget needed was to have to pay for a new door.

"Have you ever heard the voice on the answering machine before?" he asked as he lined up the screws with their holes.

"No."

"It wasn't an Oriental accent," he mused. "Other than the men you caught on camera, have you angered anyone else lately?"

"No. And for your information, only one of the men saw me, and he wouldn't know how to reach me. Oh, wait. I forgot about the man in the black Crown Victoria."

Marco stopped instantly and turned to look at me. "What man in the Crown Victoria?"

"A guy I saw taking a picture of the back of my Vette this morning."

"He took a picture of the back of your car? With your license plate on it? Do you know who drives black Crown Vics? G-men. Feds. Agency-types. Were there a half-dozen antennae sprouting from the trunk?"

Marco's reaction was really making me nervous. "I wasn't counting his antennae. Couldn't the car belong to someone in New Chapel? Sheriff's police, maybe?"

"They don't use Crown Vics. You see a black Crown Vic around here, you can bet it's government issue, and having the government looking at you is never a good thing."

There had to be some other explanation. "Maybe he's a Corvette afficionado who by coincidence works for the government."

Marco tightened the last screw and handed me the screwdriver. "Whoever he is, you've got his attention."

CHAPTER FOURTEEN

I let Simon out of his holding cell so he'd stop howling, then Marco and I sat around tossing a plastic straw to him while we tried to figure out what I might have done to put me under the microscope of the federal government. Coming up with nothing better, Marco finally conceded that it was possible the man simply had an affinity for vintage Corvettes. There were a lot of us like that.

Before he left, Marco made me repeat my promise to stay away from the spa and to call him if I saw the old man watching me or the Crown Victoria following me. Then he scratched Simon under the chin and headed for the door. Clearly, the moment for amour had passed.

To my utter astonishment, he pivoted, came back to the sofa, pulled me up against him, and planted one on me—a nice, firm kiss that told me he cared. He gazed down at me for a moment, then brushed my hair away from my face and said tenderly, "Be careful, sunshine. I don't want anything bad to happen to you."

All I could do was nod. My heart had completely melted.

I was in my pj's, washing my face, when I heard several light knocks and a whispered, "Abby, my key won't work."

I opened the door and let Nikki in. "Sorry. Marco installed the lock."

"He saw through your cover-up?"

"He saw through it *and* got it all over himself. Your new key is on the counter."

"Why are you smiling?"

"Marco cares," I said and headed back to the bathroom.

I lay awake for another hour going over the next day's hectic schedule in my mind and finally fell into a sleep so deep I barely made it to church the next morning. I slid into the back row of the balcony, put in a few prayer requests to the Big Guy, and ducked out at the end of the service so I wouldn't be spotted by any family members prowling the narthex.

I'd no sooner got into my car when Aunt Corrine came tapping across the street in her pumps and Armani suit. "Abby, I'm so glad I caught you. Have you found anything to clear Flip?"

"I'm still working on it."

She folded her hands together beseechingly, the gesture of a desperate woman. "Please, Abby. Do something soon. I've got to get Jillian out of my house." In a sudden switch of moods she said, "Oh, and that darling antique pedestal table in your display window? Would you be a doll and bring it to the country club when you come? I want to put the guest book on it."

"I can do that."

She patted my head as if I were her pet poodle. "I won't even mention to your mother that you were twenty minutes late for church this morning."

There were spies in the balcony.

My next stop was the county jail, situated two blocks from the courthouse in an unfriendly looking box of a structure five stories high, with narrow, barred windows and a flat roof. I parked in the visitors' lot across the street, put the top up on the Vette, and locked the door, then wondered why. With all the police buzzing in and out, was there a safer place to leave my car?

Inside the jail, I came to a stop in front of a steel wall with a glass window cut into it, behind which sat armed guards. I signed in and asked for Matron Patty, who turned out to be a five-foot-four, one-hundred-forty-pound, gum-snapping ball of fire.

"Great to see you, Abby!" she said, shaking my hand with a grip that could have bent iron. "You probably don't remember, but your pop brought you here when you were about this high." She held her hand to her waist, around which hung a fully equipped police belt. "Course, you didn't go any farther than this door here. You got a swell pop, you know. He was always polite to me, not like some of these bruisers. So, this is your first time here all grown up, is it?"

Patty said all this as she patted me down and ran a wand over me. Then she took my purse, made me forfeit my shoes, and pressed a button behind a counter. A buzzer loud enough to be heard at the North Pole sounded, then a thick steel door opened. I followed her through it and down a narrow hallway past a row of identical doors, stopping at the fifth one. She opened it and gestured me into a stark cubicle that was just big enough for me and a wooden chair.

"You've got fifteen minutes, honey." The door shut behind her with a snap.

I sat down at a counter facing a pane of glass with a speaker in it. The room smelled of old wood, pine cleaner, and sweat. Good thing I hadn't planned to eat lunch anytime soon. Through the thin paneled walls on either side of me I could hear the murmurs of voices, and from somewhere in the bowels of the building I heard the hard clang of steel doors being shut.

A few minutes later the door on the opposite side of the glass opened and Flip shuffled in. He had on an orange jumpsuit and shower sandals. His face was nicked from a dull razor, but his long brown hair was clean and neatly combed. He sat down in a chair identical to mine, folded his hands together on the counter, and gazed at me with the air of a beaten man.

I leaned toward the speaker, not sure how the sound would carry. "How are you doing?"

He shrugged, as if it didn't matter.

"Are you aware that Jillian asked me to help with the investigation?"

"You're wasting your time. They've already decided I'm guilty."

"But a jury hasn't. Innocent until proven otherwise, remember?"

"I appreciate the offer," he said dejectedly, "but let's be honest. What can you do?"

"What the police don't want to do—investigate other suspects." I dug in my bag for paper and a pen to take notes. I'd been so busy, I'd had to formulate questions in my mind on the way over. "I know you've been over this many times, Flip, but bear with me; I don't have access to the detectives' reports. So let's start at the beginning. Where were you last Tuesday and Wednesday?"

He heaved a heavy sigh, as if the very thought of telling it all again was too much to bear. "I went up to Lake Michigan to do some photographing."

I wrote it down. "Why didn't you tell anyone where you were going?"

"I felt like being alone."

"Did it occur to you that your friends might be worried?"

He bristled, the first real emotion I'd seen. "Is this a lecture?"

"I'm just trying to piece together everything that happened."

He didn't respond for a few moments, then he said in a tight voice, "I needed time to cool down and think."

"Were you angry?"

He lifted his shoulders, his gaze fixed on his hands.

I felt my annoyance growing. With a busy day ahead I didn't have time to wring answers from him. "Flip, I can't help you if you're going to be secretive—or maybe you don't care if they find you guilty."

"Whether I was angry then or not doesn't have anything to do with why I'm here. The reason I'm here is because of sloppy police work."

"Fine. Let's remedy that. Tell me what happened at the dunes and why you were angry. Let me decide if it's important."

For a moment he studied me, then he spread his fingers on the counter and began to recite, robotlike, "I went to the lake to take photos and get away from people. There's nothing odd about that. I've done it for years. It helps me get my head together. I didn't call anyone because I knew they would come looking for me, and I just didn't feel like explaining myself. I hiked around the park, then set up camp for the night at Clay's bird blind. I did more hiking and more photographing the next day and was getting ready to leave when Punch happened upon me."

I had been jotting notes, but at his last words I stopped. "Punch didn't happen upon you, Flip; he was looking for you."

Angry red blotches sprang up on Flip's pale face. "I

don't know who told you that, but it's not true. Punch was meeting someone there."

Had Jillian guessed right about the mystery woman? "Did you tell that to the police?"

"Of course."

"How do you know he was meeting someone? Did he tell you?"

"He didn't have to," Flip said bitterly. "I knew the signs. Punch was in love—if he understood the meaning of the word. All love meant to him was sexual attraction. When that wore off he was on to the next woman who caught his eye."

"Do you know who he was meeting this time?"

"His latest tart-of-the-week."

This man claimed to be Punch's friend? "Could it have been Onora?"

"Onora was history."

"Punch asked the hotel clerk to wish him luck before he left that evening. Any idea why he would say that?"

Flip hesitated a moment, then shook his head. Those hesitations always made me wary.

"Are you sure? Go back to when he appeared at the blind. What did he say?"

Flip shifted in his chair, suddenly edgy. "He swore at me because I'd made everyone worry. Then he tried to get me to use his cell phone. He wanted me to call Clay to let him know I was okay. I suggested we just go back to Clay's house, but he said he had other plans, and I should make myself disappear." Flip glanced away, but I caught the hurt in his eyes.

"Did Punch say what those plans were?"

"He didn't need to. We argued, and he said some terribly cruel things." Flip gazed past me, as if seeing the scene all over again. "I threw the camera at him and ran."

"Did you hear the camera hit him? Or hear him cry out?"

Tears spilled out of Flip's eyes. He immediately brushed them away. "I would never have left him if I'd known he was hurt."

I studied my notes, giving him a moment to compose himself. "Where did you go after you threw the camera?"

"Into the woods. I followed a trail for a while until I realized I had no idea where I was. I came to a small clearing where I could see the sun setting, then I headed in that direction, knowing I'd come out by the lake eventually."

Flip rubbed his forehead hard enough to leave red marks, completely unaware of his actions. "I remember thorns snagging the strap of my camera bag, and when I stopped to untangle it I must have stepped in a gopher hole, because I lost my balance and fell. That's the last thing I remember until I found all of you in the parking lot."

"Did the police recover your camera bag?"

"If they did, they didn't tell me."

"What about Punch's cell phone? Did you take it from him?"

"No."

Then the phone should have been with the body. It was another piece of information I'd have to weasel out of Greg Morgan. "Has anyone in the bridal party used your camera recently?"

"They wouldn't use it without asking. Besides, it's not an easy camera to operate. Bertie is the only one who knows how."

I gazed straight through the glass, watching his eyes. "Who do you think did it, Flip?"

He pressed his lips together and looked away.

"Does that mean you have a theory and don't want to say?"

He kept his head turned. Obviously he suspected one of the bridal party or he'd have offered an opinion.

The door opened behind me and Matron Patty said, "Time to go, kiddo."

"One more minute?" I asked her. "Please?"

I got the nod, so I waited until she had closed the door and then said, "Okay, Flip, real quick. Those terrible things Punch said to you—they must have really hurt to make you throw that expensive camera at him."

I could tell by the slight tremble in his chin that I'd hit a nerve. I folded my hands and leaned toward the speaker in the glass. "What did Punch say to you, Flip?"

He bowed his head and rubbed his eyes with his thumbs, as if to erase that painful scene from his mind's eye. "He said I was jealous."

"Of him?"

Flip's head came up and he glared at me. "Of *her*. His little *passion flower*!" He stood up abruptly, knocking over his chair in his rush to flee the cubicle.

CHAPTER FIFTEEN

Matron Patty tapped me on the shoulder. I rose and followed her out, slipped on my mules, gathered my bag, and walked into the sunlight and freedom. I got into my car and sat there a for few minutes, replaying the interview in my mind.

Flip's anger seemed to stem from two events: Punch telling him to get lost so he could meet his current lust interest; and, Punch accusing Flip of being jealous. Had Punch meant that Flip had a crush on him? Was he, in effect, calling Flip gay? The second event seemed to have been the main trigger, but had Flip been angry because it wasn't true or because he'd been found out? Most important, had he been angry enough to kill?

Bits of conversation I'd had with other members of the party the night of the murder ran through my brain. It had only been a guess on her part, but maybe Jillian had hit the nail on the head.

"I'll bet they argued about Punch's mystery girl-friend. . . . He probably resented Punch spending time with her and not us."

Then there was the odd exchange between Ursula and
Sabina, after I'd commented that a friend wouldn't have
behaved so jealously, and Claymore had retorted that a fiancée would have.

"So vould a girlfriend," Ursula had added, only to have
Sabina tell her to shut up.

Ursula and Sabina knew more about Flip than they were
letting on. I'd have to corner them at the bridal shower.

I put the key in the ignition and started up the Vette. By
habit I glanced in the rearview mirror—and caught sight
of a black Crown Victoria driving slowly down the street
in front of the jail. By the time I turned to look over my
shoulder, the car had passed the parking lot.

Quickly, I backed out of the space, pulled around to the
gate and waited for it to open, then sped out of the lot and
turned in the same direction the black car had gone, hoping to get a good look at the driver. But the big car had
neatly vanished and there was no time to search further.
The clock on the dashboard showed half past eleven, leaving me with a mere one and a half hours until the bridal
shower.

I stopped at Bloomers to pick up the pedestal table and
shower centerpiece—a big, beautiful arrangement in
shades of peach and cream (Christine roses, wild rose
vines, lily of the valley, spider mums, and baby's breath in
a deep peach ceramic oval bowl)—and from there I took
them to the country club, where I found three young
women, club employees, decorating the banquet room with
Aunt Corrine. By the strained looks on the girls' faces, I
could tell they were not enjoying my aunt's artistic direction. I was almost afraid to leave for fear I would return
later to find my aunt gagged and bound to a pillar by white
streamers.

An hour later, Nikki and I were back at the club, bearing a joint gift of a modestly priced crystal vase, which was about all our budgets could afford. Nikki looked sophisticated in a navy suit with a bright coral tank top underneath, a silver choker, and navy sling-back heels, whereas I looked, well, hastily assembled. All I'd had time for was a quick application of tinted lip gloss, taupe eye shadow, and my old standby dress, a short-sleeved, green silk, button front with matching belt, the very same dress I had worn to my college graduation. It was old, but it had good lines.

We could hear the chatter of female voices long before we reached the banquet room, and when I opened one of the double doors the noise spilled out, along with several women on a washroom run. One of them was Pryce's cousin, who stopped to tell me one of my buttons was undone. I glanced down to find that the middle bodice button had come open. I turned my back on the room full of women to fasten up, whispering to Nikki, "Why didn't you tell me?"

"I didn't notice. Why didn't you check the mirror before we left?"

"Because I was in a hurry." I spotted Mrs. Osborne heading for the door and quickly pulled Nikki into the crowd inside.

"Oh. My. God," Nikki breathed.

I clutched her arm, afraid to look. "Is it my aunt? Is she tied to a pillar?"

"No, look! The room is beautiful."

I gazed around in delight. The banquet room had been decorated to look like a white satin-wrapped wedding gift, and Jillian was the bow on top, dressed in bright peach silk and seated at a raised table in the center of the room, with her bridesmaids flanking her like the tails of a ribbon, except for the seat on the far left that was being kept open for me. My mother was perched on a chair nearby, chatting to my aunt, who bore no trace of white streamers. Obviously, her decorating crew hadn't mutinied. My mother spotted us and waved us over.

Nikki and I made small talk with them for the obligatory few minutes, then scooted off to the refreshment table in the hopes of finding something more potent than peach-flavored punch. We ended up with peach-flavored punch.

"Abby," a female voice hissed in my ear. I turned to find Jillian inches away. "Any luck?" she whispered.

"I had an interesting conversation with Flip today."

"You're not supposed to concentrate on Flip. You're supposed to *clear* Flip."

I smacked myself on the forehead. "What was I thinking? I'm so glad you clarified that."

"Don't joke about this, Abs."

I took a deep breath and forced myself to remember that this woman was my blood relative. "Jillian, you will be the first to know when I find the killer."

"Shhh!" She glanced over her shoulder. "Someone might hear you."

At that moment food was delivered to the long buffet tables, setting off a stampede that could have rivaled a herd of ravenous buffalo any day. Jillian left us to direct traffic, so Nikki and I grabbed plates and handfuls of finger foods, then stepped aside as one hundred hungry women swept down the table devouring everything in their path.

With our plates in hand we went our separate ways—Nikki to sit with my mother, and me to sit at the head table beside Sabina. Onora had planted herself on Jillian's right, with Ursula rounding out that end.

"Hi, Abby!" Sabina said with her usual enthusiasm. "Doesn't this room look gorgeous? Don't you just love all the fuss of weddings? I can't wait to get married. I'll have the fanciest wedding imaginable. How about you? Do you have any wedding plans?"

I gave her a pained smile. "Not anymore." It was not a subject I liked to discuss, especially with Osbornes in the vicinity. Besides, I had an agenda, and I needed to get busy on it before the shower got under way.

"I'm so sorry," Sabina gushed. "Me and my big mouth. You were engaged to Claymore's brother. How awful for you to have to be in the wedding with him."

I waved away her concern. "I'm so beyond that. Speaking of awful, I talked to Flip at the jail today. He's a mess, as you can imagine. But something he said perplexed me. Maybe you can explain."

Her eyes brightened with interest. She put down her glass of punch and swiveled toward me. "Sure. What did he say?"

I gave her a condensed version of Flip's story and ended with Punch's comment about his jealousy. "What's your take on that?" I asked.

Sabina turned back to her food, as uninterested now as she had been interested moments before. "I don't have a clue."

"My take is that Punch was accusing Flip of having a romantic interest in him."

She conveniently put a large bite of food in her mouth so all she could do was shrug, but I didn't let that deter me. "Now that I think about it, Ursula made a comment in that direction, too, remember? And you told her to shut up."

There was a pregnant pause, then Sabina wiped her fingers on her napkin and said lightly, "I probably told her that because she was being catty. I hate it when she gets that way."

She was trying to dodge the issue, so I decided to be direct. "Is Flip gay, Sabina?"

"Does it matter?" she said instantly. "Will it make any difference in his defense?"

"If he were in love with Punch, it could give him a motive."

"I thought you were trying to clear him."

"I'm trying to find the murderer—whoever it may be."

The last remaining traces of friendliness disappeared. "Flip's sexual orientation is a personal issue. Excuse me, please. I need to use the ladies' room." And with that she rose and headed for the door. So much for Sabina's friendliness.

I was about to move to the other end of the table to talk to Ursula when Aunt Corrine rose and announced *the game*. "All right, ladies. Put on your thinking caps. Let's see who can come up with a clever phrase using the letters in Jillian Knight Osborne."

My aunt ran through the rules, although it wasn't really necessary. The ladies were old hands at it. She rang a little bell, and everyone took up the pencil and paper beside their plates. Ten minutes later she rang the bell again, and one hundred pencils went down. Needless to say, my entry, "Kill no bones in a jig, Ruth," didn't take any prizes.

Then it was time to open the presents, an ordeal that could last for hours, depending on the swiftness of the bridesmaids. Each one of us had a duty to perform. Mine was to collect bows from the packages and fasten them to a large paper plate to make into a huge "bow bouquet" for the bride's future use. From the number of boxes stacked on the gift table, Jillian should have had enough bows to top presents well into the next century.

I positioned myself beside Ursula, who was in charge of wrapping paper disposal. With all eyes on Jillian, I took the opportunity to tell Ursula about my jail visit, just as I had to Sabina.

"What's your take on the jealousy comment?" I asked her.

"What did Sabina have to say about it?" Ursula replied. Obviously she had noticed us chatting.

I took a large pink bow from Jillian and stuck it onto the paper base. "Nothing."

"That does not surprise me. In college, Flip used to confide in Sabina all the time. She vas very protective of him." Ursula crumpled a big square of wrapping paper and dropped it into an empty grocery bag. "She is still protecting him."

Our conversation stopped momentarily when Jillian let out a high-pitched squeal over a piece of crystal that put my vase to shame. I glanced at Nikki, and she shrugged, as if to say, *That's life.*

"Then you believe Flip is gay?" I asked Ursula.

"It vas obvious to me. He vouldn't date girls, and he vorshipped Punch so much he was moody when Punch went on dates."

"Who else noticed Flip's feelings for Punch?"

"Onora. Probably Bertie, too. He always notices things the others don't."

"Not Jillian or Claymore?"

Ursula shook her head. "Too self-involved."

We paused as Jillian held up my vase and announced, "This is from my cousin Abby and her roommate, Nikki. Isn't it just so cute?" She wrinkled her nose on the word *cute,* as if that proved just how adorable it was. Then she set it right next to its bigger, more expensive cousin, kind of like putting me beside Jill.

I turned back to Ursula. "Do you believe Flip killed Punch?"

"A rejected lover is filled with powerful emotions. Could those emotions turn deadly? I think so."

"What about Onora?"

Ursula's gaze shifted to the subject in question, her face, as always, expressionless. "Onora is as cold-blooded as a snake. Yes, I believe she could have killed him."

"And Bertie?"

We paused to take care of our respective duties, then Ursula said, "Bertie is not so easy to figure out."

"Is it true Punch tried to ruin his career?"

"They had a feud, and Punch took his revenge by making terrible accusations to Bertie's boss that got him fired. Bertie says Punch did him a favor because he wasn't happy at the big firm anyway."

"Do you believe him?"

"Bertie went from making over two hundred thousand dollars a year working at one of the top ad agencies in New York, to sixty thousand dollars at a four-man firm. Would you have forgiven Punch for that?"

I was about to tell her that money and prestige didn't necessarily buy happiness, but in her mind they did, so why waste my breath? "Bertie went to a bar the evening of the murder, right?"

"He took a cab there, and we picked him up on our way to meet Punch at the dunes."

"Why didn't he drive his rental car to the bar?"

"Bertie never drives when he drinks. He's very conscientious."

Conscientious, or clever? Bertie could have taken a cab to the bar to establish his alibi. From there he could have slipped out for a short hike to the dunes, done his dirty work, then returned to the bar and pretended to have been there all evening. Means, opportunity, and motive. But that meant Punch would have had to call him, not Onora, before he'd called the others.

"Do you think there's a mystery girlfriend?" I asked Ursula.

"Punch couldn't be anywhere without a girlfriend."

"Out of Onora, Flip, and Bertie, who do you think is the most likely suspect?"

Ursula wadded up another sheet of gift wrap and tossed it. "Why not all of them? A conspiracy, you know? It vas common for Punch to pick up girls everywhere he went. Perhaps they used that knowledge so they vould have a decoy to throw the police off the trail."

A conspiracy theory? My head was beginning to ache. This investigation was getting much too complicated for my limited experience. Still, I couldn't resist asking, "Doesn't it bother you to implicate your friends in murder?"

"We were in college together. Who said they are my friends?"

Onora wasn't the only one with cold blood.

I grabbed the next bow and stuck it on the plate, wondering why I had ever agreed to help Jillian. Oh, right. The money. It didn't always bring happiness, but it did pay the bills.

I added an interview with Bertie to my list of things to do. I'd also have to take a trip out to the Luck o' the Irish bar, but I needed Marco for that because, despite its friendly Irish name, rumor had it that it was not a friendly Irish pub. In fact, I'd heard that the only thing Irish about it was the green plastic shamrock on the sign. Why Bertie chose that as his drinking destination was a puzzle. Had it been the bar's proximity to the dunes or the Irish moniker?

I really didn't want to think of Bertie as a suspect. Of all the bridal party, he was the most likeable. Not only that, but he'd defended me when Punch had gotten nasty. But I couldn't rule Bertie out just because I liked him. I'd heard him lie to the police about being Flip's cousin, and when we were first introduced he'd actually admitted that he didn't always tell the truth.

I saw Onora whisper in Jillian's ear, then slip away and head for the door, probably on her way to the ladies' room, so I asked Ursula to take over for me. Time to ask the finicky maid of honor some pointed questions. I had put it off long enough.

Onora was in a stall when I walked into the restroom, so I made a pretense of washing my hands, scrubbing them thoroughly with lots of foamy soap until she emerged.

"Those bows get sticky," I commented, reaching for paper towels.

Her gaze shifted to me briefly, then she opened her purse and retrieved a shiny silver tube of lipstick. I pulled out my lip gloss and applied it, watching her covertly in the mirror. "I've been meaning to ask you something, Onora. Where did you go the night of the murder?"

Her hand halted, the tube hovering over her lips. "Nowhere. I had a headache."

"That's odd. The hotel clerk saw you drive into the parking lot at nine o'clock."

"The hotel clerk is a moron." She threw her lipstick into her bag and snapped the little clutch shut. "Who are you, anyway, the FBI?"

Rather than fire back a smart reply I kept my cool. "Actually Jillian has asked me to—"

"I know what Jillian asked you to do. Go do it on someone else. I didn't kill Punch."

She started toward the door, so I quickly said, "Then why are you lying about going out that evening?"

Onora stopped short, her hand outstretched, ready to push open the swinging door. The room was eerily silent, save for the slow drip of a leaky faucet. Suddenly, she did a sharp pivot and, with her freshly rouged lips pressed into a hard line, she stalked over and squeezed my face between the talons of her right hand. "Listen, flower girl, what I did that evening is *my* business, so get out of my face."

"I believe you're the one in my face," I said evenly, prying her fingers off, "and since you're a suspect, what you did that evening is also *my* business."

"Oh, really? If I'm a suspect, why haven't the police told me so?"

Score one for the ice maiden. "Because," I said, trying to come up with a plausible reason, "they don't reveal their investigations to just anyone."

She sneered in my face, "Nice try."

I hated sneers; they made me cranky. "Okay, how's this, Onora? Once I tell them about our conversation the night of the murder—you remember that, don't you? You asked who killed Punch before we told you he'd been murdered?—I'm sure they'll be happy to include you on their short list."

I thought she was going to bash me with her bag. Instead, with a strangled cry of rage, she threw the little beaded number onto the floor and stamped on it. On her third stamp, the toe of her shoes came into contact with the tube of lipstick inside, her foot shot out from under her, and she went down onto her backside on the tiled floor.

"See what you've done?" she screeched, and promptly burst into tears. The woman was on one heck of an emotional roller coaster.

I held out a hand. "I'm sorry. Let me help you up."

The door opened and one of the guests came in. When she saw Onora on the floor crying, and me standing over her, the woman gasped and backed out.

Suddenly, Onora grabbed my wrist and yanked me down so we were practically nose-to-nose. Her pupils were dilated to pitch-black, radiating hatred, yet her facial muscles barely registered a twitch. "Stay away from me," she said through clenched teeth, "or you might end up like Punch."

She pushed me away, got to her feet, and glided out of the washroom, as unruffled as when she'd walked in.

Half of me was infuriated by her threat and the other half wasn't sure what to be. I didn't really think she'd try to kill me, but the fact that she had no reservations about expressing her feelings in that direction gave me pause. Sabina had been right about Onora. She had a nasty temper. She had also moved up to number one on my list of suspects.

I spent the remaining hour keeping my distance from Onora. Luckily, as soon as all the presents had been opened she left, slipping silently out of the room like a shadow. She seemed to be very good at that. I was going to follow her, but my aunt prevailed upon me to help cart Jillian's loot out to the semitrailer truck they'd hired. My sister-in-law Kathy was kind enough to take Nikki back to our apartment so I could stay and help. Nikki would have been glad to pitch in, but sitting with my mother and aunt had left her with a throbbing headache and a twitch in one eye.

After all the presents had been loaded into the truck, I secured my pedestal table in the Vette's passenger seat and returned to Bloomers, keeping one eye on the rearview mirror in case the mysterious Crown Victoria should reappear. Except for restaurants, nothing was open on the square on Sunday, so I parked directly in front of the shop, unlocked the front door, deactivated the alarm, then went back for the table.

"Hey, sunshine!" I heard a familiar voice call. "Come have a look."

Marco was standing in front of his bar, admiring a new sign, so I strolled down the sidewalk to offer my expert opinion. "Nice work. Who did it?"

"Jingles."

"The window washer is also a sign painter?"

"He did some gold lettering on the mirror over the bar, too."

I followed Marco inside to take a look. The wall behind the bar held a massive mirror framed in beautifully carved dark oak. Across the top of the mirror Jingles had painted *Down the Hatch* in fancy gold scrollwork. "Impressive," I told him.

Marco went behind the bar and held up a bottle of 7-Up. "Thirsty?"

"Not for bubbles."

"I thought you were over that bubbles phobia."

"It's not a phobia. Bubbles make me sneeze."

Marco opened a bottle of plain water and filled a glass as I took a seat at the bar. "You ought to have Jingles do something on your bay windows."

"I might be able to swing it when I get paid for the wedding flowers—if there *is* a wedding."

"I almost hate to ask, but how's the investigation going?"

"This morning I went to the jail for a chat with the police's number-one suspect and made him cry, and this afternoon Onora, the maid of honor, threatened to kill me. Other than that . . ."

Marco made a T with his hands, referee-style. "Whoa. Time out. Why did she threaten you?"

"Because I told her the hotel clerk had seen her in the

parking lot the night of the murder, when she supposedly hadn't left her room. She didn't take it well."

"Did the hotel clerk give the police that information?"

"I assume he did."

"Never assume. Call Reilly and make sure he knows. And then make sure Onora knows he knows. You don't want to be the only one holding that information. What about your interview with Flip?"

"Enlightening. Apparently, Punch was supposed to meet a girl at the dunes that night. Punch also accused Flip of being jealous, but I'm not sure of whom—Punch or the mystery girl. That reminds me, I have to pay a visit to the Luck o' the Irish bar tomorrow evening. Want to come along?" I threw that last part in quickly, hoping he'd say yes before he had a chance to reflect. It didn't work.

"You're going to that dive? No way. How about I go and you stay home?"

"This is my investigation. If you don't want to go with me I'll ask Nikki. She took karate lessons in high school. We'll be fine." I knew that would get him.

Marco glowered at me. "I'll pick you up at six thirty. And don't dress like that." He nodded toward my green outfit, which *was* rather clingy. Also, the bites on my legs had faded, and the itch had subsided enough to make shaving possible. With a little self-tanner applied for a healthy glow, I suddenly felt like a fox.

"Why?" I asked, batting my eyelashes. "Too sexy?"

His eyes raked over me in a way I found to be quite a turn-on. "Sexy isn't the right word."

"Suggestive? Alluring? Hot?"

"Churchy."

Time to go.

I returned to my car for the table, put it in the display window, adjusted the arrangements around it, and decided a finishing touch was in order. I tossed my purse on the front counter and headed for the basement via the workroom. But I'd no sooner reached the curtain when the hairs on the back of my neck rose. Something wasn't right.

I paused to listen. Other than the hum of the cooler all was silent, so I ignored that strange feeling and stepped into the workroom. To the right, the big refrigeration unit was shut, as usual. In the center, the worktable and its drawers sat undisturbed. To the left, my desk was clear—completely clear. Everything on top had been swept off, and the drawers had been emptied onto the floor.

My heart gave a lurch as I stared at the mess. Someone had broken in and rifled my desk.

The hair on my nape rose again. Why hadn't the alarm gone off? Had the robber slipped in while I was down at Marco's? Was he still in the shop?

CHAPTER SIXTEEN

My heart galloped as I backed slowly through the curtain. Quietly, I gathered my purse from the counter, noting that the cash register hadn't been touched. In fact, nothing else was out of place. Whoever had come in had targeted only the desk. But why? I never stored anything of value in it.

Keeping an eye on the curtained doorway, I felt for the door handle and was about to ease open the front door when it hit me. The Emperor's Spa photos were in my desk.

I stood there thinking hard, not sure what to do. Marco's advice would be to get out and call the cops. But if the photos were the only things taken, what would I report? That my pictures of the perverts who frequent the Emperor's Spa were missing? What was their value? Nothing. Why was I spying on them? Because the cops weren't doing their job. Wouldn't that go over well?

Instead of risking the cop's wrath, I picked up a heavy terra-cotta vase from a floor display and crept back to the curtain. Carefully, I peeked inside and did a thorough scan. Feeling braver, I slipped inside and paused again to listen.

Hearing nothing, I made my way slowly around the table to the kitchen. Still nothing. The back door was locked, too.

I peered into the darkness of the basement and decided a smart thief would never have risked being trapped there, so I went back through the shop, inspecting every nook and cranny, until I felt reasonably sure the robber had departed. Then I locked the door and went back to clean up the mess.

Scattered over the floor around my desk were pens, paper clips, lip gloss, breath mints, memo pads, nail files, and other odds and ends. I turned a drawer right side up and put it back in the bottom slot, then followed with the next two. Then I started putting back the contents. As I'd suspected, the only items that seemed to be missing were the photos.

The phone on my desk rang. I grabbed the receiver and put it to my ear, listening for a moment to make sure there was no heavy breathing on the other end. "Hello?" I said cautiously.

"Abby?" Nikki said. "You sound weird. Are you all right?"

Hearing Nikki's voice unleashed a tidal wave of emotions—shock, fright, relief, and outrage—the strongest being outrage. "Someone broke in and ransacked my desk. My personal desk! And now the spa photos are gone. The spa photos, Nikki. Okay, sure, I left the door unlocked when I ran down to look at Marco's new gold lettering, but that was an accident. What kind of person would walk right in and help themselves to my things?"

I could hear Nikki talking to someone in the background. "Nikki? Are you listening to me? *The photos are gone.*"

"Hold on. I've got Marco on my cell phone."

"Why are you talking to Marco?"

"I called him, that's why, and you should have, too.

What if you'd walked in while that madman was in your shop?" Her voice started to tremble. "You could have been killed. I might never have seen you again. I'd have to sublet your room."

Nikki was nothing if not practical.

She sniffled and said, "Marco will be right down."

At once there was banging on the front door. I peeked through the curtain and there he stood, a cell phone to his ear, a small leather bag under his arm, and a scowl on his face. I unlocked the door and stepped back as he clapped his phone shut. "What happened?"

In the face of his anger, my own faded away, replaced by an odd feeling of calm. Or maybe it was shock. "Someone came in while I was down at your bar, ransacked my desk, and stole my spa photos."

"Did you call the police?"

"To report that the pictures I secretly took of five perverts are gone? What do you think?"

Marco examined the door. "No sign of forced entry. How did he get in?"

"Remember when you asked me to come look at your sign? I'd just unlocked the door—wait a minute. This is your fault!"

"It's my fault you can't remember to keep your door locked?"

"You distracted me. All I intended to do was drop off the table and leave. Just in and out, that was the plan."

"Well, someone else had a plan, too." Marco started for the workroom and I followed. "Was anything other than your desk disturbed?"

"Not that I can tell." I stood just inside the curtain, rubbing my arms to get rid of the goose bumps that had suddenly appeared. "What if I hadn't gone down to your bar?

Would he have attacked me to get the photos? Never mind. I don't even want to think about it. I'll have nightmares."

Marco opened his leather bag, took out a brush and a small tin of metal powder and dusted the drawer pulls and surrounding surfaces. "He must have been watching you, waiting for an opportunity to get inside without setting off the alarm."

"Thank you. My nightmare video is now loaded and ready to play. Viewing times will be two and four a.m."

Marco twirled a brush over the powder, then squinted at the results. "No prints."

Smart thief. He knew what he wanted, where to find it, and how to get it without leaving evidence. "Maybe it was the guy in the Crown Victoria. I think he followed me to the jail this morning when I went to visit Flip."

Marco pondered that as he put away his kit. "The question is, why would a federal agent break in to steal a couple of photos?"

"Maybe I caught him on camera."

"That's a possibility. Have the feds been brought into the murder investigation?"

"If they have, the newspaper hasn't reported it. I'm meeting with the deputy prosecutor tomorrow. I'll see what he says."

Marco leaned a hip against my desk and studied me. "I can't help wondering how the thief knew where to find the photos."

"The only person I told was you . . . and Lottie." I turned my head to murmur, "And Nikki and Bill."

"Bill the newspaper reporter? The same Bill you didn't tell to keep your name out of it? Why didn't you just take out an ad to let the whole town know where you put the photos?"

I pushed him through the curtain. "Too expensive. Let's

go. I need some fresh air. I'm feeling light-headed. No smart remarks about that, please. It's been a trying day."

As I strapped myself into the Vette, Marco leaned his hands on the car door and said, "Don't even think about cooking up a scheme to get more photos."

"Not a problem. I'm staying away from the spa. If the salon owner has a beef with them, she can deal with it herself."

"Good girl. Don't forget to call Reilly. And one more thing. *Keep your doors locked.*"

In reply, I flattened the lock button right before his eyes.

"There you go." He gave me that little half grin and strode back to the Down the Hatch.

When I got home, Nikki and Simon were waiting by the door. Nikki threw her arms around me and gave me a hug. Simon coughed up a fur ball. It was a touching scene.

We heated split pea soup and while we ate I gave her a rundown on the theft. She thought Bill Bretton had been the most likely leak of information, and I was having a hard time disagreeing. Bill had probably gone to his editor to get the okay to do the article, and who knew how many other reporters had heard about it? One of them might have been a patron of the spa. I'd have to call Bill in the morning. I needed to let him know about the missing photos anyway.

"I almost forgot," Nikki said, licking her spoon. "Greg Morgan called."

"Please don't tell me he canceled lunch tomorrow."

"No. He verified it. Lunch at Rosie's at one o'clock. And as soon as we finish our soup, we can go find something hot for you to wear."

"It's just a lunch meeting, Nikki."

"But it's with Greg Morgan, Abby! This is the guy every woman in town drools over. You have to look good."

I scraped the last remnants of soup from my bowl. "Why bother picking out something special when he won't even notice? The only reason Morgan gazes into a girl's eyes is to see his own reflection. "

"Are you serious? I've seen the way he watches you when you're not looking."

I paused to consider her comment, the spoon almost to my lips. "What about that black off-the-shoulder blouse I found on sale last week?"

"With your black-and-white print skirt? Perfect."

Monday morning started with a fast walk around the track, a quick shower, and then the short drive to the shop. I kept an eye out for the Crown Victoria, but with the heavy morning traffic it was difficult to tell if anyone was following me. When I pulled into a space around the corner from Bloomers, I shut off the engine, glanced around for any suspicious characters, then pulled out my cell phone to call Bill Bretton. I'd decided not to say anything about the break-in to Grace and Lottie because they'd only worry more, if that was possible. With any luck they wouldn't remember that I'd had the photos anyway.

"Features desk," a man said in a bored voice.

"Bill?"

"Bill stepped away for a minute. Who's calling?"

"Abby Knight."

Hearing my name, the voice perked up. "May I tell him what this is about?"

"Just tell him I have a question for him."

"Anything I can answer?"

He was definitely fishing for information. "No, but thanks anyway, Mr. . . . I'm sorry, I didn't catch your name."

"Mike Green. I'm the features editor."

"Congratulations. Give Bill my message, will you? Thanks."

"Hold on. Here's Bill now."

The phone changed hands and Bill came on the line. "Bretton," he said.

"Hey, Bill, this is Abby Knight. Remember those photos of the Emperor's Spa I promised you? They've been stolen."

There was dead silence on the line.

"Bill? Are you there?"

"Interesting," he said.

"Very. It certainly proves something fishy is going on. If you need more photos, I'll call the owner of the salon next door to the spa and—"

"That's okay. Thanks anyway."

He was talking in a very stilted way, making me think someone was listening. "Bill, if you can't talk now, why don't you call me when you can?"

"No need."

"No need? You're not going to look into it?"

"Looks that way."

"Bill, come on! This could be a huge story."

"I understand." He covered the mouthpiece and whispered, "I was told to drop it, Abby. I'm sorry I can't help you."

"Who told you to drop it?"

"Nice talking to you." The line went dead.

CHAPTER SEVENTEEN

Someone had put a clamp on the story. An editor? The police? On the off chance that I could wheedle that information from Reilly, I dialed the nonemergency line. "I'd like to speak with Sgt. Sean Reilly, please," I said to the switchboard operator. "This is Abby Knight."

"Abby? How are you, honey? It's Georgia. Remember me? I used to babysit you and those naughty brothers of yours."

I had no recollection of any Georgia. I also had no recollection of naughty brothers. Jonathan and Jordan had been so well behaved, I'd been forced to get them into trouble just to keep from looking so bad myself. "Georgia! How have you been?"

"Just super. I hear you bought Bloomers. Good for you, Abby. You can't flunk out of that, can you?" She guffawed. A pained chuckle was the best I could manage.

"Georgia, is Sgt. Reilly around? I'd like to talk to him."

"Who wouldn't? Now there's a good-looking devil if there ever was one. But he's out right now. Is this business, or a social call?" She put special emphasis on the last two words.

"One hundred percent business. Tell him to call me when he gets in."

"Will do, hon. Pinch your brothers' freckled cheeks for me, will you?"

"With pleasure." I put my phone in my purse and got out of the Vette, checking up and down the street for the Crown Victoria and/or the little old man. I saw neither, but as I rounded the corner onto Franklin I thought I heard footsteps behind me. I swung around, but no one was there. It happened twice more before I reached the shop. Anyone watching me stop suddenly and pivot would have thought I was crazy. I was certainly starting to feel that way.

When I stepped into the shop, Grace was grinding coffee beans in the parlor, and Lottie was in the kitchen serving up her Monday morning breakfast. I stopped to check on the wire orders and saw that we'd received nine. Not a bad start for the week. My coupons had been pulling in customers, too, and I still had the contest drawing, which I hoped would garner some newspaper attention.

"Don't you look like a hot potato today," Lottie said, shoveling a mound of eggs onto a plate. "If I didn't know better I'd say you had a date with that courthouse cutie."

I adjusted my black top. "Because I'm wearing this old thing?"

"You bought it last week, hon. You showed me, remember?"

I stuffed a bite of toast in my mouth and reached for the pepper.

"Abby? You do have a date with him, don't you?"

"Not a date," I said, interrupting her dance of joy. "A lunch meeting."

"Right," Lottie said with a wink, "a meeting."

Time to change the subject. "Remind me to do that drawing tomorrow. I'm going to ask Bill Bretton to write it up for the newspaper."

The phone rang, and moments later Grace called, "It's your cousin, dear."

Was there any better way to kick off the week? A toothache? A broken heel? A flat tire? I took the call at my desk. "I want you to know you're interrupting my breakfast."

Jillian yawned, then said sleepily, "You eat breakfast?"

"Why are you up so early?"

"I can't sleep from worrying about everything. Are you going to solve this murder soon?"

"I hope you've had this conversation with the police detectives."

"They won't let me call anymore."

"I'm doing my best, Jill. Go back to bed." I returned to the kitchen to finish my meal.

"Is Jillian giving you a hard time?" Lottie asked, sitting down with her own plate of food.

"She's nervous. She's never come this close to marriage before."

"I still say she won't go through with it."

"If she backs out this time, I will hunt her down and drag her to the altar. I've got a vanload of flowers ordered, not to mention a bridesmaid dress that gives new meaning to the word *ugly*."

As I munched the last bite of toast, Lottie leaned toward me to say quietly, "Ask Grace about her dinner with Richard Saturday night. I'm dying to know what happened."

"If you wouldn't tease her, she might be willing to tell *you* these things."

"What fun would that be?"

I could see Lottie's point. "I'll have a chat with Grace before I go to the DeWitts' house."

At the sound of a distant "Yoo-hoo!" we both froze. It was Monday. My mother the Weekend Sculptress always had something new for us on Monday.

"Gotta go," Lottie said, but I grabbed her by the strings of her bib apron before she could flee out the back door.

"We're going to face this together—whatever it may be," I told her.

"Yoo-hoo, Abigail!" The sound of doom was growing closer.

"Maybe we should both leave," Lottie suggested. After a moment's consideration, we scrambled for the door, but not in time.

"Here you are!" my mother cried. "Oh, wonderful, you're here, too, Lottie. Come see what I brought." She smiled like a little girl with a big surprise. She had on a long, flowing, flowered skirt, sandals, and a lime green T-shirt. I had to admit she looked pretty good for being my mother.

Like condemned prisoners, we trudged obediently after her, through the workroom and into the shop. On the tiled floor in the middle of the room was a brown paper–wrapped parcel about a foot and a half square. My mother stuck her head in the parlor to summon Grace, then we gathered at the counter to watch the unveiling.

"Keep in mind the theme I started with the palm tree," she said, then paused, a furrow on her brow as she turned for a look at her previous creation, still in the corner next to the wicker settee. "You haven't sold it yet?"

"I may have a buyer," I said instantly, not wanting to hurt her feelings.

"Really? Who?"

I should have known she would ask that question. "It will be a surprise." For all of us.

Two female customers came in the front door and headed for the coffee parlor, but as my mother unwrapped her bundle, they paused to see what the excitement was about.

"Voilà!" my mother said, stepping back for all to admire her work. And there it stood, on all four feet. Four big, bare feet on the floor; four big, bare feet facing the ceiling, forming a solid cube of naked feet.

"Oh, look," Grace exclaimed, gingerly touching it, "you've even painted the toenails, and each one a different color, too."

The customers hustled into the parlor, pinching their lips together to keep from laughing.

"I've got it," Lottie said. "A *foot*stool."

"Of course it's a footstool," my mother said, bewildered. "What else would it be?"

Hideous?

"What do you think, Abigail?" my mother asked.

Grace slid quietly out to take care of the women in the parlor. Lottie gave me a pitying look.

"I think—you're the most creative person in our family." I gave her a hug and she beamed with pride. It worked every time.

"You look nice today," she said, pulling my off-the-shoulder top onto my shoulders.

I readjusted them. "They're supposed to be down."

"You'll get chilly."

"If I get chilly I'll put them up."

For twelve seconds it was a standoff. Then Grace peered out of the parlor and said, "Maureen, would you care for a cup of tea or coffee?" I made frantic *"No! Stop!*

I don't have time to entertain her!" arm gestures, but she ignored me.

"Thank you, Grace, but I have a hair appointment."

I slumped in relief. The bell over the door jingled as an elderly couple came in.

"Why don't I move the . . . um . . . footstool . . . in front of the settee?" Lottie volunteered, sweeping the object out of the path and into the corner as the couple began to browse.

"As long as people will notice it there," my mother replied.

"They'll notice it," Lottie assured her.

Satisfied, my mother turned to me, eyed my bare shoulders, but left the top alone. "Have you found the murderer?"

The elderly man took his wife by the arm and escorted her out the door, where I could see him hustling her away from the shop, casting worried glances at us over his shoulder.

"Mother, please don't talk about the murder in front of my customers."

"I'm sorry. But have you?"

"I'm getting close."

"So is the wedding."

"Thanks for reminding me."

"Speaking of reminders," Lottie said, sensing that things were taking a turn for the worse, "don't you have an appointment with a client shortly, Abby?"

God bless Lottie.

At nine thirty I picked up Trudee's file, slung my purse over my shoulder, and headed for the parlor. Grace was serving coffee and scones to a group of students from the university, so I waited by the coffee counter to tell her where I was headed.

"Toddle on then, dear," she said, as she put on more coffee to brew. "I'll mind the shop."

"Thanks. By the way, how was your dinner Saturday night?"

"Excellently prepared. The chef outdid himself."

Not exactly the information I was hoping for, so I took another stab at it. "The evening must have gone well. You look so . . . *happy* . . . today."

The machine stopped and Grace glanced up at me in concern. "Don't I look happy every day?"

"What I meant was that you seem to have enjoyed Richard's company."

"I wouldn't have dined with him otherwise." She made it sound so logical.

"You're missing my point, Grace. I'm trying to find out what happened Saturday night."

"I've already told you, dear. We had a lovely meal."

"And?"

"And what?"

I gazed at her serene face and knew I'd lost. "I'm going to Trudee's."

I glanced back just before I left and saw her smile secretively.

I pushed the DeWitts' doorbell and waited while it played the first two measures of "Take Me Out to the Ball Game." In a few moments I heard Trudee's stilettos tapping against the marble hall, then the door swung open and she stood there snapping her gum and smiling. Her hair, today a bright yellow, was in a Barbie doll ponytail, her shapely hips and legs zipped into pink stretch pants, and her D cups stuffed into a black halter top.

"C'mon in," she said, blowing a bubble. She tapped back up the hallway toward her kitchen and pointed to a brown leather stool at the island counter. "Put it down there."

Assuming the "it" was my posterior, I put it there and opened her file.

"Coffee?" she said, pushing a cup toward me. She filled one for herself, too, then put her "it" down on another stool to look over my plans. As I explained, she nodded sagely, blowing bubbles and popping them loudly without once getting any goo on her face. She had quite a talent for it.

"I like it," she said when I'd finished. "Only one suggestion. Something tropical in the foyer, something that will grab everyone's attention the moment they walk in."

"Okay," I said, making a note in the margin. "A tropical attention-grabber."

"Come see the backyard."

We walked out of the kitchen through sliding glass doors onto an expansive wooden deck filled with two umbrella-shaded tables, matching chairs, and two lounge chairs with cushions in bright tropical prints. Beyond the deck was a huge lawn that sloped gently down to a creek. "Right there," she said, pointing to the grassy area. "A giant flag."

"Let's measure."

Trudee held one end of my tape measure, and I walked with the other until she told me to stop. *Giant* wasn't the appropriate word. *Gargantuan,* maybe. "Trudee, you realize the cost will be exorbitant, don't you?"

"It isn't a problem."

But time was. I'd have to have my supplier deliver them directly to Trudee's house early on the morning of the party, which was not only Independence Day but also Jillian's wedding. I'd have my hands full with that alone.

"I need to make a few calls to see if I can get the flowers delivered that morning," I told her. "Why don't I get back to you tomorrow with an estimate for the flag, and then you can decide?"

"Sure, if it makes you feel better." She blew a big pink bubble and smiled through it.

Suddenly, the ground began to tremble beneath my feet, and the air around me vibrated with the sound of a bass guitar. I heard a squeal of brakes, then, two door-slams later, Trudee's pink-haired daughter Heather and her Mohawked boyfriend meandered around the corner of the house, stepped onto the deck, and threw themselves onto the side-by-side lounge chairs, tossing a black leather, soft-sided carrying case into the narrow space between them.

Pressing her bright pink lips together, Trudee marched onto the deck and went straight to Heather, who was busy setting up her portable CD player. "Where are your manners, young lady? You can at least say hello when we have company."

"Hullo," the girl said sullenly, not even glancing in my direction.

Trudee threw a frosty glare in the direction of the boyfriend, who had donned his headphones and was bobbing to the music blaring from his own CD player.

"To think I wanted to be a mother," Trudee muttered. "Think twice before having kids, Abby."

At the rate I was going, I'd be lucky to have a steady date.

We went back inside the house so I could take a better look at her foyer. I sketched it out on my notepad, promised to call her the next day, and left. But I came to a sudden stop on the sidewalk outside as I gaped at the car parked bumper-to-bumper with my Vette. It was a Volkswagen Beetle, painted to look tie-dyed, just like the one I had seen in the dunes parking lot on the night of the murder.

I did an about-face and headed around the house to the backyard.

"Hey," I said, tapping Heather on the shoulder. Like her boyfriend, she had on headphones and was listening with her eyes closed. At my tap her orbs flew open and she lifted one earphone to hear me.

"Whose VW is out front?"

She jerked her head toward Mohawk Boy in the next chair. "His."

"Does he have a name?"

"Ben."

"Mind if I ask Ben a few questions?"

Heather poked him and he opened his eyes, turning his head toward her. "Yeah?"

"She wants to talk to you."

Ben looked at me, holding one side of the headphones an inch away from his eardrum. "What?"

I walked around to his chair and perched on the end of it. "Let's make this easier on both of us. Take off the headgear." With a sharp sigh, he sat up and did as requested.

"How long have you had your VW?"

"I dunno. Maybe three months."

"Do you ever drive it out to the dunes?"

"Sometimes."

"Are you aware of the murder that happened there?" At his hesitant nod, I asked, "Were you out there that night?"

He gave me a wary look. "Are you a cop?"

"She owns a flower shop, dork," Heather said over the thumping of the bass.

"Yeah, I was there."

"Were you around when the police came?"

He made a scoffing sound. "No way. Like I want to get busted."

"Shut up, stupid!" Heather glanced over her shoulder toward the house.

I dug in my purse and found the folded newspaper photos of Flip and Punch. "I'm not interested in your illegal activities. All I want to know is whether you saw either of these two men while you were there."

Ben did a quick scan, shook his head, and resumed listening to his music. But Heather took off her headphones to lean in for a closer look. She studied them for a long moment, then tapped one of the photos. "We saw this dude. Remember, Ben? His hair was longer and kind of stringy, but this is him." She was pointing to Flip. "He was sitting down by the water, holding his head and mumbling."

"Oh, the drunk dude," Ben said, suddenly enlightened. "Man, he was wasted."

"He was holding his head?" I asked. "Could he have been hurt?"

They looked at each other and shrugged. "I guess so," Heather said. "But then we heard sirens and took off."

"Did you see this man?" I asked, pointing to the photo of Punch.

"Nope." Ben put his headphones on again and lay back, closing his eyes.

"Sorry," Heather said. She leaned over to jab her boyfriend in the shoulder. "What did you do with the White Stripes CD?"

"It's in the case."

She sat up and reached for the black leather case between them. As she pinched the brass clasp and swung the top open, I caught a glimpse of the interior.

"Isn't that a camera bag?"

"Maybe."

"May I see it?"

She turned it so I could have a look. The bag reminded me of the big leather case that held my father's old Nikon, with compartments for the various lenses, rolls of film, and all the other gadgets that an amateur photographer totes around. It wasn't the kind of case teens would buy for their CDs. "Where did you get this?"

"Found it."

"At the dunes?"

"Yeah," she said guardedly. "Why?"

A tingle of excitement raced up my spine. "Heather, you found a piece of murder evidence."

CHAPTER EIGHTEEN

The sliding glass door opened, and Trudee hurried onto the deck. "Did they hit your car? Ben, you didn't hit her car, did you?"

The car wasn't my concern at the moment. "Heather, I'd like to take that case to the police to have it examined."

She pulled it against her chest. "No way! Finders keepers!"

I appealed to her mother. "Trudee, I think this camera bag may be evidence in a murder case. I really need to have the police check it out."

"The dunes murder?" Trudee asked, steam practically shooting from her ears as she glared at her daughter. "Heather, what are you doing with that bag?"

"We found it, okay? It was just lying in some weeds, so we took it."

"Would you be able to show the police where you found it?" I asked her.

"I guess so."

"Was anything inside or was it empty?"

"Some cloth bags were inside. They're in Ben's car."

Trudee grabbed the strap and yanked the case out of Heather's arms. "Here you go, Abby. Heather, go get the things you took out of it."

As Heather clumped off to do her mother's bidding, Trudee walked around to the front with me to take a look at my bumper. Although the VW was a mere centimeter away, it hadn't scratched my car. Lucky for them.

"Here," Heather said, piling four heavy, felt bags into my arms. I could tell by the shape that they held camera lenses.

"Just to forewarn you," I told Trudee, as Heather stalked back to join her boyfriend, "the police will probably want to question them and take their prints."

"They'll be here," she promised.

I put the lenses in the case, stowed the case in my trunk, and drove away. Boy, did I have a surprise for Morgan. And an excellent bargaining tool. Marco would be so proud.

The hands on my watch seemed to move with excruciating slowness as I waited for one o'clock to arrive. Ten minutes before the hour, I alerted Lottie to my departure, picked up a shopping bag with the camera case inside, and headed across the square to the restaurant.

Time had stopped somewhere in the early 1970s at Rosie's. The walls were paneled in dark wood; the booths that ringed the room were high-backed avocado green vinyl, with polka-dotted Formica tables; the chairs and tables on the raised center platform were chrome and burnt orange plastic; and the floor was a golden brown linoleum. There was a single cash register station by the door, and a kitchen through a pair of swinging doors in the back.

The menu was classic diner food: hamburgers with a selection of toppings; chicken, turkey, ham, and beef sandwiches; a choice of three soups (one always being French onion); batter-fried fish and french-fried potatoes; meatloaf and mashed potatoes; and slices of homemade pies chosen from the glass case next to the cash register. Nothing fancy, nothing vegetarian, nothing expensive, no substitutions, and the place was always crowded. Their only concession to the new century was a selection of gourmet coffees.

I sat at a booth in the back left corner and had barely glanced at the menu when the door opened and a hush fell over the diners.

Morgan had entered the building.

I raised my hand and caught his eye. As usual, every female over the age of twelve turned to watch him saunter toward the back, waiting expectantly to see who the lucky girl was. By that cocky grin on his face, Morgan knew exactly what kind of effect he was having.

"Hello, Abby," he said, dropping his voice to movie-star range. The female sighs around me were enough to rustle the paper napkins on the tables.

"I'm surprised no one stopped you for an autograph," I said as he slid onto the opposite bench.

A thoughtful frown appeared, as if he suddenly wondered whether he'd lost his popularity. But then a middle-aged waitress in an orange blouse and black slacks materialized and practically melted onto his shoulder, reviving his flagging spirits.

"Coffee?" she gushed. "Cappuccino? Espresso? Latte? Mocha? Mocha latte?"

He gave her his toothsome smile. "How about a plain old decaf?"

"Cream? Sweetener? Sugar?"

Had she called him sugar or offered him sugar?

"Sweetener. Thanks."

She twirled and floated toward the kitchen.

"I'll have iced tea," I called, *"sugar."*

"So." Morgan glanced around the diner to see who his audience was. "How is my favorite florist today?"

"Hungry." I could have said I'd just had a third arm attached and his instant reply would have been exactly the same.

"Great. Say, I hear we're going to be walking down the aisle together."

"I've heard that rumor, too. It was really nice of you to step in on such short notice."

He leaned toward me, an angelic gleam in his eyes. "I'm a nice guy, in case you hadn't noticed."

His timing couldn't have been more perfect. Now I'd see how nice he really was. As we studied the menu, I said casually, "I have something I think you'll find quite interesting."

"Are you wearing it?" He wiggled an eyebrow at me.

Half in jest I said, "You are a shameful human being and a discredit to your profession. I should report you, but then my cousin would be left without a groomsman for the second time."

"So you're not wearing it?"

"It's a piece of evidence for the murder case. So, no, I'm not wearing it."

Morgan sat forward, all kidding aside. I knew I had his attention when he didn't even notice the waitress lean over to put his coffee and her breasts in front of him. Since I'd last seen her, her blouse had somehow come unbuttoned halfway down her chest. It was quite a display. Too bad Morgan missed it.

"What evidence?" he asked.

"I had an iced tea," I reminded the waitress. Wounded by Morgan's lack of attention, she moped off to get my beverage.

"A camera case—your prime suspect's camera case, I

believe." I pulled out the shopping bag and set it in the center of the table.

Morgan peered inside the bag. "Where did you get it?"

"From a pair of teenagers who happened to be out at the dunes the night of the murder." I slid a piece of paper toward him. "Here are their names and an address where you can reach them."

He tucked the paper in his pocket. "How did you know they had the case?"

"I have my sources." I paused when the waitress returned with my glass of tea. We put in our food orders and she stalked off, still pouting.

"I'll get it over to the detectives after my two o'clock hearing." He reached for the bag, but I pulled it back, setting it safely on the bench beside me.

"You're not going to blackmail me, are you?" he asked. "I can get a subpoena for the bag."

"And here I thought you were so nice."

He studied me for several minutes, trying to figure out my angle. "What do you want?"

I counted the items on my fingers. "One, a little information. Two, justice. Three, the satisfaction of seeing my cousin married. Four, the joy of getting paid for her wedding flowers. That should about do it."

"You know I can't divulge privileged information."

"You don't have to divulge anything. I'll ask you something, and you either nod or shake your head."

"That's still divulging."

"Come on, Morgan. I just brought you an important piece of evidence. No one has to know you told me anything. You scratch my back and I'll scratch yours—and don't take that literally."

He gave me a put-upon glance. I patted the shopping bag

and he sighed. Like it was the first time he'd ever helped anyone.

"Has the FBI joined the investigation?" I asked him.

Morgan shook his head. That was one worry gone. "Was Punch's cell phone found?"

He shook his head again. Cell phone still missing, possibly in the murderer's possession. "Did you develop the film from the camera and, if so, was there anything helpful on it?"

He broke his silence to say, "Birds and plants. That's it." Dead end there.

"Did you get any prints off the camera besides your primary suspect's?"

He took a sip of coffee, then nodded once and quickly held up three fingers.

Three sets of prints. "Have you identified all of them?"

He shook his head.

The waitress brought my grilled chicken sandwich and Morgan's mushroom-topped burger and set them down with a vengeful *thunk*. Realizing he'd been neglectful, Morgan thanked her, holding her gaze a moment longer than necessary, causing her to do a quick change in attitude. "Will there be anything else?" she breathed in his ear. I hoped she'd eaten garlic at her previous meal.

He lifted an eyebrow at her. "Maybe later."

She giggled and sashayed off, throwing him a longing glance over her shoulder.

"Shameful," I told him.

"Habit." He bit into the burger and a huge glob of mustard splattered onto his plate. I was glad the waitress wasn't there to see it. She'd be mopping it up with the front of her blouse.

"You've got three sets of prints from the camera. How many have you identified?"

He glanced over his shoulder to see if anyone was watching, then held up two fingers.

"Was Bertie McManus's one of them?"

He nodded.

Finding Bertie's prints wasn't too surprising since Flip had mentioned that he knew how to use the camera. But I couldn't rule him out without verifying his alibi. "How about maid of honor Onora?"

Morgan shook his head.

Lack of her prints was probably why the detectives hadn't pursued that thread of their investigation. They obviously hadn't thought it through far enough to realize she might have worn gloves.

"Can you tell if the unidentified prints belonged to a man or woman?"

Another shake of the head.

I paused to take a few bites of sandwich and mull over his answers. "You have an unidentified set of prints. Why are you so sure Flip is the murderer?"

"It's a classic case of revenge," Morgan said, chewing a french fry. "And frankly, his alibi stunk. Bump on the head? Temporary amnesia? Overused."

"Wait a minute. Rewind to that little bomb you just dropped. You said *revenge*. Revenge for what?"

"I can't tell you that." Morgan glanced at his watch, then signaled to the waitress for the bill. "I have to be in court in twenty minutes. I'd better go."

"Will you at least let me know what the detectives find out about the camera case? Fingerprints, et cetera?"

He covered my hand with his and said in that slick, practiced way, "For you, Abby? Of course I will."

And I wouldn't hold my breath.

The woman brought over our tab, and Morgan picked it

up. "I'll get this," he told me, "and I'll take that." He pointed to the shopping bag. I let him have both.

As we walked outside, Morgan put on his silvered shades, then patted the package under his left arm. "Thanks."

"Quid pro quo," I reminded him. One thing in return for another. It was something that had actually sunk in during my year of law school.

He smiled, and a car full of women nearly veered onto the curb. "Give me a few days, then stop by my office."

He started across the street toward the courthouse and the cars seemed to part before him like the waters of the Red Sea. If I followed, I'd be run over. My cell phone rang so I pulled it out of my purse and flipped it open.

"Abby, this is Carrie at First Impressions hair salon. Do you have time to stop by this afternoon? There's something here you have to see."

That sounded cryptic.

"Hold on. I've got another call," she said. After a minute, Carrie came back on the line apologizing. "It's a madhouse here today."

"I'll head over your way now. See you in about fifteen minutes."

As I walked back to Bloomers I thought over what I'd learned from Morgan. The key to proving that Flip wasn't the killer seemed to be identifying the third set of fingerprints. Someone else had held that camera at the murder scene, and I had a strong hunch that if I could find the missing cell phone, I'd find that person. I immediately called Jillian. "Hey, what's Punch's cell phone number?"

"Abby, he's dead."

"Whew! I'm glad you told me!" I said, emoting. "Would you just give me the number?"

"Okay, but why?"

"I'd tell you but then I'd have to kill you."

"That's not funny."

"What's all that background noise?"

"The girls and I are shopping on Michigan Avenue in Chicago. Here's his number."

I punched it in as she recited it. "Thanks, Jill. I'm going to call his phone now. If a cell phone rings in your vicinity, would you let me know when you get a moment alone?"

I hung up and dialed Punch's number. The phone rang three times, then disconnected. I tried again with the same results. Was the phone out of range or had someone ended the call? I waited a moment, then called Jillian's line again. "Did anyone's phone ring?"

"Not out here, but Ursula and Onora went into Burberry's."

"Sabina is with you?"

"Right."

"Okay, thanks. I'll let you know before I try again." I'd have to call her when the other two girls were with her.

I stepped into Bloomers and found Lottie getting ready to make a flower delivery. "I'll take it," I told her. "I have an errand to run anyway."

I placed the wrapped bundle on the seat beside me and took off. The delivery was to a home on the east side of Concord Avenue, not far from the hair salon. I dropped it off, thrilled with the elderly woman's surprised reaction, then hopped back in the Vette and drove to the salon.

"Come with me," Carrie said, and led me through the busy salon into the pedicure room, closed the door, and took a white envelope from her smock pocket. "This was shoved under our door sometime before Judy opened this morning. I didn't come in until noon or I would have called you sooner."

I peeked inside the envelope and saw photos. Three of

them, to be exact. I pulled them out to take a look and went cold all over. They were all of me. One in my car. One walking into my shop. One coming out of my apartment building. I was being stalked.

I felt light-headed and decided I should sit down before I ended up out cold on the floor. I sat with my head between my knees while Carrie ran to get me something to drink. She returned with a cup filled with dark coffee. I took a sip and shuddered. It was dark, all right—about five-hours-old dark.

"What's going on?" Carrie asked, nodding toward the photos.

"Someone is watching me and wants me to know it."

"Why were they left here? Why didn't they send them to you?"

"Good question."

Her face paled. "It's because you took pictures for me. This is a warning to both of us. I'm so sorry, Abby. I never meant to drag you into it."

"Don't be sorry. I offered to help."

Carrie's eyes widened as something occurred to her. "Maybe they gave the pictures to me to lure you here."

I gasped in alarm. "My Vette!"

With Carrie on my heels, I dashed through her shop and out to the parking lot. It wouldn't have been the first time my car was a target for someone with a bone to pick.

The Corvette was sitting between a minivan and an Audi, facing the Emperor's Spa parking lot, which was empty, as usual. I checked inside the car, under the hood, and in the trunk, but nothing seemed out of the ordinary.

Carrie cast a nervous glance at the old house next door. "I think we'd both better keep our distance from the spa."

I was thinking along those same lines myself. I told Carrie to be careful, then I tucked the photos in my purse and slid into the Vette. My phone rang and I fished it out. "Hello," I said, keeping an eye on the spa.

"Remember those Chinese symbols written on your bedroom window?" Marco asked. "I got the translation back."

"You're going to tell me it's not a good-luck wish, aren't you?"

"How did you guess?"

I spotted a wrinkled face staring at me from a corner of the spa window, just as before. "Marco, are you at the bar?"

"Yep."

"Stay there. I have something to show you."

Without saying a word, Marco took the envelope from me and went to sit at his desk. He put up his feet and pulled out the photos to study them, tossing each one in turn onto the top. Then he leaned back and rubbed his eyes, in pondering mode.

While his brain was otherwise occupied, I pulled the pictures toward me and lined them up along the edge like little soldiers. An Abby army. "You know, all things considered, I don't look half-bad."

His eyes opened into slits as he glared at me.

"No need to lecture," I told him. "I know I shouldn't have gotten involved."

"A little late for that, isn't it?" He swung his feet down and pulled his chair forward. "The problem is how to get you uninvolved. How do we let this stalker know you're out of it?"

"By staying away from the spa?"

He studied me, his fingers drumming the desk. "I can't think of anything else to do, other than hiring a bodyguard."

Marco could guard my body any day. But Marco wasn't in that business, and I couldn't afford to hire a real one. "I'll just be very careful."

He snorted. "I've heard that one before."

"Here's what else I found out today." I told him about the camera case, the squashed newspaper story, the new information from Morgan, and calling Punch's number. "Someone has that phone, Marco, and that person may be the killer."

"Before you get arrested for making harassing calls to that number, talk to Reilly. Find out where they are on the investigation."

A waitress tapped on the doorframe. "Telephone, Marco. About your car."

"Thanks."

I scooped up the photos and rose. "Did something happen to your Jeep?"

"I sold it. Too many of them on the street. I wanted something different."

I smiled, imagining myself seated beside him, hair flying as we sped past throngs of envious women in a hot red sports car. "What did you buy?"

"Dark green Impala. Previously owned. Perfect for PI work."

My fantasy dissolved. "Are you going to drive this dream car when you go with me to the Luck o' the Irish bar tonight?"

"Are you going to dress like that?" He nodded toward my short skirt and black top.

"Didn't we have this conversation already? The one where you tell me my outfit is too churchy?"

"That's not the word I was going to use today."

"Square. Dowdy. Fashion mistake."

"Sexy."

I would never figure that man out. "You think I'm sexy?"

"Come down here after work and we'll take my car."

"You didn't answer my question."

He got up and came around the desk, fixing me with a look that made me quiver like a jellyfish. He took my hands in his big, strong ones, then he pulled me to my feet and straight into his arms. Or maybe I propelled myself there.

Nevertheless, we were standing knee-to-knee and he was gazing down at me with an expression that said, *Cara Mia*—men always speak in foreign languages in my fantasies—*I find you utterly and totally desirable. In fact, I've never met anyone as alluring as you, so let's run away tonight and get married.*

What he actually said was, "Yes."

A man of few words.

"What are you going to do about it?" I asked, hoping for a kiss.

"Go with you to the Luck o' the Irish bar to make sure no one lays a hand on that skirt."

"Sounds like a plan to me."

He glanced at his wristwatch. "See you in four hours."

I had just finished an arrangement of a dozen red roses for a walk-in customer needing a quick fix for a marital spat when the phone rang. Grace answered it in the front and in a moment poked her head through the curtain. "Phone call, dear. Someone named Maria Mendoza."

The hotel housekeeper. Maybe my bouquet had paid off after all. I took the call at my desk. "Maria? This is Abby Knight. How are you?"

Obviously not in the mood for friendly chitchat, judging by her brusque tone. "You asked me if I saw a woman with the guy that got killed. I didn't exactly tell the truth."

I nearly jumped up and down with excitement. "Can you describe her?"

"She had long black hair and a tight red dress. She was kind of skinny."

Bingo! That fit Onora to a T. "Was her face kind of frozen-looking, like a mask?"

"She didn't have no mask on."

"What I mean is, did it look like she couldn't smile or frown?"

"Are you trying to ask me if she was Chinese? 'Cause that's what she was. Chinese."

CHAPTER NINETEEN

Punch's mystery date was Chinese? I was stupefied. "Are you sure about her race, or was she just wearing an Oriental-style of dress?"

"Look, lady, I've worked in hotels all my life. I know Russian from Polish. I know Spanish from Argentine. I know Korean from Thai. I know Japanese from Chinese. I'm telling you, this woman was Chinese."

"Was this the woman you saw naked?"

"How did you know about that?" she asked warily.

"Todd mentioned it."

"That *pendejo*! It was his fault."

I was afraid to ask what *pendejo* meant, so I just let her rant.

"He told me room four twenty was out of towels, so I took up towels. I knocked on the door and no one answered, so I opened it and went in and this Chinese girl came running out of the bedroom screaming at me, holding a red dress in front of her."

Room four twenty was Punch's room. "What time was this?"

"Maybe six thirty."

"Could she have been a masseuse?"

"How would I know?"

"Do you remember anything else about her? Did she leave with the guy in the room?"

"She left the room by herself but there was an old man waiting for her outside the hotel. That's all I remember. Now I gotta go."

I sat there with the phone in my hand, thinking about her surprising revelations, until Lottie came by, took the handset, and set it in the cradle. "Everything all right, sweetie?"

"Just fine." Right. More like upside down, sideways, and inside out. Questions were piling up so fast my head spun. Was the young Chinese woman Punch's mystery girlfriend or a masseuse from the Emperor's Spa, or both? Had Onora found out she'd been to see Punch? Had Onora been so overwrought with jealousy that she'd lured Punch to the dunes and killed him?

Given Onora's temper, it was the best theory I'd come up with so far, and it would explain her sexy outfit.

I reined in my spinning thoughts. Before I could pin the murder on Onora I had to eliminate the others. I glanced at the spindle to see how many more orders needed to be finished and saw that it was empty.

"Lottie, would you mind if I stepped out for fifteen minutes or so?"

"You go right ahead, sweetie. Are you sure you're all right? You seem jumpy."

"You're not putting yourself in harm's way, are you, dear?" Grace said from the other side of the curtain.

"Certainly not. I'm fine. Everything is fine. Fine and dandy." I picked up my purse, slipped through the curtain, and aimed for the door, but I didn't move quickly enough. Grace struck her pose and began to quote the bard.

"'The lady doth protest too much, methinks.'"

I hate when I do that.

I did a quick walk to the jail, asked for Matron Patty, then did a little begging. All I could say was thank goodness my father had made so many friends.

It took over ten minutes for the prison guard to bring Flip down. When Flip saw me he hesitated, and for a moment I thought he was going to ask to be taken back to his cell. But he finally sat, though he continued to gaze at me with suspicion.

I decided to get right to the point. "You knew Punch had been seeing a young Chinese woman, didn't you?"

Flip's upper lip curled slightly. "*Seeing* isn't quite the word I would use to describe it."

"Why didn't you tell me about her?"

"Because her identity had no meaning in Punch's world. One woman was the same as another."

I couldn't believe he had withheld the information. It was almost as if he wanted to be found guilty. "Was she with him when he met you at the dunes?"

"No."

"But that's who he was meeting?"

"I assume so."

"Did Onora know Punch had arranged this meeting?"

Flip shrugged. "I have no idea what Onora knew."

I knew he wouldn't like my next question, but I had to ask it, so I braced myself for his reaction. If I touched a nerve, he'd be angry. If I was completely wrong about him, he'd be even angrier. "Did Punch threaten to expose you, Flip?"

He abruptly stood and turned to pound on the door. "I'm done in here."

"Flip!" I called through the speaker, deciding to take the full plunge, "I know you loved Punch. I understand how it feels to be betrayed by someone you care for." Or, in my case, someone I *thought* I cared for.

Flip turned to give me an incredulous stare. "You understand how I feel? Give me a break. So your wedding was called off. Big deal."

"It was a big deal to me. I was, and am, terribly humiliated."

"Then imagine your humiliation if Pryce had posted naked photos of you on the Web for the whole world to see."

My mouth nearly fell open. "Punch did that?"

Tears filled Flip's eyes. He quickly swiped them with the back of his hand. "He said it was time I came out of the closet and found myself a *proper* boyfriend. Do you still think you understand how I feel?"

I couldn't even begin to imagine that kind of humiliation, and I failed to see why so many women, and at least one man, were attracted to Punch. Had he been the "bad boy" everyone wanted to tame? "Did Punch tell you about the Web photos when you saw him at the dunes?"

Flip gave a quick nod.

"And that's why you threw your camera at him?"

He nodded again.

"Did you kill Punch?"

Flip gazed at me through a blur of tears. "I loved him. How could I kill him?"

That was a no-brainer. It was called a crime of passion.

The beautiful June weather had brought out the shoppers, filling the stores and sidewalks around the square, making it necessary to dodge them as I hurried back to the shop. I didn't mind at all. It was great to see the downtown so alive, especially since there were malls springing up all around.

I came up to the corner of Franklin and Lincoln, ready to turn left and head up the street to Bloomers, when I noticed Sgt. Reilly coming out of the courthouse across the street.

"Hey, Reilly!" I called, waving my arms. As soon as the light changed, I started toward him.

"What happened now?" he asked, swaggering toward me as only a policeman could do. "Someone try to kidnap you?"

"Don't you wish. Actually, I wanted to give you an update on the murder case."

"You're going to give *me* an update?"

"My being one step ahead of you looks bad for the force, Reilly. First of all, did you know that the maid of honor, Onora, was seen returning to the hotel the evening of the murder when she supposedly hadn't left her room?"

"Yes."

"Oh. Then I'll bet you *didn't* know that Onora asked us who had killed Punch *before* we'd told her he'd been murdered."

He took out his notepad and pencil and began to jot. "What else?"

"When I mentioned that little slip to Onora, she threw a fit and said if I reported it, I might end up like Punch."

"Huh."

So far Reilly hadn't seemed either impressed or surprised. "Here's something you should like. The former housekeeper at the New Chapel Inn saw a young Chinese woman in Punch's room around six thirty the night of the murder."

"I need the name of the housekeeper."

Ha! He hadn't known about Punch's mystery girlfriend. Now I had him right where I wanted him. "Her name? Sure, if you'll answer a few questions for me."

"I should have known there'd be strings."

"Is that a yes?"

He scowled at me. "Yes. Go ahead."

"Her name is Maria Mendoza. The hotel can give you her address. Now, did you or someone above you tell the newspaper not to look into the Emperor's Spa?"

"What is it with you and that spa, anyway?"

"I take it that's a no?" At his scowl I asked, "Has Punch's cell phone been recovered?"

"No."

"Did you try calling the number?"

"Now, why didn't we think of that?" he asked, heavy on the sarcasm.

The police were more on their toes than I'd thought. "Did you get the records from the wireless company?"

"Is there a reason you need to know this?"

"I'm trying to help you solve this case."

I heard him mutter something that sounded like "interfering busybody," but a noisy truck rattled past so I couldn't be sure. I decided not to pursue the matter and instead gave him a big smile. After a heavy sigh he said, "Yes, we got the records."

"Did the victim make any calls to the Emperor's Spa on the night of the murder?"

He gazed at me pensively, as if he couldn't decide how much to reveal.

"Yes or no, Reilly."

"I can't say."

Translation: Yes. "Haven't I been telling you something fishy is going on there, like prostitution in the disguise of massage therapy? If this were my case—"

"It's *not* your case. We're handling it. Go arrange some petunias, will you?"

Steamed, I turned around and marched away. The idiot.

I never used petunias in an arrangement. They wilted too quickly.

Just because Reilly had irked me, I parked myself on a bench facing Lincoln, took out my cell phone, and dialed Punch's number. It rang three times, as before, but this time it didn't disconnect. "Hello? Is anyone there?"

After a moment a voice whispered, "Wong numbuh."

"Pardon me?"

"Wong numbuh!" the voice whispered louder, then we were disconnected.

That voice sounded Oriental. Was it Punch's mystery girl? I dialed again, and this time the call went directly to his voice mail. I hung up. It would be too eerie to hear a dead man talking.

I put my phone in my purse and glanced up to see a slight figure in sweats and a hoodie draw back between two minivans parked on the opposite side of the street. Was it the little old man? Was he spying on me? I jumped up and ran to the curb, determined to find out what was going on, but traffic was heavy, so I had to wait for the light to change before attempting to cross through the lines of cars.

As I stood there craning my neck to catch a glimpse of the man, he shot out from between the vans, sprinted down the sidewalk across the street, and dashed around the far corner. At that same moment, a black Crown Victoria drove past, several antennae waving from its trunk. The driver's side window was down, and through it I caught a glimpse of a man sporting a ponytail and short beard.

Hadn't the man I'd photographed at the spa had a pony-tail and short beard? The cars were different, but couldn't it be the same man?

I turned and spotted Reilly about to climb into his squad car, so I waved my arms and shouted his name, trying to get his attention before he drove away. I got the attention of a dozen passersby instead. "Go back!" I called, as they came hurrying toward me. "It's nothing."

I glanced around and saw the black Ford slow down for a red light. "Reilly!" I shouted again. "Come quick!"

This time he heard me. He slammed the door and came running across the lawn, his hand resting on his holster, causing more people to gather around me.

"What is it?" he asked, breathing hard.

I pointed down the block to where the black car was at that moment turning the corner. "That black Crown Victoria has been tailing me."

He strained to see over the SUVs jamming the street. "I don't see it."

I gnashed my teeth in frustration. "It just turned the corner. Can't you go after it?"

"For what?"

"For tailing me."

"It's not tailing you now."

"It was!" I glanced around at the throng of curious faces, then moved closer to Reilly and said quietly, "Just tell me honestly, is the FBI on the murder case?"

"What does that have to do with a car tailing you?"

"Everything."

"What's happening?" Marco said, striding up. "You're drawing a crowd."

Reilly turned with a frown. "Okay, folks, move along."

As the people scattered, I said to Marco, "I was followed by the Crown Vic again. You were right about the antennae."

"What's going on, Sean?" Marco asked. "Why is there a tail on Abby?"

"Marco, I'm telling you straight out, if the feds are working on the murder case, they haven't shared it with me." Reilly turned to me and said, "If you see the car again, call us immediately and we'll see if we can catch him."

"This is starting to freak me out," I told Marco, leaning my forehead against his chest as Reilly headed back to his car. "I could swear the driver of that Crown Vic was the same man I saw going into the Emperor's Spa, only then he was driving an ancient Chevy. It has to be a cover. He has to be with the feds."

Marco put an arm around my shoulders and said quietly, "Listen to me, sunshine. If this guy is a federal agent he's not going to hurt you. He's watching you. So you must be doing something that's sending up red flags."

"Like what? Going to the jail to talk to Flip?"

"Could be. Didn't you see that car the last time you went to see Flip?"

"Then maybe they *are* investigating the murder. Maybe I'm on to something and I don't even know it."

"Another reason to leave police work to the police." He saw I was about to argue and held up a hand. "I know. You promised your cousin you'd help. But after this is over, no more!"

"Something else happened, too, Marco. I thought I saw the old man spying on me again."

"Why didn't you tell Reilly?"

"I'm not sure it *was* the old man. I only caught a glimpse, and then he ran away."

"Running doesn't sound like an old man's behavior."

"I think I'm becoming paranoid," I said, rubbing my temples. "One of these days you'll see me walking around with an aluminum bucket on my head."

Marco checked his watch. "Isn't it about time for you to close up shop? We have a dive to visit tonight, remember?"

As I walked back to Bloomers I was stopped a number of times by people wanting to know if I was okay and if my attacker had been caught. It was amazing how fast gossip traveled around the square. Even Lottie and Grace had heard the reports. They were standing in front of the shop, wearing anxious expressions, and quickly ushered me inside to ply me with a cup of Grace's comfort tea. I assured them I was fine, then filled them in on the Crown Victoria sightings. I didn't mention the old man.

"Trouble just seems to find you, doesn't it, sweetie?" Lottie said sadly.

Grace cleared her throat and lifted her chin, going into lecture position. "There's an old Chinese proverb that says, 'Trouble doesn't seek people; people seek trouble.' I think in your case that applies, dear."

Just what I needed—something else Chinese. I dropped my head with a groan.

An hour later I was sitting in the passenger seat of Marco's green Impala, sharing a bag of roasted peanuts with him as we headed for the Luck o' the Irish bar. I gave him a description of Bertie so he could ask the appropriate questions, then I said, "Can I ask you something?"

"Can I stop you?"

"Tell me honestly, do I seek trouble?"

"That's a trick question, right?" He eyed my skirt. "Why don't we swing by your apartment so you can change?"

"What do you have against this skirt?"

"The answer to your question is yes, you seek trouble."

The bar was a squat, rectangular, brown cedar structure that had weathered to a muddy gray. A yellow wooden sign with a faded green shamrock hung over the door. The sign looked as though it dated back to the early 1900s, possibly when the bar was actually Irish. There were no windows in the building, so the only natural light came from a small pane of glass in the door.

We walked in to the sound of an old-fashioned jukebox blaring out the Beach Boys' "Help Me Rhonda," and the smells of sour beer, tobacco smoke, and odors I didn't care to identify. The bar itself took up most of the room, running from left to right with wooden stools all around. On the stools sat men and women who looked as if they'd been there for some time—decades, perhaps—possibly without ever bathing.

Nearly all the men had on some type of black leather—boots, vests, jackets, even some spiked collars. Several men were bare-chested but for their open vests and heavy gold chains that lay in thick mats of chest hair. There were heavily tatooed arms, piercings in areas of flesh that looked painful, and bellies that hung over belts. All of them needed a shampoo and a shave. Desperately. Even some of the women.

There were a few younger women working as barmaids, wearing khaki-colored shorts and tight white T-shirts. Then there were the middle-aged women with pasty skin, no makeup, extra-roomy cotton shirts, and drab stretch pants, and a few older women in too-bright lipstick, floral-print dresses, and bony arms and legs that were shriveled like prune skins.

We immediately found ourselves the center of attention—the women sizing up Marco and the men turning hungry gazes on me. Marco laid a comforting hand on my arm and led me to a pair of vacant stools. "Now do you understand about the skirt?"

I took the stool next to a woman with pockmarked skin and brittle white hair, leaving Marco the stool next to a slumbering pile of human fur on the other side. The fur stirred briefly and lifted his head, revealing a puffy, haggard, male face, then went back into hibernation.

The woman raised a leathery hand to take a drag on the

cigarette clutched between two stained fingertips, then gave me a knock in the arm as she leaned toward me. "You got a real looker there."

The fumes from her breath rolled over me like a tsunami, shriveling the hair in my nose. "Thanks," I said, trying not in inhale.

The bartender, a thick-necked, former football player–type with a droopy mustache and gray ponytail, ambled over, taking swipes at sticky puddles on the counter. "What can I getcha?"

"A can of Lysol," I said, trying not to touch anything.

"What did you say?"

"She said a can of light beer." Marco nudged my knee in warning. He asked for a draft for himself, and when the man returned with our drinks, Marco slid money across, double what the drinks cost. "Listen, man, I need some information."

The bartender took the money with a snort. "Listen, *man,* get in line."

Unfazed, Marco said, "A guy came in last Wednesday— Irish accent, clean-cut, short brown hair, friendly. Remember him?"

"What are you playing, twenty questions? You know how many people come in here? I'm no memory bank, ya know."

"The thing is—" Marco put his hand on the counter. Between his index and middle knuckle was another twenty dollar bill, neatly folded. "Me and my buddy here," he nodded toward the money, "would appreciate your cooperation."

The bartender eyed the money. "How much cooperation?"

Marco wiggled the money. "This is it, pal. You're not a memory bank and I'm not Bill Gates."

The bartender hesitated a moment, then reached for the twenty, which Marco promptly removed. "Like I was saying, I need information."

"Okay, okay. I remember him. Yeah. He was quite a storyteller. He sat at that table over there in the corner. Everyone in the bar was over there, listening to his jokes."

Marco took his hand away, leaving the twenty, which the bartender instantly snatched.

"What time did he get here?"

"Like I watch the clock. Some time around six, maybe?"

The hairy snoozer beside Marco lifted his head and mumbled, "Six thirty."

"How do you know it was six thirty?" Marco asked him.

"M' wife comes t' get me ever' night at six thirty." He sank back into oblivion. I felt instant sympathy for his wife.

We glanced at the bartender for verification and he said, "Like clockwork."

"What time did my Irish friend leave?" Marco asked the bartender, just as the jukebox began to wheeze out "Woolly Bully." Considering the clientele, it seemed an appropriate tune.

"Couple of hours later. He took a phone call, then his friends came to pick him up."

"Did you get a look at any of these friends?"

"Only one, when she got out of the car to let him in. Tall blonde, a real babe."

That had to be Ursula.

"What make of car?" I asked.

The bartender scratched his ear. "It was silver . . . a Lexus, I think."

I whispered to Marco, "That's Claymore's car."

"Did you happen to notice how he arrived?" Marco asked.

"I got better things to do than watch the door."

"Hey, sweet thang," I heard a gravelly voice say. I swiveled to see one of the collared animals grinning at me, his full, graying beard coated with the remnants of his last meal. "Wanna dance?"

Marco put his arm around my shoulders. "Sorry, man. She's mine."

In my *dreams*. I gave the bearded beast a shrug and said, "Maybe next time."

In *his* dreams.

Marco took a few sips of beer and looked at me. "Ready to go?"

Was I ever. Once we were back in Marco's car and I had cleansed my hands with a disinfectant wipe from his glove box, Marco said, "Looks like Bertie's story checks out."

"I'm taking his name off my list of suspects. The next one up is Onora. I need to get into her hotel room to search for the red dress and black gloves the hotel clerk saw her wearing that night. If she killed Punch, there would have to be blood splatters on them."

Marco looked at me with new admiration. "Very good, sunshine. You're starting to think like a PI. How are you going to get in?"

"With a key," I replied with a smile, feeling extremely proud of myself, "which I will get from Jillian." New Chapel Inn and Suites hadn't yet graduated to the age of computerized key cards. Cutting-edge technology wasn't a phrase most people were familiar with.

He nodded approvingly. "And how will you prevent her from telling the others about your proposed room-snooping?"

"I'll threaten to reveal an embarrassing secret. No, that won't work. She doesn't embarrass. I know. I'll threaten to tell her mother about a certain boy she entertained when she was sixteen and her parents were in London. Damn. That won't work either. She could retaliate." My smugness dissolved as I frantically searched for the answer to Marco's pop quiz.

"How about reminding her that her wedding day is coming up and you haven't found the killer yet?" He turned the corner onto Franklin and pulled up beside my Vette. "Rule of thumb. Stick as close to the truth as you can. It makes life a lot easier. I'm going to give you a head start, then follow you home. I want to see if your shadow comes back."

"Since you're coming out my way, do you want to stay for supper? I can whip up a mean grilled cheese sandwich—with real American cheese."

"Is there any other kind?"

Was it any wonder I liked this man?

"Tempting," he said, "but I have to get back to work. Thanks anyway."

No snuggling on the sofa tonight. I slid into my car, started the engine, glanced in my rearview mirror for signs of the black car, checked for the little hooded figure, then pulled out and started home. It was getting to be a ritual.

I caught a glimpse of Marco's car at the next street, waiting for the light, but that was the last I saw of him. Ten minutes later I pulled into my parking lot, locked the car, and started for the building's entrance. My cell phone rang.

"No shadow," Marco said.

"Where are you?"

"Sitting at a corner watching you walk toward your door."

"Do you like the way I walk?"

"Are you going to start that now?"

I had to laugh. Marco was one of the few men who could make me laugh. I liked that in a guy. I wanted to thank him for bribing the bartender and defending my honor—if not my skirt—and taking time out to go to a stinky dive with me, and just for putting up with me in general, but I knew he'd tune me out after the first five words, so that's what I gave him—five words that said it all. "Hey, Marco, thanks for everything."

"Not a problem. Be careful, okay?"

As I put away my phone, the door to the apartment building opened and Peewee the snarling taco dog made straight for my bare ankles. Luckily, Mrs. Sample scooped him up before he did any damage. I bid her a good evening, then jumped inside and pulled the door shut behind me, wondering if it was just me, or if Peewee hated everybody's ankles.

Upstairs, Simon was waiting patiently beside his food dish. I had barely locked the door behind me when he started mewing, a pathetic cry designed to bring on instant guilt, as though he would expire from malnourishment at any moment. Oddly, his dish was still full from morning.

"Sorry I'm late," I said, giving him a quick scratch behind the ears. I cleaned out his dish and gave him a fresh glob of cat food from a can in the refrigerator. Simon sniffed it, then turned and walked away. I glanced at the label and saw the reason for the cat's attitude. Nikki had tried a new variety. It always took Simon one meal to decide if he liked it, which he never did. After that first sample, a week of starvation wouldn't force him to eat it.

"Okay, Simon," I called. "I'm getting out your old favorite—kidneys in gravy." I ran the can opener and Simon materialized at my feet, nearly tripping me as I stepped over to fill his bowl. He finished it before I had a chance to cap the can and put it away.

I consumed a grilled cheese sandwich in record time and was cleaning up in the kitchen when the phone rang. I grabbed the handset on the wall.

"Hi, Abs," Jillian said in her Little Miss Innocence voice.

"No, I haven't solved the case yet."

"How do you know that's what I was calling about?"

"Isn't it?"

"Fine," she said petulantly. "Bye."

"Wait, Jill. I need a favor. Are you going shopping with the bridesmaids tomorrow, and if so, can you get me a key to their hotel room without them finding out?"

"Is this about the murder investigation?"

"No, actually I'm planning a burglary. Of course it's about the investigation."

"Then yes, I can."

"Great. I'll stop by in the morning to pick it up."

"How early in the morning?"

"Seven forty-five."

"Too early. How about, say, noon?"

"That's not morning."

She huffed impatiently. "Eleven fifty-nine, then."

Talk about splitting hairs. "Fine. What time are you leaving to go shopping?"

"I have to shower," she said, thinking aloud, "do my hair, pick out something to wear—"

"So around dinner time?"

"One o'clock, smart-ass."

I rolled my eyes at Simon, who had just dropped a wet rubber band on my bare foot and was gazing up at me patiently. I plucked it off and tossed it down the hallway. "Remember, Jill, don't say a word to anyone—unless you *don't* want me to find the killer."

"My lips are sealed."

That would be a first. I hung up just as Simon came trotting back with the rubber band. Before I could stop him from dropping it on my foot again, the phone rang. "Now what?" I asked, expecting to hear my cousin's voice again. But there was no sound at all.

"Jillian? Hello?"

There was muffled noise in the background, as if some-one had put a hand over the phone. I expected the heavy breathing to start at any moment. "Who is this?" I asked, digging in the junk drawer for my whistle.

"Abby Knight?" a man said in a hushed voice. "They're on to you. Be careful."

Goose bumps sprang up on my arms. "Who's on to me? Who are you?"

The line disconnected. I hit the code to find out the caller's number and was told it was blocked. Someone was on to me? What did that mean? Who was I supposed to watch out for? A light tap on the knee made me look down. Simon sat at my feet, a paw on my leg, waiting. I tossed the rubber band as far down the hallway as I could. He started after it and, halfway there, plunked down on the floor to give himself a bath.

I poured myself a glass of V8 Splash and stood at the window scanning the parking lot and the homes across the street from the apartment building. The problem was that I didn't know who or what to scan for. The FBI? The little old man? My only hope was that the guy would call back so I could get more information.

But by eleven o'clock that night no more calls had come in, so I hit the sheets and fell into a restless slumber filled with eerie dreams. At five o'clock in the morning, tired of tossing and turning, I got up, deciding I might as well get an early start on the day. My to-do list was as long as my arm.

I did my walk in the predawn light, showered, ate break-fast, and was in the Vette on my way to work by the unheard-of time of seven o'clock. As I passed the alley that ran behind Bloomers, I took a glance down it, as I usually do, expecting to see it empty. Not today. Today the black

Crown Victoria was parked there, directly behind my shop. If that was someone's idea of being discreet, someone needed to go back to spy school.

I made a sharp turn into the alley and roared up behind the black car. The driver didn't even turn. Ready to do battle, I got out of the Vette and marched up to his window, pushing aside the thought that maybe confronting this man wasn't the wisest thing to do.

Then again it really didn't matter. The man was dead.

CHAPTER TWENTY

I jumped back with a gasp. His face was a mottled purple, his eyes bulged from their sockets, and his tongue lolled—yet still I recognized him. Dark blond ponytail, light brown goatee—the man I'd captured on camera at the Emperor's Spa, and most likely the man who'd driven past when I was chasing the old Chinese guy. This guy had to be with the feds.

My hands shook as I dug for my phone and called 911, all the while glancing around to make sure the murderer wasn't lurking nearby. "There's a dead man in my alley," I said, trying not to hyperventilate. "I think he's with the FBI." I gave them the location, then called Marco.

"Hey, sunshine," he said sleepily. I could hear the stir of sheets in the background. "What's up?"

"Not too much," I said with false lightness. "Just a Crown Vic behind my store with a dead man inside."

I heard the sheets whip back as he murmured a curse, then he said, "Where are you now?"

"In the alley waiting for the police."

"Get away from the car. Go inside the store and lock the door behind you."

Up to that moment I hadn't decided whether to be mildly or completely freaked out, but the urgency in his voice tipped the scales in favor of completely freaked. I backed up all the way to the big iron door, but my hands were trembling so hard I had trouble unlocking it.

"Okay, I'm inside," I reported at last, trying to sound calm and collected rather than completely unhinged. "And here come the police."

"Good. I'll be down there soon. Put your head between your knees and take deep breaths."

How well he knew me.

Four squad cars arrived from either end of the alley, with sirens blaring and lights flashing. I watched from the doorway as they got out, drew their weapons, and cautiously approached both my Vette and the Ford. An ambulance arrived next, and within minutes the police had swarmed the black car and were taking photos and collecting evidence—with the corpse still in the front seat. Another squad car pulled into the alley and Reilly got out. He walked up to one of the officers on the scene, got the scoop, spotted me, then headed my way.

"Tell me how this happens. You report a black Crown Vic tailing you and the next morning a man in a black Crown Vic ends up dead."

I massaged my temples, which were starting to tighten. "Ironic, isn't it?"

He scowled at me as he reached for a notepad and pencil. "Is this the same car you said was following you yesterday?"

"And the day before that, and the day before that."

"Have you ever seen this man before?"

"Yes, at the Emperor's Spa."

He stopped writing. "The spa thing again?"

I planted my hands at my waist and tried to look indignant. "If your people would investigate, there would be no need for a private citizen to have to do it."

He ignored the lecture. "Are you positive this is the same man?"

"Yes. I took photos of him."

"You took . . ." Reilly made a strangled sound that could have been the word *photos*.

"How else could I convince the newspaper to do an exposé on the spa? But then someone killed the story, which is another fishy aspect to this whole deal. Have you ever been out to the spa, Reilly? You ought to drive by sometime, like on a raid. They won't wait on women customers, there's paper covering the windows so you can't see inside, their female employees are guarded by an old Chinese man, and there are no ads on the marquee, just a phone number. Now what does that sound like to you?"

He didn't take the bait. "Let me get this straight. You were spying on the spa's customers, one of whom you believe to be this victim, who was, in turn, tailing you."

"That about sums it up."

He shook his head in exasperation. "What time did you get here this morning?"

"Seven o'clock."

"Do you always get here at seven?"

"No, usually eight."

"Why did you arrive early today?"

"Because some idiot called last night and scared me and I couldn't sleep."

"So today of all days you arrive early and find the man you claim has been following you dead. Behind *your* store."

I stared at him in amazement. "What are you implying?

That *I* might have strangled him? Me? Abby Knight, flower shop owner, upstanding citizen, and daughter of a cop?"

"I didn't tell you he was strangled."

"I found the body! Anyone who's ever watched a cop show on TV knows what a strangled person looks like."

Reilly looked a bit sheepish as he scratched his neck. "Well, then someone wants it to look like you killed him."

"It's a warning," Marco said, walking up to us. "It's too obvious to be a frame-up."

Reilly gave Marco a skeptical glance. "How is it you always show up right after something happens to her?"

"I'm psychic." He put his hand on the back of my neck and rubbed it. "How are you doing?"

"If you keep doing that, I'll be a lot better." I turned to Reilly. "This might be a good time to mention that the man who called me last night told me that *they* were on to me and warned me to be careful. That was all he said. Nothing about who *they* were. His phone number was blocked. Do you think the caller could have been him?" I pointed to the body in the car.

"I'll get your records from the phone company to see where the call came from, and I'll have them tap your line while I'm at it, in case you get any more calls. It takes about twenty-four hours to put on a tap, so you might want to let your machine pick up until then."

"Tapping her line is fine, but it isn't enough," Marco told him. "Abby needs police protection."

I glanced at Marco in surprise.

"I'll put a detail on her." Reilly stopped writing when one of the officers brought him a wallet and a computer printout of the license registration, along with the news that a reporter was waiting to talk to him. I glanced over and saw the photographer readying his camera, so I quickly averted my face. I didn't want my parents to read about me in the newspaper again.

"Nothing unusual here," Reilly said, studying the printout. "No arrests, no tickets." He opened the wallet and pulled out an ATM card. "No license, no credit cards, insurance cards, or Federal ID."

"The better to protect his identity," Marco said.

"When I photographed him he was driving a rusty Chevy," I said. "Doesn't that sound to you like he was working undercover? Maybe the feds caught on to the spa's illegal activities before your guys did, Reilly."

I got a frown for that remark.

The coroner came over and spoke quietly with him. After he left, Reilly said to us, "The victim seems to have been strangled with some kind of garotte, possibly the thickness of a rope, but smooth, not rough like hemp fibers would be. We'll know more after the autopsy." He pointed to me. "I'll have a detail on you within the hour. In the meantime, keep your nose clean. Don't talk to reporters. And get that Corvette out of the way."

With that he strode off to deal with the press.

"Why don't you give me your keys?" Marco said. "I'll move your car and you can go have a cup of java and de-stress."

"Abby?" I heard Lottie call from inside the store. In a moment she and Grace came hurrying outside.

"Good heavens!" Grace exclaimed. "What happened?"

Marco snatched the keys from my hand. "See you later," he said, and headed toward my Vette, leaving me to face the next round of interrogations alone.

We sat in the parlor drinking cappuccinos while I told Grace and Lottie what had happened. They were so sympathetic that I felt compelled to come clean about the spa investigation. I braced myself for Grace's lecture, but nearly fell off my chair when she exclaimed angrily, "A house of prostitution! In our town! And the mayor knows about this? Let me have the name of that features editor. I want him to tell *me* why that exposé was canceled."

Go, Grace!

She made the call, but the editor wasn't due in until ten o'clock, so we decided the best thing to do would be to resume our normal duties and try to forget about what had happened behind the shop. Grace began her usual routine of setting out her bud vases, Lottie went to place orders to the suppliers, and I held an impromptu drawing for the "What's My Vine?" contest.

Of the seventeen entries I'd received, only one came close to being creative. For the picture of a Swedish ivy sprouting from a tole-painted watering can, the winner had titled it, "Ivy Leak." For that she would get a fifty-dollar arrangement of fresh flowers on the day of her choice, and hopefully I would get free publicity on local radio and in the newspaper.

I gave the information to Grace so she could notify our winner while I turned my attention to Trudee's party. After putting together an estimate for the floral flag, I thumbed through a wholesale catalog looking for that special tropical accent for her foyer. Yet no matter how busy I kept myself, I couldn't shake the image of that body in the car. Someone wasn't beyond killing to make a point. But what *was* the point?

The bell over the front door had been jingling all morning, although most of the business had been on the parlor side. I heard it jingle again and went up front to see if Grace needed assistance. There I found my aunt Corrine standing in the middle of the room, holding her hand over her open mouth, staring at my mother's coatrack.

I greeted her, and she immediately gave me a hug. "I'm so sorry," she said.

"Someone will buy it. Eventually."

Still staring at the tree, she handed me a paper sack. "This is from Jillian. She said it would save you a trip."

I glanced inside and saw a pair of black leather driving gloves. Either Jillian had hidden the key inside a glove or she'd misunderstood my request. *Room key. Driving gloves.* Nope. Not even Jillian could get those two mixed up. "Thank you, Aunt Corrine."

She barely heard me. Her gaze had shifted to my mother's footstool. "I'm so, *so* sorry," she muttered, and hurried away.

As soon as she left, I pulled out the gloves, shook them, and a key fell to the floor. "Thank you, Jillian," I whispered, and slipped it into my pocket. At the very least, the room search would take my mind off the scene in the alley.

I phoned Jillian at twelve thirty and learned that she was on her way to the hotel to collect the girls for their trip to Chicago. They had to finish their grand tour of the Magnificent Mile, she informed me. They had only reached the halfway mark yesterday.

"You're sure they're *all* going—Ursula, Sabina, *and* Onora?" I asked.

"I'm sure. Wasn't that clever of me to hide the key in the glove?"

"Very. Just remember, not a word to anyone."

"It's burned into my brain."

That and her credit card number. I grabbed a quick sandwich at the deli, giving Jillian plenty of time to round up the girls, then I took off for the hotel, automatically checking for the Crown Vic before realizing that there wouldn't be a Crown Vic tailing me anymore. Then I remembered that there *would* be a cop, and he probably wouldn't be too

happy to find me snooping around in someone else's hotel
room. I glanced in my rearview mirror and, sure enough,
there he was, two vehicles behind me. I'd have to lose him
for at least an hour. But how was I to hide a bright yellow
Corvette?

I scanned the streets as I drove through town, searching
for a way to shake him. At the next intersection I knew
there would be a large grocery store to my right, with a car
wash in the side parking lot. Taking a chance that there
wouldn't be a line of dirty cars, I waited until I was almost
at the corner, then I cut over a lane and made a hard right
turn. The cop didn't have time to follow and had no choice
but to sail on through the intersection.

I flew down the street to the parking lot entrance, made
a left turn, and drove straight up to the car wash. There was
one car just starting through, so it was only a matter of seconds until I was able to pull forward. Once inside, I put the
car in neutral, pulled the top up, and sat back with a
chuckle. Not bad for a law school flunk-out.

A few minutes later I pulled out with a gleaming car and
took off, no squad car in sight. When I reached the New
Chapel Inn and Suites, I drove slowly past the parking lot
to make sure Jillian's car was gone, then I parked the Vette
and went into the lobby. There was a different clerk at the
reception desk, this one a middle-aged, paunchy male with
a comb-over, reading a newspaper. I pretended to be a guest
and walked straight to the elevators, hitting the button for
the fourth floor and shooting up the hallway to the girls'
room. I let myself in, calling, "Hello? Anyone home?"

Hearing nothing, I hung the DO NOT DISTURB sign on the
doorknob outside, shut the door, and charged through the
sitting room, past the kitchenette and bath, and into the bedroom. The girls had unpacked their belongings, so I started
my hunt for Onora's clothing in the closet. Finding nothing

incriminating there, I moved to the bureau drawers, then hauled out the three suitcases from of the back of the closet. Not knowing which was Onora's, I had to go through each one, but I still found nothing. Had Onora disposed of the dress?

Acting on a hunch, I picked up the phone and punched the button for the laundry service. "Do you have any laundry for room four twelve?" I asked.

"Jus' a meenit," a woman said. Several minutes later she said, "Jes, I hab red dress."

"What about gloves?"

"No glubs."

"Has the dress been cleaned?"

"Not jet."

"Perfect. Would you send it up, please?"

"But ees dirty."

"Yes. That's great. Don't touch it."

"Joo strange, lady."

I've been called worse. While I waited for the dress I decided to look around one more time, just to be sure I hadn't missed the gloves. I checked the bottom of the closet and under the bureau, then took a peek under Onora's bed, finding dust bunnies large enough to warrant rabies vaccinations.

Then I spied something dangling from the mattress up near the headboard. I slid under the bed, clamped two fingers around the mystery object, gave a tug, and a long black glove fell free. I pulled it out and stood by the window to examine it. Were those blood splatters on the fingertips? It was hard to tell on dark material.

I was in the process of moving the mattress away from the headboard to hunt for the second glove when my cell phone rang. I dug it out of my purse and answered.

"Abby," Jillian said. "Bad news. Onora didn't come with us."

My stomach gave a lurch. "Where is she?"

"She went down to the hotel dining room to have breakfast. She said she had a headache and needed to eat something, then go back to bed."

I sat down hard, clutching the glove in a hand that was growing damp. "Why didn't you tell me this sooner? She could come barging in here any minute."

"I had to wait until I could stop at the toll road oasis so I could call you in private. I'm sitting in a bathroom stall right now."

"I think, given the circumstances, you could have managed to come up with a reason to call sooner, Jill!" I stuffed the phone and the glove in my purse and sprinted for the door.

Too late. Someone was inserting a key into the lock. I came to an abrupt halt and glanced around for a place to hide. There was no time to run back to the bedroom and jump into the closet. There was nothing to crouch behind in the sitting room, and there was no way I could squeeze into a cabinet in the kitchenette. There was simply no place to go.

CHAPTER TWENTY-ONE

The door swung open and there stood Onora, clad in high-heeled pink sandals, designer jeans, and a pink chiffon blouse. She took one look at me—guilt plastered all over my face and my purse clamped under my arm like a quarterback making a run for the goalpost—then she stepped inside and shut the door.

"What are you doing here?"

I stood my ground and maintained eye contact, which wasn't easy given the difference in our heights. The worst thing to do would be to show fear. "I came to pick up—" *Came to pick up what? Think, Abby!* "A necklace. Ursula said she had a necklace I could borrow."

"How did you get in?" she snapped, her face drawing up tighter than usual.

I considered admitting Jillian's part in the scheme, but on the off chance the wedding still went on and Onora was cleared, I couldn't see ruining their relationship. "I—um—borrowed a key."

"Whose key?"

"That's not important."

Onora's smooth features tightened even further as she advanced on me. "Why don't I believe you?" Before I knew what she was planning, she had grabbed my purse and was holding it over my head as if I were a five-year-old and she'd taken away my ball.

"That's private property!" I cried, trying to get it back.

"You invade my space, I invade yours. That's fair, isn't it?" Then she proceeded to shake the contents onto the floor. Out fell my cell phone, wallet, keys, lip gloss, pen, pack of tissues, and the wadded glove, which unfurled as it dropped.

Onora snatched it up. "What's this?"

"My glove," I said instantly, trying to snatch it back.

"No, it's not! It's *my* glove." Her pupils darkened as she gave me a shove backward. "What are you doing with it?"

For probably the second time in my life I was speechless. I stood there rubbing my shoulders where she'd pushed me, trying to come up with a viable reason for having someone else's formal glove in my purse.

Her pupils widened. "Omigod. You're looking for evidence. You're trying to prove I'm the murderer!"

I eyed my phone on the floor, calculating how many seconds I'd have to grab it, dash down the hallway, and lock myself in the bathroom to call for help. All I had to do was push Onora off balance.

"Where's the other glove?" she demanded.

"I didn't find it."

"Liar!" She started to shove me again, but I dodged her and dove for my phone. Before I could get away, she grabbed me around the waist and flung me onto my side. I rolled onto my back and drew my legs up to kick back, but she neatly sidestepped me, picked up my phone, and stuffed it into her back jean pocket.

"Get up," she said.

Keeping a wary eye on her, I got up and dusted off my backside.

She tossed the glove onto the table, then pointed to the small sofa. "Sit."

"Gosh, I'd really like to, but I have to get back to my shop or my staff will be worried and come looking for me. And by the way, there's also a cop parked outside." Right. A cop I'd foolishly managed to evade.

Onora's hands clenched and unclenched, and I could see she was gearing up for one of her emotional rages. "Will you just sit down and shut up?"

I sat.

"Do you think I don't know I look guilty? I have an IQ of one hundred seventy-six and an MBA from Wharton. I'm not an idiot!" She had screeched the last part, then must have realized how unbalanced she sounded. She scraped her hair back from her face, pulled a chair up to face the sofa, and sat on the edge, leaning toward me. "The truth is, I *can't* tell anyone where I went last Wednesday evening. It's too embarrassing."

"I'd rather be embarrassed than accused of murder."

"Are you serious?" She thrust her face in mine. "Look at me! Look at my face. Look at my eyes. Do you understand now?"

At the risk of making her even more deranged I said, "Understand what?"

She straightened with a huff. "Don't pretend you don't see them. *Wrinkles!*"

"Onora, I am not lying when I say that all I see is smooth skin."

She jumped up and paced to the door, rubbing her arms as though she were cold. "You're afraid to tell me the truth. Everyone is afraid to tell me. I look horrible and I know it. My skin is aging faster than my body and I'm powerless to stop it. *Powerless*. By the time I'm forty I'll look like an old hag!"

"I understand your concern," I said to placate her, although in truth I thought she was nuts, "but I don't see what this has to do with the murder."

She dropped down onto the sofa beside me, a frantic tone in her voice. "Punch broke up with me because he couldn't stand to look at my face. I tried to win him back. I even dressed up like his little Chinese tart. Know what he did when he saw me? He laughed."

Onora laughed, too, but not in a natural way. More the way a maniacal murderer might laugh just before she chops someone into bite-sized wedges. "Do you know how humiliating it is to dress in the sexiest outfit you can find and throw yourself at a man, only to have him laugh at you? Do you know how it feels to be made to look like a fool?"

"On more than one occasion," I told her somberly. If this woman didn't have a motive for murder, no one did. She was crazy, and I was beginning to wonder if I was going to get out of that room without one or both of us suffering bodily harm. I decided to try to reason with her, if that was possible.

"You know, it might help to talk to someone. In fact, I know the very person you need, so why don't I call him?"

"A therapist? I don't need a therapist. I need a plastic surgeon!"

Actually, I was going to suggest a cop, but at that point I'd do anything to get out of there. "Okay, that'll work. Let's call a plastic surgeon right now. Would you hand me my phone? Please?" I gave her a tentative smile.

"For God's sake, will you stop acting like I'm going to kill you?"

"I will if you're not."

"I didn't kill Punch!" she cried, banging a fist on the sofa. "What will it take to make you believe me?"

"Calming down would be a good start. Then you could tell me where you went in your car that evening."

She glared at me for a moment, still seething, then turned her head and began to rub her forehead, smoothing all those nonexistent lines. Her lips started moving as if she were having an internal debate, so I gathered my scattered belongings and put them back in my purse—gingerly, so as not to interrupt her discussion.

Finally, in a resigned voice she said, "Okay, fine. What have I got to lose except my dignity? The truth is I got the name of a New Chapel doctor from my dermatologist back in New York—in case my last injection wore off—which it did! I went to his office that night."

"Your last injection of what?" I asked stupidly.

She pointed to her eyes. "Botox! Bo. Tox. There! Are you happy? Now you can tell everyone that Onora gets Botox injections!"

What she needed was a sanity injection. "There's a doctor in this town who keeps evening hours?"

"Believe me, I paid dearly for it."

"Can you prove you went to see him?"

"Call his office. I've got his card in my purse."

"Let me make sure I understand. You went to Punch's room and tried to seduce him. When that failed you went for a Botox treatment."

"What was I supposed to do? Punch said he couldn't stand to look at my face. I thought if I could just smooth out these horrid wrinkles maybe he'd take me back." She looked at me with such sad desperation that I almost felt sorry for her. I also had a sneaking suspicion that if Punch had said he couldn't stand her face, he hadn't meant it literally.

"What did Punch do after you left his room?"

"I don't know. When he told me to get out, I ran back to my room, called the doctor, and left."

"Did you see Punch's—um—date in the room?"

"Passion Flower?" Onora's upper lip tried to curl back but had to give up the struggle. It wasn't a pretty sight. "I *wish* I'd run into her."

"Is that her real name? Passion Flower?"

"That's what Punch called her. I had another name for her."

"Do you think he went to meet her at the dunes?"

She shrugged. "He only said he had to leave."

"Just one more question. Why is there blood on your glove?"

"Because that dermatologist was a hack," she said bitterly. "When I got back in the car, I looked in the mirror and saw spots of blood where he'd injected me. I must have touched them."

"Why did you hide the gloves?"

"I didn't hide them. I threw them."

Probably in the throes of another temper tantrum.

Onora toyed with a lock of her hair, looking suddenly like a little girl. "Are you going to tell the others my secret?"

"Not unless you want me to. What you do to your skin is your business."

She blinked rapidly. I think she would have cried if she could have moved the right facial muscles.

"But you're going to have to tell them something about that evening," I warned her, "because everyone is wondering where you went."

"Well, I did have a terrible headache, and I did stop at a drug store. I'll just say I went out to get a pain prescription filled."

"That'll work. Now I suggest you call Sergeant Reilly and get your name off his short list." I held out my hand. "Phone?"

"Why don't we just ask that cop to do it?"

"What cop?"

"The one you said was parked outside." With a wry smile, which was about all a stiff-faced person could do, she reached into her back pocket and pulled out the phone. As I opened it and hit the police's number she said, "You're okay, you know?"

I wished I could say the same for her. I got Reilly on the line and quickly explained the situation.

"How the hell did you get away from your detail?" he bellowed. "I've got half the police force out looking for you."

"All six of them? Just kidding. I think I lost him when I stopped to get my car washed. I'll be more careful from now on."

He muttered a few words under his breath that I chose not to hear, then he told me Onora would have to come down to the station to give a statement. I relayed the information to Onora, but she wasn't happy about it. She'd had the crazy notion that the police would come to her.

I left her in her room and started for the elevator just as a maid got off carrying a red silk dress. Deciding to play it safe, I gave the girl a tip and took the dress with me. I believed Onora's story, yet I'd been fooled before. Let the detectives do what they wanted with it.

Now I was down to the last suspect on my list: Passion Flower. If she didn't pan out, then I'd have to admit that Flip was most likely the killer. But how was I going to find her?

Sitting in my car in the hotel parking lot, I put the top down, then tried Punch's number again. It rang six times, and I was about to give up when I heard it connect. "Hello," I said quickly. "Who is this?"

"Wong numbah."

"Wait! Don't hang up. What's your name?"

"Wong numbah," the whispered voice said again.

"How did you get Punch's phone? Are you Passion Flower?"

There was a slight intake of breath, then the call disconnected. It had to be her. But where was she?

Since I couldn't get inside the spa to look for her, I settled for my second option, which was to check out the new Chinese restaurant to see if she worked there. As I pulled out of the lot, I saw a squad car come up the street toward me. The officer stopped even with my car and rolled down his window.

"A car wash, huh?" he said with a scowl.

"Yes, sir. Doesn't this baby shine? And just so you know, I'm on my way to the China Cabinet." I gave him a friendly smile and drove away.

The Chinese restaurant smelled pleasantly of sweet-and-sour sauce, fried pork, and garlic, and was decorated in the standard red-and-gold color scheme, with hanging paper lanterns over the tables, red cushioned chairs, hand-painted folding screens, jade statues, and a small water fountain at the entrance. Most of the tables were filled, so I grabbed a vacant one near the door and ordered an egg roll and green tea.

"Nice place," I told the young Chinese waitress when she brought my order. She looked to be about twenty, with pretty, dark hair pulled into a twist at the back of her head. Her name tag said KIM.

"How is business?" I asked her.

"Good," she said blandly, not paying much attention. "You want to order something else?"

"No, thanks. Do you know a young woman by the name of Passion Flower?"

"Passion Flower?" she asked, looking genuinely puzzled. "What kind of name is that?"

"Oddly enough, that was my next question."

The waitress stepped aside as her boss, who also served as the host, seated a group of college kids at the table behind me. "Sounds like someone from the old country," Kim said. "Who is she?"

"That would have been my third question. I don't know who she is and I need to find her. I have a sneaking suspicion that she works at the Emperor's Spa."

There was a look of sympathy in Kim's eyes. "If she does, then I feel very sorry for her."

Her boss snapped out something in Chinese, then she said, "I have to get back to work."

I ate my egg roll and took a few sips of tea, then went to the cashier to pay. When I returned to the table to leave a tip, Kim paused behind me to whisper, "The spa is a very bad place. The girls come from China and are guarded like prisoners. The owner is a very powerful man in Hong Kong and he doesn't like anyone interfering in his business. I wouldn't go near there if I were you."

I turned to thank her, but she'd slipped away.

An absentee owner and a guard. If that didn't sound suspicious, nothing did.

As I hurried back to Bloomers, I glanced at the clock on the dashboard and groaned at the amount of time I'd spent working on the murder. I needed to put everything else aside for the rest of the afternoon and concentrate on business, especially Trudee's party. I still hadn't come up with an idea for her foyer or figured out the logistics of the floral flag. Thank goodness I had Lottie and Grace to help.

Once the wedding and the party were over I'd have to take my assistants out to eat. It would strain my checking account, but they deserved a bonus.

When I stepped into the shop the first thing I saw was Lottie trying to squeeze around the outstretched palms of my mother's coatrack to retrieve a silk fern on a shelf behind it. "It hates me," she grumbled, rubbing her arm where a "hand" had jabbed her. "And it doesn't fit in this tiny corner. It needs space. Like in the basement."

I was on my way to the workroom, but stopped instantly and turned. "What did you just say?"

"I said it needs space."

I swung around and stared at the sculpture. "That's it! Lottie, you're a wonder. I've been searching for the perfect tropical eye-catcher for Trudee's huge foyer and it's been sitting right in front of me." I stood back to admire the tree. "She's going to love it."

"Baby, if you try to sell her on that thing, she's more likely to give you a Hawaiian punch than a check."

"Trust me; it'll fit perfectly in her foyer."

"If I were you," Grace said from the parlor, "I would ask Trudee to come take a look at it before you haul it out there. 'Tis better to be safe than sorry, as the saying goes."

I called Trudee on the spot and got her daughter Heather. "Hi. This is Abby. The florist. Is your mother there?"

"No." Noncommittal tone.

"Would you leave a note that I called?"

"Yes." No change in voice.

I didn't even try to make further conversation. If I ever got married and had kids, I'd have to sell them off before they hit their teens. I poured myself a cup of Grace's excellent coffee and went to the workroom to do what I loved best—arrange flowers. I pulled an order, gathered my tools, chose my theme, and began.

This was going to be spectacular. A summer feast for the eyes. A combination of scarlet pyracantha berries, apple green spider mums, yellow chili peppers, purple anemones, dusty pink hellebores and Lollo Rosso lettuce leaves. I wasn't going to think about the missing cell phone, or Passion Flower, or the little old man, or Punch, or even Trudee's flag. Nothing but the fresh new creation that was taking shape in front of me. Tomorrow I would resume the murder investigation and try to tie up all the loose ends.

Or so I had planned.

CHAPTER TWENTY-TWO

Lottie and Grace waited outside while I set the alarm and locked up, then both women insisted on walking me to my car even though there was a cop parked across the street. "Go straight home and put everything that happened today out of your mind," Lottie told me. "Don't even think about the murder."

Up to that moment, I *had* put it out of my mind. Now that she'd brought it up, it was firmly back in place.

"Don't forget to lock your door," Grace said.

I took their advice graciously because I knew they cared. I turned the radio to a rock station, put the car in Drive, waved to the cop parked behind me, and headed for home. At the apartment, Simon was parked on the coffee table licking his paw. Around him lay the scattered remains of a dried flower arrangement, which he had apparently attacked and subdued.

"Simon!" I cried. He paused in his ablutions to gaze up at me.

"Don't give me that innocent look. Who's going to clean up this mess?"

He resumed his bath. He knew who the cleaning crew was, and it wasn't him. I shooed him off the table and took the decimated flowers to the trash can in the kitchen. "It's a good thing I was going to replace this," I called, "or you'd be next one to go." Wherever he was, I was positive he wasn't quaking in his boots.

The phone rang, and it was Reilly, wanting to know if I was in for the night and had locked the door. I told him yes on both counts. He said he was pulling the detail until morning, but if I had any problems to call 911.

The phone rang again while I was using the portable hand vacuum on the coffee table, but I didn't know it until after I'd shut off the vac and saw the light flashing on the answering machine. I pushed the Play button and heard a female voice whisper, "Prease ansah."

Could it have been Passion Flower? I replayed the message three times, certain the caller had been the same one I'd heard earlier say, "Wong numbah." How had she known my home phone number? I dialed Punch's cell phone, hoping that's where the call had originated, but it rang and rang until the voice mail picked up. I hung up with a shudder.

I sat by the phone, waiting for another call, until my stomach began to growl for its supper. I put away the vac, changed into shorts and a yellow T-shirt with the *Bloomers* logo on it, fed Simon—who was still unapologetic—and made myself a quick version of huevos rancheros with the last of our eggs, tomato, chili powder, and dried onion flakes.

I took my plate to the living room and turned on the TV. Simon perched beside me, purring loudly to show that, despite my earlier behavior, he still loved me and therefore deserved a bite of egg. When the phone rang I set the plate on the coffee table and sprang to answer it.

"Hello!" I said. "This is Abby."

"Prease," that same voice whispered, sounding very terrified, "help me."

"Okay. Yes. I'll help you. Tell me who you are and what I can do for you."

In the background, I heard a man's voice bark a command in an Asian tongue. The caller hung up. I paced, nibbling my lower lip, remembering what the waitress had said about the girls at the spa being kept like prisoners. Was the girl on the other end trying to escape?

The phone rang and I jumped. "I'm here!" I said hurriedly.

"Abby!" Jillian wept on the other end. "I'm ruined!"

That was *not* what I wanted to hear. "What happened?" I asked irritably. "Did you break a nail?"

"Worse. The wedding is off," she sobbed loudly.

"Did the Osbornes call it off? Damn! I should have figured they'd do it to you eventually. At least I had two month's notice."

"Not the Osbornes. The hotel! I just got a call from the events manager at the Peninsula. The President of the United States is coming to Chicago, so they need the ballroom. Do you believe that? I got bumped!"

"If it's any consolation, you were bumped by the President."

It wasn't a consolation. She wailed louder. "For crying out loud, Jill," I shouted over the noise, "find another place."

"It's too late. Everything is booked. Why did this have to happen to *me*?"

"Should it have happened to someone else?"

"Well, duh! Abs, what am I going to do?"

"What about that new banquet center, the Garden of Eden?"

She sniffled. "Is it in Chicago?"

"It's about ten miles east of New Chapel, just off the highway. I did flowers for a birthday bash there a few weeks ago, and it was very nice."

"Nice? I don't want *nice*. I want spectacular."

"At this late date you'll have to take whatever you can get. I'll call them tomorrow to see if they have an opening on the fourth."

"You will? Abby, I wub you."

I heard the call-waiting beep and said quickly, "Gotta go." I hung up on her second *wub*.

"Hello!" I almost shouted into the phone.

"Help me, prease," came the whisper, a little louder than before. "I must leave now or he kill me."

"Wait. Who's going to kill you? Are you Passion Flower?"

"Yes. Come now. Behind beauty parlor."

"You want *me* to come get you? I really think you should call the police."

"No call police!" she said in a frantic voice. "He kill me I call police."

I wanted to believe her, but I just wasn't sure. "Why did you call me? You don't know me."

"You friend of Punch. You call his phone. I see your numbah. He say I need help, call friend." I heard a hiss of breath, as if something had frightened her, then she ended the call.

I couldn't remember if I'd called Punch's number from my apartment phone or not. I stood there with the phone in my hand, trying to make a quick decision. If I called Reilly, he'd either send an officer to check out her story, which the old Chinese man would most likely deny, or he'd blow me off. *"Not the spa thing again."*

Either way, it wouldn't help Passion Flower and might even get her killed. So I called Marco instead. His cell phone sent me directly to his voice mail. I left a message saying I needed to talk to him, then I phoned his bar.

"Hold on while I look for him," the bartender told me.

I tapped my toe; I paced; I pulled back the curtain and stared out into the darkness. What was taking so long? I glanced over and saw Simon licking the last bits of egg from my plate. "You are so grounded."

Simon began to wash his face, pausing to glance at me like, "Are you talking to *me*?"

"Can't find him," the bartender said at last. "Want to leave a message?"

Damn! "Tell him Abby has new information and needs his advice ASAP."

"Will do."

I hung up and stared at the phone, my insides in knots. Did I dare try to call Punch's number again? If Passion Flower was in danger, would the ringing phone jeopardize her even more? Should I sit it out until Marco called me back? What if he didn't call for hours? What if I ignored Passion Flower's plea for help and she ended up dead?

I had to do something. I knew better than to go to the Emperor's Spa, but the beauty parlor was a different story. What danger would I be in if I were to drive through their parking lot? It couldn't hurt, and it might just save a life.

Traffic was light, typical for a Monday evening, so I made it to the salon in less than ten minutes. I shut off my headlights as I turned into the lot, then I slowed the Vette to a crawl. The parking lot was empty as I rolled slowly through it, and the salon was dark. The only illumination came from a street light on the opposite side of Concord Avenue and the occasional passing car. I shivered in the darkness, starting to feel creepy. My cell phone rang, startling me.

"Abby, I'm glad I reached you," Marco said. "I've got some new information."

"Just listen, Marco," I said quietly. The top was down and I wasn't sure how far my voice would carry in the empty lot. "I got a call from Passion Flower. She's in danger and needs to get away from the spa."

"Why did she called *you*? Wait a minute. Is that an engine running? Where are you? Don't tell me you're on your way to the Emperor's Spa. Even you wouldn't be that foolish."

"I'm not *on* my way to the spa. I'm in the beauty salon parking lot *next* to the spa."

"For God's sake, Abby, turn that car around and get the hell out of there."

"I can't. The girl said someone would kill her if she didn't leave now. She pleaded with me to come get her."

"Listen to me," he said in a firm voice, "I just spoke to Reilly. The dead man was a federal agent investigating a Chinese sex slave ring operating out of the spa. Somehow his cover was blown and he was killed. And you're probably next on the list, so get out of there. Let the police come for her. I'll call Reilly and have him send a car."

As Marco talked, a slender figure stepped out from the shadows behind the salon, her long hair blowing in the breeze. "She's here now, Marco," I whispered. "I can't leave. I'll pick her up and drive straight to the police station. I promise."

"Did you hear what I just said? You could be walking into a trap."

"Stop worrying. I'll be out of here in a minute." I closed the phone, gave the Vette a little more gas, and inched forward until I could see the pearly complexion and shiny black dress of a Chinese woman. There was a look of distress on her face and she kept glancing back at the spa, as if she feared being followed.

I reached across and swung the passenger door open. "Don't be afraid. I'll take you somewhere safe."

She looked over her shoulder again as she started for the car, only to step wrong on one of those four-inch heels and go down in the gravel with an *oomph*. Instantly, I shifted into Park, and opened my door, ready to hop out and lend a hand. Then Marco's warning ran through my head. Was this a trap?

"Help me, *prease*!" she sobbed, trying to stand. "He kill me! Hurry, before he come."

There was no way I could ignore her desperate cry for help, nor could I count on the police to get there quickly. I had to trust her. Leaving the engine running for a quick get-away, I got out and did a quick visual sweep of the parking lot as I ran around the back of the car and stooped to help her up.

Just as she took my hand, J felt something silken loop around my neck from behind. I let go of her and grabbed it with both hands, struggling to free myself. The silk loop was drawn tighter, making me gasp for air as I was dragged into the shadows behind the salon. I tried to twist around to fight back and found myself on the verge of blacking out.

Surely this wasn't how I was supposed to die. Strangled in a back alley? Cut down in my prime? I had a sudden vision of my parents receiving the news, a cop at the door, solemn faced, hat in hand. Then I saw Nikki red eyed and weeping as she hand-lettered a "Roommate Wanted" sign at the kitchen table. And Simon, sitting at her feet, head tilted to one side, with a look on his little pointed face that said, *"I miss her, too."*

Just when my life began to flash before my eyes, the silk loosened and I could breathe again. My knees buckled and

I sank to the gravel, gasping and coughing. Before I could recover my wits, I was yanked to my feet and shoved forward. I stumbled through a rear doorway and into a dimly lit hall that smelled of new lumber.

Ahead of me I could make out the oval face and black dress of the woman I guessed to be Passion Flower. My eyes were watering so much I had to blink to clear away the blur of tears. Even so, she didn't look as young as I'd imagined her to be. She also didn't appear as frightened as she'd seemed only moments ago. In fact, she looked rather smug.

My stomach dropped. It *was* a trap.

A voice behind me barked something in Chinese. I swung around to see an old man in a black kimono, loose trousers, and thong-style sandals. He was small in stature, maybe two inches taller than I was, with the round, wizened face of a capuchin monkey. It was the same face that had glared at me from the spa's window and had watched me from inside the hood of a sweatshirt. I would have guessed him to be over seventy years old, yet he had the strength of a much younger man. He stood with arms akimbo, blocking the exit. He snapped at me again, pointing toward a doorway near where I stood.

"He want you prease to go in room," the woman translated.

Polite request or not, I wasn't in favor of that plan. I tamped down the fear that was turning my muscles to mush and gave the old man my fiercest glare, putting my hands on my hips to mimic his posture, pretending it were no big deal to be pushed around by a little monkey-man. "Tell him I'm not going anywhere but out the back door," I whispered hoarsely.

As the woman translated, I started to move past him, but before I could blink, I was sitting on my rear on the floor. How had that happened? I started to scramble up but he shoved me down again, pointed to the doorway behind me, and barked another order.

"I know, I know," I said, when the woman started to translate, "he wants me to go into the room." I rose and dusted myself off, trying to think of a way to get past him, half expecting to be tossed again. But this time he waited to see what I'd do. I turned so I could keep one eye on him and still see the woman and said quietly, "Did you call me? Are you Passion Flower?"

Before she could answer, the old man pushed me through the doorway, where I found myself in a windowless room paneled in light wood, with a pale blue ceramic-tiled floor. On one paneled wall, white terry-cloth robes hung from a row of white ceramic hooks. Against another wall, beneath a big white clock, was a wicker table that held thick, navy towels. Long redwood benches lined up along a third wall, and in the far corner was a glass-enclosed shower.

The main attraction, though, was a small, sunken pool in the middle of the room, no doubt the custom-designed hot tub the girls next door had mentioned. The pool was made of white ceramic tile onto which had been painted figures of naked women. There were four steps leading into the pool and tiled benches around the sides. It had not yet been filled with water.

The old man snapped something again, and I swung to face him. In his hands was a long black sash, pulled taut. The smooth garotte.

My heart raced. I took a step back. "Don't even think about it!" I yelled, pretending to be angry instead of scared witless. "You have no idea the trouble you'll be in. I told a dozen people where I was going tonight, not to mention that they'll see my car in the parking lot. Keep in mind that the police will be here any minute, too, because I called them five minutes ago."

I wasn't sure if the old man understood, but I knew the woman did. She looked up at the clock and said something to the old man, and I could tell they were both doing some quick calculations. It certainly didn't take a mental giant to figure out that if I'd called the police they would have arrived by now. So where were they? I knew Marco had called them. Where was Marco, for that matter?

"Car has been moved," the woman said.

I swallowed hard. If my Vette was gone, Marco would think I was, too. In desperation I tried appealing to the woman's conscience. "You called me to come help you, and I did. At least you could return the favor by getting me out of here."

"You came to help Passion Flower," she corrected.

"Aren't you her?"

The woman muttered to someone standing outside the door, and suddenly an even younger woman stepped into the room, bringing the scent of jasmine with her. Where had I smelled that recently? Of course. At the murder scene. Jasmine didn't grow at the dunes. That should have tipped me off that a woman had been there.

"*Here* is your Passion Flower," the other woman said spitefully.

The girl was small and graceful, and wore a tight, red silk dress. Her head was bowed, her long black hair falling like a satin curtain over her face, her hands folded together at her waist. She raised her head, revealing a young, frightened face. She couldn't have been over seventeen years old.

She smoothed one side of her hair back, exposing her ear. From her right lobe dangled a gold earring in the shape of a punching bag. I stared at the earring, causing the girl to finger it nervously. Had Punch given it to her? Was she trying to signal something to me? Or had she killed him and removed it as some kind of macabre souvenir?

The old man snapped the sash between his hands and commanded me to do something which the woman translated as, "Hold out wrists, prease."

My stomach plummeted so fast and hard I thought I was going to be sick all over his thongs, which actually might have improved my chances of getting out. I took another step backward, my mind racing for a way to stall until help arrived. My only option was to distract them. "Why are you doing this? Why did you bring me here?"

"You try take Passion Flower," the woman said curtly. "Chou have to stop you. You very dangerous."

Chou being the old man, no doubt. And Chou apparently was prepared to kill me for being dangerous. I pointed to my yellow T-shirt with the Bloomers logo on it. "Look! I run a flower shop. I'm not a danger, except to myself sometimes. You keep Passion Flower and I'll walk out of here and not say a word about this to anyone. Tell him that. Tell your boss." I nodded toward the old man.

"Chou not boss. Kuon-Liu boss. Passion Flower belong to him. No one take her from Kuon-Liu."

Marco's words echoed in my mind: *"The dead man was a federal agent investigating a Chinese sex slave ring operating from the spa."*

I glanced at Passion Flower, who was watching me with terrified eyes. She was merely an asset to Kuon-Liu, an investment to be guarded by the old man to the point where he'd kill anyone who threatened to take her away. Poor, lust-driven Punch. The old man must have thought he wanted to help her escape.

"You met Punch at the dunes last Wednesday night, didn't you?" I asked Passion Flower, keeping a nervous eye on the other two. "And Chou followed you."

At her quick nod, I gestured toward the old man. "Did Chou kill Punch?"

She gave another brief nod, and in halting English said, "Chou follow me to lake. He find out Punch ask me to marry him. Punch want to elope that night." She started crying softly.

I stared at her, stunned. They were going to *elope*? No wonder Chou had gone after her. He didn't dare lose Kuon-Liu's merchandise. At least now I understood why Punch had asked the clerk to wish him luck. He couldn't have had a clue what kind of hornet's nest he was stirring up.

I saw Chou start toward me and I swung to face him, edging back even farther. "Keep away from me. You won't get away with another murder."

"You not murdered," the woman behind him replied. She pointed to the empty pool. "You drown. All an accident."

CHAPTER TWENTY-THREE

There was a blur of motion and suddenly Chou had the sash wrapped around my mouth and knotted behind my head. He was ready to bind my wrists with yet another sash when Passion Flower threw herself at his feet, crying and chattering away in Chinese. He tried to push her away, but she hung on for all she was worth. I hoped she was pleading for my life. Chou snapped something at the older woman. Instantly, she took the sash and came toward me.

I yanked the gag out of my mouth and held out my hands like I actually knew some karate moves. "Don't mess with me!"

I immediately found myself lying on the hard tiles with a bump rising rapidly on the back of my head and the wind knocked out of me. As the room swam in dizzy circles, she straddled my waist, pulled my hands together, looped the sash around them and was about to tie it when Passion Flower let out an ear-shattering scream.

The woman looked around in alarm, and the momentary distraction allowed me to press my wrists as hard as I could against the material so I'd have some wiggle room. Chou hissed something, then the girl went silent, whether from his words or a well-placed karate chop I didn't know.

As the woman knotted the sash I heard what sounded like a body being dragged from the room. She stood and pulled a thin, nasty-looking knife from a sheath strapped to her leg. "Get in tub, prease," she said, gesturing with the weapon.

What was the point of her politeness when she was about to kill me? I muttered something of that nature through my gag as I struggled to my feet and walked down the tiled steps into the empty tub. My gaze darted about the room as I searched for a way to escape.

She gestured with the knife. "Sit, prease."

Shooting her glares, I sat on a bench. She grabbed the ends of the sash and pulled them through a ring at the bottom of the tub, bringing my wrists down to my ankles and my face to my knees. From that vantage point I saw several more rings around the perimeter, probably used for some kind of bondage games.

Her feet climbed the stairs—that was all I could see—then I heard the sound of beeps, as if she were programming a microwave. I tried to raise my head to see what she was doing, but the sash wouldn't give an inch. Suddenly, warm water began to rush into the tub from three different inlets and swirl around my feet in a frothy foam.

"Good-bye now," I heard her say, and then the door closed.

In a panic, I yanked repeatedly on the knot at the bottom, pulling as hard as I could, until I thought I'd snap my wrists. It held firm. My stomach roiled in terror. The rushing water now covered my hands. When my knees were submerged, my face would be, too. At that thought I started to hyperventilate.

Breathe, Abby. In and out. Slow and steady. You're not going to die here, damn it!

Precious minutes flew by as I worked my hands against each other to weaken the soggy material, but the bubbling water, now halfway up my arms, made it impossible to see what I was doing. I pushed and pulled and twisted, again and again, as the water crept higher. I had to keep reminding myself not to panic, but as the level neared my knees my prospects for getting out alive were looking grim.

Within minutes my chin was submerged. I lifted my head as high as it would go and pressed my lips together, concentrating on the binding around my wrists. My neck ached from the awkward position and my back wasn't feeling so hot either. When the material began to roll I nearly cried. With a little more effort I would be able to slip it down over the widest part of my hand.

The water bubbled under my nose. I strained my neck up as far as I could, but moments later even that didn't work. I separated my knees, took a deep breath, and plunged my head underwater so I could see what I was doing. Blinking to see through the froth, I folded my right thumb in close to my palm and pulled down. My lungs burned, and I knew I had seconds left. Just when I thought I couldn't make it, the material rolled the rest of the way down my hand. I was free.

Quickly, I raised one side of my body high enough to gulp air. And then I plunged under again, pushing the material down until my other hand was free. I sat up, yanked off the gag, and filled my lungs with precious air, then scrambled out of the pool, grabbed a towel, and ran for the door.

It was locked.

I stood there with the towel wrapped around me, water dripping from the ends of my hair, wondering how I was going to get out. I had no tools to use—no purse, no phone, no keys. I'd left it all in the car. And I didn't dare bang my fist against the door. If the police weren't there, Chou would only return and finish me off.

I looked around the room for a weapon, but there were only towels and benches and a wall clock. I could barricade the door by dragging the benches in front of it and wedging them there until the police arrived. But what if the police never arrived? With my car out of the picture, I couldn't count on their help. The clock wouldn't be much of a weapon either. That left only the shower stall.

I ran toward it, slipping and sliding on my waterlogged sandals. The showerhead was chrome and looked heavy enough to use as a weapon, but it was way above my head. How was I going to detach it?

I glanced around and spotted a bench. Quickly, I threw off the towel and half carried, half dragged it across the tiles to the shower, trying not to make noise. I stood on one narrow end and examined the showerhead, which appeared to be held to the base by a thick nut. I wrapped my hand around it and tried to turn it, but it wouldn't budge. I finally wrapped an end of the damp towel around it and used that as my grip. After practically hanging on it, slowly it began to turn. I doubled my efforts and finally the head broke loose, nearly clattering to the hard floor.

With the heavy piece of chrome in one hand, I leaped off the bench and scurried to the door, trying not to slip on the way. I started pounding on the wood and calling for help. If Chou was the one who responded, I'd stand behind the door and strike him as hard as I could.

Within minutes I heard footsteps running toward the room, then the lock turned and the door swung open. My heart was beating so hard, the blood hammered in my ears. I held my breath, the chrome head raised high, clamped in my sweaty hands. I didn't dare miss or I was as good as dead.

"Abby?" Marco called, looking around the door.

The showerhead had started its descent when I realized

who it was. Marco jumped out of the way just as I aborted my attack. I dropped the metal and ran into his arms. It clattered noisily on the tiles, but I hardly heard it for all the crying going on.

"It's okay, sunshine," Marco said, stroking my hair as I burrowed into his shirt. "You're safe now. Don't cry."

Was that me crying? I gave him a final hug and stepped back, wiping my eyes, not wanting him to think I was a wimp. "Did you come all by yourself?"

"Reilly is here with five of the town's finest. They're taking away the old man and the girls right now, including one with a mustache and European accent. I think she was their front lady—or man, as the case may be."

"Did you find my Vette? Is it okay?"

"Your baby is fine, and your purse is locked in my car. I found the Vette parked behind the deserted car wash down the street. The yellow paint stood out like a beacon. That's when I knew you'd been had."

I gestured toward the pool, feeling a fresh batch of tears build. "Th-they t-tried to dr-drown me."

He went for a dry towel, wrapped it around my shoulders, and hugged me close to stop my shivering. All that male warmth soaked through to my damp skin, relaxing my tensed muscles and soothing my jitters. "How's that? Is that better?"

"My neck hurts," I said, hinting for a rub. Marco, ever the gentleman, complied, his fingers working deep into the muscles at the nape.

Reilly came around the door and cleared his throat. I looked up, surprised to see him in a cotton shirt and jeans. He must have been off duty. "Am I interrupting anything?" he asked.

"Just a little TLC," Marco replied. "Abby went for an unplanned dip in the pool."

"You okay?" Reilly asked me.

"Sure . . . now. What took you guys so long?"

Reilly held up his hands. "Blame the legal system. We had to get a search warrant."

"Where was the judge? In Alaska?"

"Listen, you ought to be grateful we got it as quickly as we did, and that's due to Mr. Salvare here." Reilly nodded toward Marco. "He kept insisting that you'd been kidnapped. If he hadn't found your car with your purse inside, we wouldn't have had much to go on."

"It was a team effort," Marco said modestly.

Reilly aimed his index finger at me. "Maybe next time you'll leave the investigations to us."

"Take the *maybe* out of it," Marco said. "Didn't I warn you it was a trap? Didn't I say to get out of there? Did you listen?"

"Yes, yes, and no, and I'm very sorry about all of it. But at least I found Punch's murderer, and probably the FBI agent's, too. It's the old man, and don't be fooled by his size. He's as strong as an ox. I have the bruises to prove it. He murdered Punch to stop him from eloping with one of the girls." My teeth started to chatter again, so Marco suggested I save my story for later so I could go home and put on dry clothes.

Reilly started to leave, so I said, "Hey, Reilly, the youngest girl in that group—her name is Passion Flower. Go easy on her, okay? She was trying very hard to get out of here."

"I'll see what I can do."

I massaged my wrists and said to Marco, "You know what I could use?"

"A psychiatrist?"

"Chocolate. Dark chocolate. Any form. That's what I could use."

"How about a nice glass of wine to go with it?"

I flung the towel across the room. "I'm ready."

Marco wrapped an arm around my sodden shoulders and ushered me to the back door. "Let's go get your car."

We rounded up my Vette, a bar of dark chocolate, and Nikki. I changed into jeans and a T-shirt, then we gathered in the last booth at the Down the Hatch, where Marco treated us to a perfectly chilled bottle of Clos du Bois chardonnay with a side of french fries, the latter because Nikki had just gotten off work and was famished. Reilly stopped in to give us an update on the spa investigation and ended up joining us for a beer.

"The feds had been looking into this massage parlor for about a month," Reilly told us. "The owner, Kuon-Liu, heads a crime organization in China that, among other things, buys girls from brokers to ship overseas and use as prostitutes. They're watched closely so they don't escape and are beaten if they try. Most simply resign themselves to their fate, but some take their chances with sympathetic men who are willing to help them. Unfortunately, most men are afraid to get involved because they have wives at home. They want to see these girls as exotic playthings, not as frightened little girls who need help."

"I can't believe parents willingly sell off their daughters," Nikki said in disgust.

"Money talks," Marco said, "especially in a poor country."

"In all fairness," Reilly said, "they might not know what's in store for their daughters. I'm sure they're painted a rosy picture of the wonderful life they'll have here."

"What's going to happen to Chou?" I asked.

"Once the feds are done with him, he'll be prosecuted and sent to prison. When his term is up, he'll be deported.

Kuon has several massage parlors in the Chicago area that are still under investigation. This is the first time he has branched out our way."

"And the last, I hope," I said.

Reilly took a pull of his beer. "Don't bet on it."

"I just remembered something," Marco mused. "Two days ago a sign went up in the window of an old house down on Lincoln Street, right next to my barber."

"And the sign said?" Nikki prompted, when he wasn't immediately forthcoming.

"*Massages.* With a phone number underneath. The way they slipped that business in—no advertising, no grand opening—I'll bet it's the same kind of place." He drummed his fingers on the table. "Maybe I'll make an appointment to check it out."

"Excuse me, Mr. Salvare," I said, trying to keep a straight face, "are you planning to do some meddling?"

I could almost hear the wheels spinning in Marco's brain as he tried to come up with a better explanation. But the best he could do was, "It's not the same thing."

Nikki, Reilly, and I burst out laughing.

Marco scowled at me. "You're a bad influence."

"How bad?" I asked with a flirtatious bat of my eyelashes. The electrified look he sent me made me tingle all over. I glanced at Nikki to see if she'd caught it, but she was deep in thought.

"Poor Punch," she said with a sigh. "He finally did a good deed and got murdered for it."

I broke a piece off the chocolate bar and nibbled it. "Why wouldn't the police look into the spa, Reilly? Was someone at the top bought off?"

"Not bought off. Warned off. The FBI wanted to handle the investigation. When you started poking around, they got nervous, afraid you might tip their hand. They're the ones who took your photos and squashed the newspaper story. They didn't want their guy exposed. But it happened anyway."

"Why did the FBI wait so long to inform you?" I asked.

"They're territorial," Marco said. "It happens all the time."

Reilly took another pull of beer. "From what I gather, he'd been tailing the old man, and when the old man started watching you, so did the agent."

"See there?" Nikki said to me. "You're not paranoid after all."

"Thanks. I feel so much better. Someone refill my glass."

"I think you would have been left alone if you hadn't kept trying to contact Passion Flower," Reilly said. "She was very helpful, by the way. She told us about the old man following her to the dunes and killing Punch. She also said the old man strangled the federal agent after discovering his true identity."

"That must have been just after the agent called to warn me," I said.

"How did Passion Flower get to the dunes?" Nikki asked Reilly.

"Taxi. Punch had apparently paid a driver in advance to pick her up."

"How did the old man get there?" I asked.

"He's not talking."

"Then the third set of prints on the camera should match the old man's," I said.

"Correct."

"And Flip is in the clear."

"You got it."

"Will the old man be charged with murder?" I asked.

"Among other things. As will the woman who lured you to the salon."

"What about the girls?" Nikki asked.

"INS will deport them," Reilly said.

"Poor things," Nikki said sadly. "Their parents abandoned them, and now we're sending them back to who knows what kind of life."

"Think of it this way, Nikki," Marco said. "Whatever is waiting for them there can't be worse than what they've been through here. And they speak the language."

My cell phone rang. I turned away to answer, while the others continued to talk.

"Abby?" Jillian cried excitedly. "Claymore just called. Is it true? Has Flip been cleared?"

"Yes. In fact, we were just—"

"That's wonderful!" she gushed. "Now I can get married. Too bad I still have *no place to hold the reception*."

I held the phone away from my ear while Jillian ranted. Nikki laughed at something Marco said, and I had missed it, so I told Jill good-bye and ended the call.

Marco held up his glass. "It's time for a toast."

We raised our glasses to his and he said, "Here's to murderers being caught, slave rings being broken, and Abby returning safely back to us."

"Hear, hear," we all said, then clinked rims, took sips, and sat back with satisfied sighs.

"Who was on the phone?" Marco asked, reaching for a chunk of chocolate.

No need to spoil the party with Jillian's complaints, especially since I hoped to talk Marco into having a private celebration with me afterward.

I looked him straight in the eye and said with a mysterious lift of an eyebrow, "Wong numbah."